A New Life in Amsterdam

Helga Jensen is an award-winning British/Danish best selling author and journalist. Helga holds a BA Hons in English Literature and Creative Writing, along with a Creative Writing MA from Bath Spa University. She is currently working on a PhD.

HELGA JENSEN

A
New Life
in
Amsterdam

hera

First published in the United Kingdom in 2025 by

Hera Books, an imprint of
Canelo Digital Publishing Limited,
20 Vauxhall Bridge Road,
London SW1V 2SA
United Kingdom

A Penguin Random House Company
The authorised representative in the EEA is Dorling Kindersley Verlag GmbH.
Arnulfstr. 124, 80636 Munich, Germany

A CIP catalogue record for this book is available from the British Library.

Print ISBN 978 1 80436 933 3
Ebook ISBN 978 1 80436 937 1

This book is a work of fiction. Names, characters, businesses, organizations, places and
events are either the product of the author's imagination or are used fictitiously. Any
resemblance to actual persons, living or dead, events or locales is entirely coincidental.

Printed and bound in Great Britain by Clays Ltd, Elcograf S.p.A.

Look for more great books at
www.herabooks.com | www.dk.com

For the wonderful Alun Gibbard. Thank you for everything.

Prologue

I don't like the way Hannah's looking at me. She's been pacing up and down the living room all morning. Every now and then she sneakily glances over at me, looks at her phone, then goes to say something but stops herself. I know her so well that I can always tell when something is bothering her. I just don't know what.

'Are you okay, Hannah? You've been acting weird all morning.'

She hesitates, gazes at the floor and then clears her throat.

'I've something to tell you and I don't know how you'll react. I thought I could just come out with it but...'

'Come on, spit it out. I'm your mam, you know you can tell me anything. I won't be cross. Well, I might be for a moment, but whatever it is I'm sure I'll soon calm down.'

'See, that's what I mean. You might go bonkers.'

'I won't go bonkers, I promise. I'll always support you no matter what.'

'I know, it's just I'm worried you'll be sad.'

'You never make me sad. I'm always proud of you. Come on, you'd better just tell me. Whatever it is, I promise I'll understand.'

I try not to let my mind go into overdrive. Has she had bad news? What could be so bad that she is afraid of telling me in case it makes me sad? I have to take a deep breath to stop myself from panicking. Whatever she is about to tell me, I have to be strong in front of her.

Hannah bites her lip and looks down at her phone, which is ringing in her hand. She ignores it, placing it down on the table, looking at me seriously.

'Okay. Please don't burst into tears.'

'I won't burst into tears, I promise.' I try to smile even though she is unnerving me further.

'I'm moving to be closer to Dad.'

'What?'

'I'm moving to Melbourne.'

'Right.' I nod my head approvingly. I know that I have to show my support, no matter how devastated I am that she is moving so far away from me. That's what mams must do. It's part of the job description.

I try hard to remember that I must not show any reaction on my face other than a smile; although I have to grab the arm of the sofa to steady myself as I take in the news.

If I'm honest with myself, I always had a feeling she would move to Melbourne eventually. I just didn't expect the decision to come today as I am standing in the middle of the kitchen making a morning brew. As I absorb the news by staring out of the kitchen window, I notice the dip in the grass where Hannah used to dig as she attempted to get to Australia when she was small. Hannah was absolutely convinced she would get to see her grandparents and cousins in Oz if she dug deep enough. If only it were that simple. I think back to those long flights we used to take. I even used to believe that if my marriage to Paul could survive a long-haul trip like that with a busy toddler, it was surely bullet-proof.

The problem is that when we get older everything changes. Our children grow up and leave us to start their own lives, and people want different things. While Hannah may have always had that yearning to live in Australia among Paul's large family, I didn't think Paul felt the same way. He had been living in Abergavenny for thirty years and while he missed the outdoor Aussie lifestyle over the years, I never suspected that one day he would return there for good. Then he started reminiscing about the Christmases he had on the beach, the family barbecues, the views from Mount Dandenong overlooking the Melbourne skyline, the Vegemite toast and even the witchetty grubs. In all our visits to Australia over the years, I had never seen him go anywhere near witchetty grubs. He was hankering for his homeland more than I ever realised, and with my mam not well I couldn't join him on his trip home. Just like Hannah standing in front of me now, it was time for our lives to take different directions. As he turned fifty, he reconnected with the outdoorsy person he was when we first met. A five-hour hike and foraging for food were now his idea of fun. Whereas walking around Waitrose for twenty minutes was enough foraging for me.

I may have married a gorgeous Aussie who had been working his way around the UK until he stopped in my local Welsh bar in his twenties, but Paul has gone for good and now our only child is running off to join him in Australia. I feel utterly bereft. How on earth am I supposed to pretend I'm happy? Those baby books I read about motherhood when I was pregnant never prepared me for this period in my life.

I plaster on my best pretend smile and try to say the right words.

'Wow. Well, I'm so happy for you. This is incredible. Just what you've always dreamed of.'

'Are you really happy for me?'

'Yes, of course. I mean, I know you have some good friends here, but we don't have much family left. You have cousins and aunties in Oz and, of course, your dad. I'm super happy for you, really. I expected you to make this decision one day, and what better time than now you've finished uni.'

Hannah rushes over to me and gives me a big hug.

'Oh, Mam. Thank you for being so good about it. I hate the thought of leaving you here on your own. At least you've got Debbie though.'

'Yes, Debbie's only next door. Thank goodness for besties. I'll be fine. Don't you worry about me.'

'So, when are you planning on leaving?'

Hannah gives me that nervous look again.

'Soon, I'm guessing by that look on your face.'

'Yup. Next week. It's taken me ages to pluck up the courage to tell you. You know I'll miss you so much.'

'Yeah, I know. Me too, my lovely girl. Oh, come here and give me a hug.'

Hannah's eyes are filling up as I hold her.

'I'm sorry, Mam.'

'It's okay. It's the right thing for you. It'll be the best thing you ever do. Better not to have too long to think about it. I'll just have to cancel that dinner reservation I made for us next weekend.'

'Oh, Mam. Now I feel guilty. Maybe it's also time for you to have a new start – that's what you need.'

'Please don't be guilty, I'm fine here. I don't need a new start. Come on, shall we open a bottle of wine and celebrate? We've got to make the most of our last moments together for a while.'

'Oh, go on then, thanks, Mam,' says Hannah with a grin. The relief on her face at my calm demeanour is palpable. Mentally though, I am already working out whether they do parental visas in the Australian embassy. Although, even as I seriously consider it, I realise that I can't be one of those mams who doesn't give her daughter the freedom to find her own feet. I have to let her go. My only child, my world, my everything, is moving to the other side of the world and I don't know when I will see her again. I am the mother hen who is being left with an empty nest, and I have to hide the sadness of this loss.

Chapter One

Six months later

Hannah's words echo in my head: 'A new start – that's what you need.' It's alright for her, she is young and living her best life on the other side of the world. My empty nest is so different from the home that used to be filled with Hannah's friends popping over and girly pyjama parties that I would get the house prepared for. Without the chaos of her lovely mates popping in, my home feels bare. I keep myself busy with my felting hobby, making cute felt animals for pet lovers, but when that goes quiet, my life just feels empty. My home doesn't even feel like the same place any longer and so, as I think of Hannah and how far away she is, I do what I always do when I feel lonely. I pop to the shops.

'Hello, good to see you back so soon, Sandy,' says Janice at the boutique down the bottom of the road.

I smile and joke about how you can never have enough clothes, but really, I don't need anything, although that doesn't stop the excitement I feel as I reach the rail with the fancy jackets with their luxurious fur collars. I suppose the boutiques are getting ready for winter now. I don't need another winter jacket, but these have fake-fur collars! I can't possibly resist and promptly remove one from the rail.

I shove my arms into the blue suedette jacket and snuggle into the comfort of the cream-coloured fur trim. It practically hugs my face. It is so soft and sumptuous.

'That looks stunning on you,' says Janice.

'It is rather lovely, isn't it?' I say, admiring the jacket in the full-length shop mirror.

'You can't resist that, surely? It was made for you,' says Janice.

'No, you're right. Oh, go on then, wrap it up.'

I feel warm and fuzzy and smile as Janice wraps up the jacket. I watch closely as she folds the arms and covers my new clothing in tissue paper. I love watching her wrap my – many – purchases. She does it with such care. She places one of the shop stickers on to seal the package and pops it inside a fancy paper bag, handing the rope handle over to me. Before I leave, she tells me about her new grandson's latest antics and asks how Hannah is getting on in Australia. We chat as though we are friends, but I know I am not really her friend. I am merely someone who spends a lot of money in the boutique she owns. As I walk out of the shop with my bag swinging from my arm, I have a moment of happiness, but when I open the door of my empty home once again, I realise that nothing has changed. I throw my bag down as my smile is quickly replaced by a frown. With nobody to hear me, I let out a big sigh.

Yet again, I have filled my cottage with *things* instead of people. After all, material goods don't leave you. They don't get sick and if they break, they can generally be fixed or replaced, unlike the human brain or a husband who wants to live out the rest of his days a million miles away. I am only too aware that I take solace in new *things*. And when I spend money, people are nice to me. Friendly shop assistants, and owners like Janice, smile and wish me a pleasant day as I leave the store. It gives me a hit of endorphins as I walk out holding a bag full of stuff. Perhaps the carrier bag is like some kind of comfort blanket, just like my mam holding my hand when I was small. The only problem is that when I get home and unpack my goods, I am alone again.

I am intelligent enough to know that shopping solves nothing. Looking at my purchases in the shop might make me happy for a moment, but I am slowly beginning to realise that all these material goods only serve as a temporary comfort blanket. It is the loneliness at home that is the problem and, as the cottage is becoming fuller, I am feeling emptier. Truthfully, it is Hannah I want and not another coat or handbag but, with nothing else in my life, that is my only solace. Although it is not so comforting when my bank statement arrives.

As I consider the high that shopping gives me and wonder how I can get those endorphins in a more economical and healthy way, I hear the thud of the Saturday morning post in the hallway. That will be the magazine subscription I impulsively signed up for. It had seemed absolutely necessary at the time, since the heading on the March issue was *How to Live Your Best Life over Fifty*, so, of course, I had to buy it. Again though, that compulsion was short-lived; by the time I got to the end of the article, I realised that none of it applied to me. I didn't want to get up at five a.m. each morning to start a yoga session in my living room, and I didn't like the idea of blending kale smoothies for breakfast to stave off the years either. Give me a lie-in, a chocolate bar and three strong coffees in the morning instead. Who cares if it adds a couple of wrinkles? Life is for living. What sort of advice is that? Unfortunately, though, I am now subscribed for the whole year with no chance of cancelling it for another six months. I try to remain positive about the needless subscription and open the magazine, skim-reading it for the sake of the extortionate price I have paid.

With a fresh brew, I sit down at the kitchen table and flick through. Fancy clothes and the latest beauty products catch my eye. I try to tear myself away from the beautiful jade evening dress that I would never be able to wear around here. It takes all my willpower to stop myself ordering it though, as I consider the excitement I would feel when it arrives. I remind myself of what would happen next, since I know it would be the usual scenario. Just like today, after a small moment of euphoria, my next step would be to put it away in the cupboard knowing full well that it will never be worn. My mother would be horrified to see me spending the inheritance that is meant to keep me in my early retirement on these impulsive purchases. I am so incredibly fortunate to have the money from my mother's estate and I don't ever take it for granted, but then the guilt eats away at me as I see it being frittered away. I already feel awful enough about what I am doing, without considering what my mother would think of me. I don't need that judgement too.

While I am not someone who passes the blame, and I take responsibility for my behaviour, there does need to be more done about consumerism. Everywhere I look there is encouragement to spend. My social media knows exactly when to target me – on a lonely evening when I am doomscrolling in bed. After all, I am their target market. A woman on her own in her empty nest with nothing to do but scroll through adverts. If I don't stop, I will be buying a steam cleaner on a shopping channel next, or signing up for a gym membership I'll never use. I bought a crisp picker-upper once because I saw it on TV. I ordered it especially from Japan and I used the little hand-shaped tool to eat three of my crisps before I gave up; it was much easier to use my fingers. It's a slippery slope, and I want this to be the end of it.

When I put my beautiful new jacket away and spot a nearly identical one in my wardrobe with its labels still intact, I quickly close the cupboard door in shame. That's it. No more. I am going to stop all this crazy shopping right away. It is time for me to downsize my life and, if I am being honest with myself, my home. Do I really need four bedrooms when I am here alone? All this house does is remind me of how full it once was, and has since become so empty. Perhaps there are too many memories here and it is making me miserable. Maybe it's time for new memories to be made.

With my new resolution in mind to stop buying so much, I rip out the page of the magazine that has the dress on and throw it in the bin. I don't need any encouragement. But, as the page flips over on the top of the bin, a headline grabs my attention.

Decluttering! Is it Time You Decluttered Your Wardrobe and Your Life?

As the article hovers in my hand above the bin, I can't help but notice the words.

Decluttering is the new spending! What happened to that old adage 'less is more'? In today's world of consumerism, we seem to have forgotten that we don't need everything we are being sold. Imagine if one day all that clutter you've been collecting fell on top of you and you didn't even need half of it.

I picture the horror when the day comes, and I get squashed by all my clutter. What if Hannah has to fly back from Melbourne and clear out the stuff I have been ordering from Ann Summers recently? This thought alone stops me in my tracks, so I move away from the bin and read on.

Chapter Two

I hate to admit it, but I quickly discover that this article is perhaps one of the more sensible features I have read in years. For once, I'm being told to get rid of stuff instead of accumulating and buying into a lavish fancy lifestyle that the average person on the street cannot possibly afford. I am soon engrossed and need to know more about decluttering and downsizing. The article quickly fascinates me. It makes so much sense. Do we really need all the clutter we have in our homes? It is something I have been grappling with more and more recently. I have a feeling that I am about to throw myself into the latest buzzword – decluttering!

I look around at all the things I have picked up over the years. The first thing I notice is the pair of Delft china clogs I picked up in Amsterdam, which need a good dusting after being sat on the kitchen windowsill for over twenty years. Then I turn to the cuckoo clock on the wall in the kitchen; a memory from a trip to Switzerland that the three of us went on when Hannah was small. The cuckoo hangs lamely from a spring after Hannah managed to get up on a chair and pull at it, not long after we returned. She yanked it out with all her might with her tiny little hands before I caught her. It should have gone in the bin years ago, but I couldn't bear to throw it out. That cuckoo clock was the reminder of our special family holiday and so it has remained on the wall for all these years. Sentimentality is a particular problem of mine. After all, when the trip is over, only memories and souvenirs remain.

I turn my attention to the copper pan collection that is displayed in a glass cabinet beside the oven. There is zero sentimental value attached to those. I bought them at a designer outlet on a whim. They seemed like a spectacular bargain, even though I knew I would only be cooking for one and not entertaining people like this set suggested. As I look at the pans with hindsight, and the thought of clearing out my life in mind, I begin to realise that this was another purchase I certainly didn't need. After all, I eat a ready meal from a plastic tray most nights. How could I possibly think that shopping could replace the family unit that I miss so much? I need to get a grip. None of this can replace the yearning for my family. I begin to resent all this clutter and decide that those pans will be the first thing I need to let go of – along with the left-handed golf clubs I inexplicably bought at a charity shop, despite not being either left-handed or interested in golf.

I look at myself in the huge silver mirror – a recent online purchase – and admit the truth to myself: 'Sandy Davies, you have become a shopaholic.'

I stare at my reflection, realising that I have to resolve this problem. I am committed to stopping, although I have never been one to do things by halves. Paul always said it was everything or nothing with me. When I get an idea in my head then I tend to become totally engrossed in it. When I shop, I shop a lot, so when I clear out, I can imagine I might not have much left by the end of it.

Galvanised, I spring into action. No time like the present, as my mam used to say.

I roll up my sleeves, grab some bin bags and prepare to start. I look around and the full scale of the task assaults me. How on earth am I going to get through all this junk?

Do people follow feng shui nowadays? Looking at all this clutter, I imagine there is probably a lot of stagnant energy in this home. No wonder I am feeling a little overwhelmed and stuck in a rut at the moment. Maybe having a clear-out will release the flow of positive energy and my life will become more exciting overnight. I can always hope! From the thought of feng shui, my mind starts to wander and I consider whether I should fill my house with crystals to attract some of that positive energy. I saw some lovely ones for sale recently. A heap of rose quartz could do the trick…

'Nonsense, you need to get rid of things, not buy more!' I shout at myself. I try to refocus and not get carried away down a rabbit hole of crystal healing, returning to the task in hand.

With the copper pans in a bag ready to sell, the next thing I do is remove the cuckoo clock from the wall. I have a bit of a wobble and wonder if I can really bear to part with it. I tell myself to think rationally and not emotionally. This clock hasn't worked for over sixteen years – why do I need to keep it? *Memories*, my brain shouts at me! I tell my mind to shut up and throw the clock in the bin before I can be persuaded to put it back up. Removing it leaves a small, faded patch of paint on the wall where it has hung for all these years. It will need something new to cover it, unless I want to start redecorating. I could go out and buy something new to hang there – perhaps an art print or a mirror – but then I remember again what the clear-out is in aid of and a better idea strikes me. I have been looking for the perfect spot to put up a recent photo of Hannah. I am filled with joy as I replace the broken clock with a photo in a frame that was hidden among some ornaments. My gorgeous girl smiles down at me and already I feel better. Perhaps decluttering will be easier than I thought.

I feel an immense sense of satisfaction as I continue my clear-out and carefully put a glass decanter on top of the saucepans in the bag. The decanter was never used either and I wonder why I even bought it. Then I remember that I picked it up in the outlet, when I was out shopping with Debbie. Since she wanted one and told me how they were all the rage, I bought one. At the time, it felt like a bonding session with my bestie during our shopping trip. Now, as I look at the stuff already piling up in the bag, I feel disgusted. None of this was ever going to be used, and looking at it makes me feel so ashamed.

The doorbell intrudes on my self-loathing, and I remember Debbie had promised to come over with some fresh tomatoes from her greenhouse. Amid the stack of blue and black bin bags that are waiting to be filled, I desperately try to make some kind of space in the kitchen so we can have a catch-up.

I always look forward to our Saturday morning chats. Even though I can pick up the phone and speak to a few friends dotted around the UK, apart from retail staff Debbie can sometimes be the only person I see for a week or two. Hannah's having far too much fun settling into the glamorous Melbourne lifestyle, so although we are in touch regularly, we don't tend to ring each other more than once every couple of weeks.

'Hello, I come bearing tomatoes,' says Debbie, with a big smile on her face. The first time I met Debbie at a village fete when we first moved here, she was selling her prize tomatoes and was joking and smiling then. She is always such a positive person.

'Ooh, lovely. They look delicious. Maybe the microwave can have a night off. Come on in, but please excuse the mess.'

Perhaps I was a little too eager with my clear-out and should have at least waited until after Debbie had been over. I do have a habit of being a bit disorganised and overwhelmed, but the kitchen looks like a tip with all this clutter being redistributed around the floor. It is quite the struggle to search around for the cast-iron Japanese teapot I picked up in a fancy furniture store in Cardiff to make Debbie her brew.

'Not thinking of moving out, are you?' says Debbie, looking around at all the mess.

'Not seriously. Even though Hannah thinks I should have a new start in life, and I should probably downsize. But, no, I'm not planning on going anywhere quite yet. Besides, I have nowhere to go.'

I tell Debbie about the feature on decluttering that I just read, and she immediately agrees that it sounds like a great idea.

'I need to do that myself. Although,' she pauses, looking around, 'I've nothing like the amount of stuff you have.'

Has she noticed all along that I have a problem and not said anything?

'Yes, well. I've gone a bit over the top with my shopping recently, so I'm going to put a lot of it up for sale.'

'That's brilliant. You should put all the money together and treat yourself to a holiday or something. When was the last time you got out of here?'

'Good question.' I try to think. The furthest I've been in the past year or two was an Abba Voyage concert in London with Debbie. Paul, Hannah and I were always travelling. I suppose I stopped because I no longer had anyone to go with.

'You know, there are holidays for single travellers with no supplement. Why don't you plan an organised trip? That'd be nice.'

'I don't know. I'm not sure I fancy anything organised. I wouldn't want to go on a bus tour or anything. I've always liked doing my own thing. I'm happy enough with my own company, to be honest.'

'Well, if you don't mind me saying, you don't seem very happy in your own company. Since Hannah left you've been, well…'

'Well, what?'

'Miserable? Lonely? Umm, I don't know. You just don't seem your usual bubbly self.'

'I'm fine. I keep myself busy. In fact, it's super busy with my needle felting at the moment. I'm making fifty miniature labradoodles for a group on Facebook. They've already paid and everything. I've a load of new customers and I'm always getting new enquiries.'

'That's great. Although maybe you need to get out a bit more. Felting isn't going to introduce you to new people. It doesn't get you out there.'

'I don't need to meet anyone. Like I said, I'm very happy with my own company. I've got you, and I can always pick up the phone to friends.'

'Yup, I know. It's not always the same over the phone though, is it? You should go out and meet people. Maybe even start dating.'

'Absolutely no way. Nothing would be worse than going out on a date with someone I don't know. I'd much rather stick to my felting and early nights, thank you.'

'I understand. It's just that I heard Rachel, who works with Nigel, is dating again after Tom's death and it got me thinking.'

'I remember when Nigel said about that. It was quite a while ago now that Tom died.'

'I suppose. Anyway, talking of Nigel, he's being a right pain.'

'Oh, what's he up to now?'

'He's saying he doesn't want my mother over for Christmas this year.'

'But she comes every year.'

'I know. He's getting more cantankerous as the years go by. Bloody men. Imagine telling an eighty-year-old that she can't come this year.'

'No, that wouldn't be nice. I hope you manage to persuade him.'

'Yeah, I will. He can give me the silent treatment for all I care. He always does when something doesn't suit him. I'll have peace and quiet then. He does my head in, but I suppose at least he isn't as bad as Adrian. Did you hear what happened?' asks Debbie.

You can always guarantee she has the latest gossip on every one of our neighbours.

'No – unless Janice from the shop knows the gossip, I wouldn't hear anything.'

'You wouldn't believe it. He's only gone and stolen money from the cricket club. Adrian's been helping himself to the petty cash. No wonder he's got a new car on the drive.'

'Goodness, that must have been a lot of petty cash. I noticed he's also got one of those robot lawnmowers out the front.'

'Well, they're not cheap. See, rumour has it that he's been dipping his hand into the church roof collection too.'

'That's terrible. It's not surprising he's always first to volunteer for everything then.'

'Well, I'm not saying it out loud, but you've basically said what everyone's thinking.'

Debbie sits back with her tea; the silence and our imaginations are more powerful than any gossip about Adrian. This is mostly as deep as conversation goes on our street. We must all know everyone's business, but, on a positive note, if things go wrong, we are also there for each other. Nobody would ever get away with breaking into someone's house because a busybody would soon spot them through their window. Although I don't think Adrian will be getting much support from anyone after stealing from the local community.

'Oh, well, I hope Leanne will be okay. I bet she's embarrassed to show her face.'

I do feel sorry for Adrian's wife, even though she sometimes boasts about her new quartz-topped kitchen. I bet she's also got matching copper pans and a decanter.

'Yeah, well, we can't control what our partners do. She may have enjoyed the trappings of the money, but I don't believe she had a clue. She had to go straight down the doctor's for medication the moment she found out. Well, that's what one of the receptionists in the clinic told me.'

'Are the receptionists allowed to go round saying stuff like that? Isn't that confidential?'

'Yeah, of course it is, but you know how it is round here.'

I roll my eyes.

'Anyway, talking of errant husbands, I'd better be off and see what Nigel's up to. And you've got all your stuff to sort. I can't wait to hear where you decide to go on holiday with all the money when you sell everything. You could even do a Caribbean cruise with all this lot.'

'Oh, I don't know that I'll be going on holiday anywhere. Depends on how much I make, I suppose.'

We hug goodbye and Debbie makes me promise that I will sort some kind of holiday plan out. Spurred on by Debbie's enthusiasm for the clear-out, I start making a list of the items to go on auction sites. I may have lost quite a bit of money buying everything new but I'm sure they will still be worth a small fortune second-hand after everything has been put together.

I place things in piles and make a special stack of things I could never bear to part with; my mother's beloved crocheted christening blanket for Hannah for one. Then I make a heap of items that must go, which sadly includes my grey ceramic Dusty Bin from the Eighties. I put it in the pile for the charity shop. I'm pretty sure this will bring back memories for someone, but it's time for me to let go of mine, even though I have fond memories of picking it up at Neath Christmas Fayre with my mam.

By the end of the day, the spare room is crammed full of nearly-new stuff ready to sell. This one room alone looks like a hoarder's paradise. Like it belongs on one of those programmes where a whole team of people have to come in and help someone who has lost all control. A feeling of self-loathing and shame washes over me in a wave once again. I try to remind myself that this is why I am doing this. I am going to stop. I know it is wrong.

With photos taken of stuff to sell, I decide to start listing a couple of items before bed so that I can judge how much interest there is before spending days listing everything else. Sorting out clutter is tiring work, and I am almost done for the day. I rub my eyes, which are aggravated by the dust mites that I have unearthed, along with the tiredness that is creeping in.

However, as I am about to log off the auction site something grabs my attention. I can only assume that I have been targeted for this advert since I have just listed an assortment of rubber ducks that I pointlessly bought on a trip to the Netherlands, along with the Delft clogs, many years ago.

As my mouse hovers over the button to shut my computer down, I read the words over and over: 'Houseboat in Amsterdam for sale'. I love Amsterdam, and since I don't live too far away from Brecon, I have always been obsessed with houseboats. What a combination!

Despite my exhaustion and my resolution to not allow myself to be enticed by anything remotely material, my heart skips a beat as I look at the photo of the houseboat situated on a canal in the middle of Amsterdam. There isn't much detail in the small thumbnail advert, but it invites me to click for more information. My mind is telling me to ignore it, but my heart is beating fast. It is too late; the adrenaline is already pumping through me. It is as if I have a little devil on my shoulder shouting, 'Open it. Take a quick look! What harm can it do?'

I wrestle with my conscience but, as usual, listen to the naughty devil on my shoulder and open the advert up. I feel the endorphins immediately. My pulse rate quickens further. I am almost breathless and the tiredness has quickly dissipated.

Hannah's words ring in my head as I read over the advert. 'A completely new start, Mam. That's what you need.' In the past, when she was younger, this time of year always brought exciting new beginnings. September came with a new term at school, new teachers, new uniform, new pencils: everything was shiny and fresh. As the leaves fell off the trees, the autumn season felt like a time for renewal. A time to start over. The advert makes me wish for that new start. However, as I told Hannah when she tried to give me her advice, and I tell myself now, 'I'll be fifty-six next month. What if I'm too old for a new start?'

Despite my fears, I can't resist reading through the specifications of the houseboat. I mean, it is only window shopping. I am not actually buying it. I haven't spent a euro. It is just curiosity. And what could be wrong with that?

I put my reading glasses on for a closer inspection and stare at the screen in front of me.

> Environmentally friendly houseboat for sale.
> Constructed from sustainable materials, this stunning Nordic houseboat is available immediately.

My eyes skip past the bits about how it's equipped for harsh winters with its 123 mm wall insulation and the solar panels on the roof. I am too mesmerised by the fact that it's sustainable and I'd be doing my bit for the planet while also relishing my favourite words – *available immediately*!

There is only one thing to do and so, before I head to bed, I complete the online enquiry form. Only then can I shut down my computer as my mind starts to become consumed with thoughts of what it must be like to live on a houseboat. I'm sure it would be amazing. After all, I watched *Rosie and Jim* enough times with Hannah when she was small to know that life on a houseboat is utterly idyllic. I realise that's a kids' show, but I've also seen lots of those lifestyle TV programmes about people living on houseboats. They all seem to live the dream. And those ones in Brecon always look lovely…

I might have promised myself that I would stop spending, but it was Debbie who suggested I needed a holiday. Why don't I do better than that and heed the advice of both Hannah and Debbie? Being half Irish, I have an EU passport and don't have to worry about the immigration side of things.

A new start in a new country would beat any two-week holiday. I mean, it is better than coming back to a cold and empty home with a few tacky souvenirs for the kitchen and a couple of extra kilos on my waist. Instead, I would be living the houseboat dream, and the holiday would never end! Besides, the thought of downsizing has been in the back of my mind for a while, and how much better could it get than downsizing to live on a barge? Surely this could be one purchase that is worth every single euro.

Chapter Three

For someone who has spontaneously sent a sales enquiry to a company advertising on the internet, my inbox is remarkably quiet. I thought companies were only too keen to get sales enquiries, and I am surprised I am not already on their database. I am on edge each time my email pings, which is frequently, since I have been automatically subscribed to newsletters every darn time I have bought anything online. At least I manage a productive morning when I unsubscribe from four clothing companies that I don't remember subscribing to.

Another email pings into my inbox, clearly from some other database that I didn't know I was on. Appalled, I press delete and shout at the computer that I really don't need an over-fifties funeral plan! The cheek of these companies once you turn fifty. I am not quite ready to pop my clogs. Talking of clogs makes me think of Amsterdam again. I am starting to get impatient and decide to call the company selling the houseboat. Even as I dial the number, I tell myself this idea is absolutely ludicrous, but I still can't help myself. The sensible part of me is almost fearful of what I will come out with on the phone. With this level of overexcitement, I am going to be handing over my credit card details to some random person. I curse myself for not having more self-restraint.

Anyway, I find myself disappointed when I am transferred to a recorded message. That is when I remember what day it is: Sunday. Of course! That's why I haven't heard anything. In my eagerness, it completely slipped my mind that it is the weekend.

Fortunately for me, the internet is available all day, every day, and so I start searching online to see what else is out there. Now that the idea is in my head, I want to learn everything I can about life on board a houseboat. I look at some of the sales listings but they are all way beyond my budget. I start to lose hope of fulfilling this dream, but when I find the blog of someone who sold up everything and moved to a houseboat in Brecon, I can't stop reading about her experience. She's a single woman, like me, although a bit younger. I read her words as she describes waking up on the canal with the sound of birds for company.

'I should have done it years ago. Living on a houseboat in Brecon is pure heaven,' she writes.

I have always liked Brecon, and it would be a lovely place to live, with a great theatre and all those lovely country pubs, but I am looking for a completely new start. I can easily drive there in half an hour. What sort of adventure would that be? I quite like the idea of going somewhere further away and now I am consumed with the idea of Amsterdam.

I look at the photos of the blogger's bright green houseboat. She has a silver watering can on the front of the boat, filled with sunflowers. The houseboat windows are decorated with pretty little nets and there is an abundance of leafy green plants on the roof. She even has hanging baskets. It really is a home from home and I can see why her lifestyle feels so heavenly to her. I consider commenting on the blog and asking her lots of questions. I would love to know all the practical things, like whether it is safe to live on a barge, or if you could drown in the middle of the night while fast asleep.

However, before I can start racking up my questions, I am surprised to hear my phone ring. Hannah isn't due to call today so I hope everything's okay. I notice that the number calling is from overseas but it's not an Australian dialling code.

'Goedemorgen,' says the voice.

'Hi, sorry, English?'

'Yes, of course. Good morning, you called the office? I'm Gerrit from the *makelaar*, umm, the agency.'

'Oh, yes. I was expecting an email. I didn't realise you'd actually call.'

'We're closed today, but I went into the office to collect something and could see we had missed a call. I thought I'd call you back. How can I help you?'

His Dutch accent makes me picture Amsterdam as he speaks.

I clear my throat and explain about the enquiry I sent.

'Ah, let me see which houseboat you're talking about. They sell very fast.'

As Gerrit does his search and remains silent down the phone, I am full of adrenaline. What if it's no longer available? My heart sinks at the thought of that beautiful boat having been sold and I decide that if it's still for sale then I am going to take a leap of faith and go for it. How bad a purchase can it be if they sell that fast? It already sounds more like an investment than one of my silly purchases. This could be like shares, or bonds. It is technically property, after all, and that is always a wise investment. It could double in price in no time…

'Ah, I see your enquiry now. It is the Nordic thirty-six-foot one, right?'

'Yes, yes, that's the one. Please tell me it hasn't been sold.'

'Ah, I'm sorry. It's gone. It was a beautiful barge.'

I sink back in my computer chair in disappointment. How could I be so downhearted about something I didn't even know existed twenty-four hours ago?

'Damn. It's so gorgeous.'

'Don't be disappointed. If I can take the particulars of what you're looking for then I can put you on a list and let you know if we get anything similar.'

'Oh, well, I was looking for something like that and I wanted it now, really. I don't know that I want to wait.'

'Are you looking for a narrow boat in particular, or a wide beam?'

'Sorry, I don't really know the difference.'

'Umm, okay. So, the wide-beam barges, as the name suggests, would be wider. It would give you more living space. They can be around twelve feet wide.'

I can't decide if it matters at this stage since I am decluttering and downsizing so will only take my absolute essentials with me. The whole idea is that it is time for me to simplify my life. Do I want to go for the bigger size? Would it cost more to run? Who knows?

'Goodness, I don't know. How wide is a narrow boat? Perhaps I need to do a bit of homework about all of this, after all.'

'For a narrow boat you're looking at six foot ten inches. I suggest you also start by thinking about the mooring. Do you want a permanent mooring, or are you looking to sail the barge around the Netherlands?'

'No, I definitely don't want to sail it around. I want it as a houseboat to live in. I certainly won't move it. I won't even drive down the M4; I'm never going to drive a barge down a canal in Amsterdam.'

'Right, um. Okay, because there are no more fixed houseboats allowed in Amsterdam. Did you know this?'

'Well, um, no.' I realise I sound such a novice as I speak to him. I know nothing and am literally out of my depth here. I hadn't thought too much about the technicalities, only the allure of a houseboat.

'So, you see, the canals are completely full now so you can't find a space and just put a barge on there. You have to buy a houseboat like you would buy a flat. It comes with the mooring and you have to wait for one to come up for sale. It's not as easy as people think.'

'Oh.'

'The houseboat you were looking at didn't come with the mooring. You need the houseboat with the space to keep it if you are certain that you want to be in Amsterdam.'

'Yes, I definitely want Amsterdam, and I want it to be like a home that I live in. I know that much.'

'Okay. Well, that's very hard to find, although I do have...' I hear Gerrit rustle some papers. 'Umm, no, maybe not.'

'What do you mean, maybe not? Do you have something there?'

'Something's going on the market tomorrow. The mooring's in Lijnbaansgracht, a very pleasant residential neighbourhood but...'

'But what? Oh my gosh. How much is it?'

'Well, it's not as expensive as the others, as it's not quite as sustainable or eco-friendly as the one you saw. In fact, it is nothing like the one you enquired about. This one is more traditional, shall I say.'

The mention of traditional intrigues me. I do like traditional things. I mean, I kept that cuckoo clock for years.

'It needs some work, so it's priced to be sold quickly. It will go tomorrow for sure, even if it's just for the mooring.'

'Well, how much is it?'

'It's a bargain price. That's why I know it will go right away.'

'Like how much of a bargain?'

'Two hundred and fifty thousand euros.'

I would hardly call a quarter of a million euros a bargain. That amount of money is still a fortune. I mean, it is not exactly in the same league as that pair of black flares I bought in the sale the other week. It was obvious why those hideous things were a bargain. However, as an only child, with the sale of my mother's house not long having gone through, I do have the finances available to go ahead. I wouldn't need to arrange any loan that could halt the purchase. But still, it is a huge amount of money.

'Many of the houseboats are 450,000 euros and above. This is a good price,' says Gerrit.

I suppose if they usually go for that sort of amount then it is a bargain. In fact, it sounds as though the mooring alone could be an investment for retirement.

'Can you send me some photos? I'm seriously interested. Please, this sounds absolutely perfect.'

'I can send you photos, but you must remember that it needs some attention. Although, for peace of mind, we will get a survey report done for you if you wish. But we do believe that structurally everything is fine.'

'Well, as long as the structural report is okay then I don't mind having a project. This sounds like just what I need.'

I'm quite crafty, and love giving things a new lease of life. I am a dab hand with a paintbrush and my needle felting. The thought strikes that this will be a much bigger undertaking than making a felt dog or unicorn, but I push it aside.

'I'll send the photos over now then, yeah?'

'Yes, Gerrit, please do send them over. Oh, and also, if you have any information like a structural report, recent sales prices of similar houseboats, whatever you have, can you send it all over to me?'

'Right. Will do. It's going to be a big file so it might take some time to upload, but call me back once you've seen them and let me know what you think. Just remember that it will be live on our website tomorrow at nine and I expect it to be gone within the hour.'

'Okay. I'll call you the moment I have them.'

'Ah, I am just going through the file now and I think I have a video of the boat, so you can have a virtual walk around it. Shall I send that too?'

'That's brilliant. Yes, please and thank you so much. You're so helpful.'

I rush to the kitchen and attempt to make a strong coffee, but I am almost shaking with delight as I spoon in the coffee granules. My head feels like a complete whirl-wind of excitement. A horrible thought occurs: what if it is terrible? Manky and rotting? I am going to be so disappointed. But then again, what if it is exactly how I dream it could be? Even if I fall in love with it, it is a big risk buying something in another country without having actually seen it. There is so much money at stake if something goes wrong here.

I turn to look at the fridge magnet I picked up with the other souvenirs from when I went to Amsterdam on a girls' weekend many years ago. Like the shade of blue on the dusty clogs, it was so long ago that the image of a red windmill has faded away with time. Perhaps it is the memory of that fun and carefree trip that is spurring me on right now. It was a fantastic city break. We were young, with the world at our feet. Nicky was my best friend in those days, and she and I shopped until we dropped and bought the wildest matching cowboy boots. Then we ate Dutch pancakes and waffles until we nearly burst.

The memory of the trip still means everything to me as Nicky died of breast cancer four years ago. She was only fifty-four and had been my best friend since we first worked together at the local council offices when I left school. We bonded from the start and when she went through her treatment, I really thought she'd be okay. I was there beside her every step of the way. I just couldn't believe that with the advances in modern medicine she wouldn't get better. I promised her that we'd go back to Amsterdam when she was clear of the cancer. But we never did. So, this is also for Nicky. She'd have loved the fact that I was spending the pension I paid into over all those years at the council to run off to live on a houseboat in the city we enjoyed so much. This would be just the kind of thing she'd have done if she'd had the opportunity. Life is so short, and thinking about how Nicky was far too young to get sick spurs me on. We only get one chance at life, and I have to take a brave leap; just as Nicky would have done if she was here. It's sad to think she can't enjoy any more adventures with me, but the thought of

Nicky and our wonderful Amsterdam trip motivates me to find out more about this houseboat. I can already picture myself walking along the canals, bunch of tulips in one hand and a bottle of wine to sit back and relax on the boat with in the other. Right now, I have never wanted anything more.

As I walk back to the computer with my coffee, so that I can stare at the screen, willing the photos to arrive, I hear the ping of an email. I almost trip over the corner of my rug as I rush to the screen. If it is junk mail, the whole neighbourhood may hear me scream in frustration.

I am relieved when I see the email is from Gerrit with some specifications and the first few photos.

Okay… I must admit that it is a bit shabbier than I expected. It certainly doesn't have the modern sleekness of the Nordic barge I fancied but it doesn't deter me. It's not hideous or anything, just a bit unloved. The red paint is peeling, the blue window frames are possibly a bit rotten, but if it was on one of those DIY programmes, I'm sure they would say that there isn't anything too untoward. The damage all looks pretty superficial. Hopefully there isn't a big hole hidden somewhere, but on the surface it appears as though I could get it back to its former glory with some TLC. Aside from all of that, the coveted mooring in central Amsterdam is enough to make me want to agree on the spot. However, I manage to wait long enough for the virtual show-around to download. I click on the link and watch closely as the door opens into an open-plan living area and kitchen. Just like on the outside, it all looks unloved and run-down, needing a new lick of paint, but nothing that I can't resolve. It still looks so cute and dinky. I can just see myself living there.

I ring Gerrit back, who answers right away.

'Hi, so what did you think?'

'It's beautiful. Well… umm, it needs work, as you said, but I can see past all of that. How fast can you do the survey on it?'

'It just takes a couple of days. I can arrange it tomorrow and it will probably take the surveyor a few days to write it all up. So, by the end of the week it should be with you. You'll need to pay a deposit first, I'm afraid.'

'Okay, but what happens if the report's really bad? Can I get my money back?'

'Usually, it's a case of losing the deposit if you back out. Since I'm quite positive there won't be any issues that come up, I can give you half of it back, excluding the fee for the survey. Would that be fair enough? I'll put my money where my mouth is, so to speak.'

I think for a moment. It seems fair since he is taking it off the market so no one else can sneak in and gazump me. Worst-case scenario, I lose a surveyor's fee plus a bit more, although the sensible part of my brain tells me surveys are never cheap. However, I really need to know the figures before I can commit.

'Okay. Well, that sounds fair. If you can send me a breakdown of all the costs, then I can send the deposit to take it off the market.'

'Well, umm, that's great. But I would prefer it if you, or someone you trust, saw it first. Do you have a friend in Amsterdam who I could meet tomorrow morning? I'm happy to show them around.'

'No, I don't know anyone there.'

'Okay. I mean, it's a rare opportunity but, as much as I love a sale, I want you to be happy. I don't like to sell something without a buyer viewing it.'

'Oh, I'll be happy. I take full responsibility. I promise not to blame you for anything.'

Although as I say it, I realise this isn't going to be like some of my impulse purchases that I return to the shops the following day. If the figures all stack up, this is a huge commitment. There is no fourteen-day return on a houseboat, but I do have the survey clause. If it's a dreadful mistake then I only lose half the deposit. And Gerrit is quite confident that the survey will come back fine.

'Okay, I'll send all the fees and the paperwork you need right away. Thank you very much.'

Gerrit sounds as astounded as I am that I have just tentatively agreed to such a huge purchase without even seeing it properly, but I've never been one to dilly-dally about anything. I might get things wrong, but I don't want to miss out either. This sounds like an opportunity that is far too good to miss, provided the report is okay.

As I finish my now stone-cold coffee, I am both elated and nervous. I have never made this big a purchase on the spur of the moment before and I am aware that what I am about to do is ridiculously risky.

The last time I made such a big investment was for the cottage. When Paul and I bought this place, it took heaps of viewings and talks long into the night about whether it was the right place to start a family before we committed. This time, there isn't anyone to discuss the pros and cons with. It is my decision alone. As I zoom in to the photos and watch the video one more time before going to bed, I can't help but wonder if that is a big crack that I see down the side of the barge. I pop my reading glasses on once more for a closer inspection. I manage to convince myself that I am seeing things and dismiss any concerns.

After checking out the agent's details and making sure it is all legitimate, I press send on a deposit to a bank in Amsterdam so that it will be there for Gerrit in the morning. Now all I can do is hope for the best.

Chapter Four

I once read that self-control wanes in the evening. This is why, if you're on a diet, you often break it by the end of the day as you are more impulsive. I have found this to be the same with spending. I can have the best intentions all day and then in the evening buy something utterly ridiculous.

As I wake up the next morning the first question I ask myself is did I really shell out a huge deposit on a houseboat without seeing it last night. When I remember that I did indeed pay that deposit, my nerves start to get the better of me. It is a huge commitment, but what was I supposed to do when I had the pressure of knowing that if the deposit wasn't received by the morning, someone else was going to snap it up? I try to calm down by reminding myself that the fear of missing out on a spot in the heart of Amsterdam was way stronger than the idea that I could make a mistake. After all, life would be boring if we were afraid to take risks. This is one risk I have to take. Besides, if it is as great a mooring as I am told it is, then surely I can always sell it on if it doesn't work out for me. I might even make a large profit.

By the time I get out of bed, an email has already arrived from Gerrit with some paperwork I need to look through. As I read it, I can clearly see that I need a lawyer. It's in Dutch and my Google Translate can't keep up with all the jargon. I decide that, even if the structural report is all okay, I will find a lawyer to check over the paperwork before parting with the rest of the money. I may have been a little impulsive with the deposit, but I am not that reckless.

I sit back and look at the computer screen in front of me. Buying this houseboat before it went on the open market makes me feel as though I belong to some exclusive club. I can already see how my emotions were swayed by the thought of getting a good deal before anyone else. This is exactly what I need to stop doing, although I persuade myself that this isn't like my normal purchases. This is a new life I'm buying. It's not a new kettle, or a handbag to be tossed aside, but a life. This is the new start Hannah wanted me to have. Excitedly, I decide to call to tell her that I have taken her advice. I want Hannah to be the first to know.

'Mam, do you know what time it is here? It's the middle of the night,' she answers sleepily.

'Oh, I'm sorry. I did think it might be late, but I was too excited to wait.'

'What is it? Everything okay?'

'Yes, yes! I took your advice. I'm getting a new start.'

'You're on Tinder?'

'No, a completely new start! I'm going to sell up and move.'

'Really? You haven't mentioned anything about moving before. Please tell me you've not been looking at those retirement flats they just built, have you? You're not that old yet.'

'No, don't be silly. Far from it. I'm off on an adventure to another part of the world.'

'What? Are you moving to an island in Greece? Like, doing a Shirley Valentine?'

'Good gosh, no. I'm off to Amsterdam. I've just put the deposit down on a houseboat there.'

'Amsterdam? Seriously? Woah. Wait a minute. This is a joke, right?'

I can imagine Hannah sitting up sharply now I have her attention.

'Nope. It's not a joke. I've just put a deposit down on a houseboat on a beautiful part of the canal. It has so much to offer and…'

'Stop right there. Mam, you can't be serious. Amsterdam? You can't live in a city on your own. I don't want to be horrible but you're not the most streetwise person I know. I mean, you've lived in Wales all your life. It's not like you're from a big city. You've never even lived anywhere apart from Abergavenny.'

'Well, neither had you until you left for Melbourne. What difference does it make for me?'

'It's different. I'm here with Dad and all my cousins. Who do you know in Amsterdam?'

'Nobody, really. The agent who's selling the place is very nice though.'

'Mam, please be careful. You don't know who this guy is and besides, won't it be cold on a houseboat? You know how you can be a bit of a sun-worshipper.'

'Yes, but that only ages your skin. I finally understand that, in my fifties. Imagine, Amsterdam! It's going to be wonderful. I'm going to snuggle up by the fire on my houseboat and do my felting. I'll get through all the books I bought and never had time to read. This is how to spend retirement. It's going to be sheer bliss.'

'Bliss? You might think it sounds lovely on paper, but you'll be lonely there all on your own. You've got friends at home. You don't know anyone there.'

'It won't be lonely when I have all my hobbies. Anyhow, I found a houseboat in a lovely area that is apparently very friendly. From what I've read on the internet, life on a houseboat is less lonely than being here. They say it's like one big community.'

'Wow. It sounds like you've made your mind up and nothing I can say is going to change it. It's like you're brainwashed! Is it definitely legit?'

'I'm not brainwashed. I know what I'm doing. I've made sure to get a survey and I've checked out all the information. It all adds up. I have to say I'm very disappointed you have so little faith in me.'

'I do have faith in you. I know you're not stupid, but you know what some of these things are like on the internet. Sometimes they're too good to be true and there might be some kind of catch. Look, if you're sure, I can't exactly stop you. It's not what I expected you to announce, but if you're sure this is a good idea…'

'Yup. I haven't felt more excited about something since…' I try to think back to when I was this excited, but nothing springs to mind.

'Then I guess I'm kind of happy for you. But please make sure you can lock the doors properly and stay safe.'

'I promise I will.' I smile as I think how Hannah sounds like she's the parent here. Although her words do sit a little uncomfortably with me. What if I am being irresponsible by spontaneously buying a houseboat in the middle of Amsterdam? As I think about it like that, I realise I am being *incredibly* irresponsible! I remind myself that it's too late to get all the deposit back but it's not too late to back out completely. Even if the survey is fine, there is still time if I have buyer's remorse at the last minute.

But, by the next day, my dream is back on track. I have zoomed in to and inspected every photo of the houseboat and watched the video repeatedly with my spectacles on and I don't think it was a crack I spotted. The houseboat needs painting, yes, but the sun that shines through the wheelhouse makes up for any shabbiness. I can see past all of that and, with a little bit of imagination, can picture myself in the evening with a steaming hot chocolate, living my best life. With that thought in mind, any buyer's remorse I had is soon forgotten. I print out a photo of the houseboat and pin it on the fridge with my special magnet. I think of lovely Nicky once again. She would be so excited for me right now. That makes me think of Debbie – she is not going to believe what I have done, and I can't wait to tell her next.

I rush around to her home next door to break the news. Nigel answers the door in his slippers. He looks ready for bed.

'You alright? You don't usually pop round in the evening. Aren't you watching one of those boring soaps? Or is it all this *Strictly* stuff nowadays?' he says.

'Oh, I don't know. I'm not one for much TV.' Now that I think about it, I probably won't even bother with one on the houseboat.

'Oh, of course. You do that thing where you stuff animals.' He makes it sound like I'm a taxidermist!

'Felting,' I correct him.

'Yeah, that. You'll be looking for Debs then, I expect? Come on in.'

I wipe my feet on the doormat that always make me smile. I read the familiar words as I step off it. *Please Hide Packages from Husband*. If I still had a husband, I'd have definitely got one of those for the house. I wonder if I'll need a doormat on a houseboat? There are so many things I don't know yet.

'This is a nice surprise. I wasn't expecting you,' says Debbie.

'I hope it's not inconvenient.'

'No, not at all. I've just put the kettle on. How about one of my pomegranate tea bags infused with hibiscus shells?'

'Sounds very fancy. Go on then.'

Debbie loves to be adventurous with her tea bags. I am more of a PG Tips fan myself.

'So, what's happening then? And why have you got the biggest smile on your face? I've not seen that look in a long time. Don't tell me you've gone on one of those dating sites and met someone lovely after all? It'd be quick work if you have changed your mind.'

'No! You're as bad as Hannah. A man is never going to make me smile again, believe me. I've had my lovely family – those days are over. I'm content being single because it also means I can do whatever I please, which is something I just did.'

'Huh, what're you on about?'

'I've just bought a houseboat!'

'A houseboat?'

'Yup, like a barge.'

'Really? Wow. Well, that's just fabulous. I've always thought those boats going up and down the canal in Brecon looked gorgeous. What a great idea. Will you spend weekends on it? It's not far for me to come up and visit. We could go to the pub up there that does those lovely Sunday lunches.'

'Oh, it's not a barge in Brecon that I'm buying.'

'A barge. You're going to buy a barge?' interrupts Nigel.

'Yeah, I'm so excited.'

'Oh, I'd think twice if I were you. Is it too late to back out? I used to work with a guy who lived on a houseboat. He always smelt of damp.'

'Don't listen to him. You won't smell of damp,' says Debbie.

'She might.'

'Oh my gosh, I hope not.'

'So, where's the barge then? If it's not Brecon it must be Monmouth way,' says Debbie.

'No, it's actually on a canal in Amsterdam.'

'Amsterdam? Isn't that full of people on wacky baccy?' says Nigel.

'My goodness, Nigel! Can you be happy for Sandy, please? Oh, he's a right miserable so-and-so.'

'I'm just realistic.'

'It's okay. Amsterdam is amazing. Have you ever been there, Nigel?' I ask.

'No, I've been to Denmark, though. Danish, Dutch, it's all the same, isn't it? It's the same language and everything.'

'No, it's not,' says Debbie. She rolls her eyes at him in disgust. 'Ignore him. He's so ignorant. Honestly.'

I know Nigel isn't the worldliest person on earth, so I am amazed he has even been to Denmark, although if I remember correctly that was for an organised football club event. If the rest of his club hadn't gone then I'm sure he wouldn't have bothered getting a passport.

'Well, Nigel, I'll have to show you around and you can find out for yourself how fabulous it is. You'll both have to come and visit when I'm all sorted. There's a lot of culture in Amsterdam and around the area, actually. Did you know there's a fantastic Van Gogh museum? Then there's the Rijksmuseum, which is full of masterpieces by Rembrandt, and...'

'The only masterpiece I want to see are those roast dinners Debs makes me.'

'I give up. How could I marry such an uncultured human being?' says Debbie.

Nigel winks at Debbie and I can't decide if he's teasing her or being serious. But it does make me think how nice it is to be single and not have any man showing me up in front of my friends. Not that Paul ever did, to be fair, but I've noticed a lot of older men undermining their wives recently. Is it a midlife thing?

'Anyway, the houseboat is going to be fabulous, I'm sure of it. Look, here's a photo.' I take out my phone, scrolling past the beautiful screensaver I have of Hannah on an Australian beach and showing them both a photo that I have already saved.

Nigel peers down at the photo.

'I hope you didn't pay too much for it. You do know what they say about boats of any kind, don't you?'

'Umm, no.'

'Bring Out Another Thousand. B-O-A-T. Get it? They're bloody expensive things. Never stop costing money.'

'Well, this one seems to be a bit of a bargain. I've got a video here if you want a look.'

'Perhaps that's because it needs a lot of money spending on it.'

'No, it isn't. Look,' I start playing the video but Nigel still doesn't seem keen.

'Is that a big crack I see down the side?'

'No, you're wrong! I checked myself. It just needs a lick of paint. They don't think there is anything structurally wrong, but to be certain I asked the agent for a survey. I'm not a complete moron, you know.'

'It looks beautiful. Seriously, Nigel, will you go away? This is women's talk. We really don't need you and your mansplaining.'

Sulkily Nigel finally walks off and leaves us alone.

'We should have told him we were going to discuss my endometriosis, that would have got rid of him,' says Debbie, laughing. Then she lowers her voice.

'I must admit, I'm so jealous of you. What I wouldn't do to run off and have a new start. Marriage isn't all it's cracked up to be when you're menopausal and everything your husband does gets on your bloody nerves.' She takes a sip of her tea and rolls her eyes. I do feel for her as they've been bickering for some time now.

'Well, just remember that you can visit anytime. You'll always be welcome. If you ever need a break, just come over and I'll be there for you.'

'That means so much. Thank you. I might just take you up on that. Oh, Sandy, it's going to be so amazing for you. Like I say, I envy you so much.'

'Well, there's a lot of work I have to do before my new start. I've still got to get rid of all the clutter I've accumulated over the years. Not to mention finding a buyer for the house. I know it might be risky selling up before I know how it's going to go out there, but either way it's time to downsize, even if I hate life on a barge and end up coming home.'

'Why would you hate it? You've always loved Amsterdam. You always said how it reminds you of Nicky.'

'Yeah, I know, but that was one weekend a very long time ago with some very special memories. When I stop for a moment, I realise quite how bonkers and irrational this decision sounds.'

'You can always come back and, selfishly, I'd be happy if you do. What will I do without my bestie next door?'

'We'll manage. We can still have our Saturday morning catch-up. We'll just have to do it on the phone or whatever.'

'Well, I'm certainly going to live vicariously through you. I can't wait to see what you make of your new home. I just know it's going to be gorgeous.'

'Thank you. I'm not sure I have the faith you have in me, but I'll try my best to make it a cosy home.'

As I bid farewell to Debbie, and Nigel who is sulking in his armchair, I look back at their beautiful Abergavenny cottage with its ivy climbing up the walls, just like mine. I watch as Nigel gets up to close the curtains as I walk down the path. There might not be a lot of love going on inside there right now, but it certainly looks like a loving, happy home on the outside. I only hope the houseboat can be just as cosy by the time I put my stamp on it and that it won't be the damp place that Nigel envisions. I pray that I am not making a mistake and remind myself that I still have a get-out clause if the survey shows anything unexpected.

Chapter Five

Less than forty-eight hours later, a full seven-page survey lands in my inbox. Before I can open the report, Gerrit's email explains that, as he thought, everything is okay. I open the survey to inspect it for myself; it all looks professional and has been signed off by the surveyor. Gerrit has gone to the trouble of getting the Dutch report translated into English for me. I scan through it, noticing phrases like 'bilge pumps' and how there is 'soft wood in an area starboard aft'. I don't really get it, but I guess the most important part is the final line. 'Summary: Satisfactory – good.'

With everything satisfactory, it means that my purchase will go ahead and, since I am not one to hang around, I excitedly decide to start on tackling the downsizing. I soon learn that it is not only hard work that is involved. It seems that downsizing comes with a barrage of emotions I had never thought about. I have only gone through the first drawer when I find myself getting emotional as I come across hospital photos of Hannah on the day she was born, my wedding to Paul, pictures of my parents, and also my grandparents who are long gone. Four generations all stuffed in one drawer. Photos that are becoming faded memories.

On the first morning alone, I am reminded how much has changed in my life. Looking at photos of my parents and grandparents is a reminder of how fragile our lives are and why I need to make the most of my time remaining on this earth. Buying a houseboat might be my wildest idea yet, but if I don't do it then what will my life be like in a few years? I could be sat here alone apart from my felted animals, gossiping about who is doing what in the village and hoping I have enough money left to heat this large house, cursing myself for the money I've frittered away over the years. It would be my fault entirely if I couldn't afford heating because a friendly shop assistant had persuaded me that I needed the latest kitchen gadget or fashion accessory.

I have never needed a new start more than I do right now. Although, as I look at the amount of work I have ahead of me, I realise that moving to another part of the world, buying a houseboat and imagining my cosy nights indoors through the autumn were the romantic parts. Looking at this unnecessary stuff that I have accumulated over the years like some sort of deranged magpie, knowing I will have to sort and shift it all, is something else.

With a strong coffee in hand, I can see that this is a job I am going to need a little help with. I call Debbie to see if she's doing anything, and since she wants to escape Nigel whingeing about the football results, she tells me she will gladly help me with this mammoth task. While I wait for her to arrive, I find a clearance company online and book them in for a week's time, when I will have been able to sort out what I will keep – which will have to be very little – from what is to be sold or thrown out. As with any huge job, I will have to take this step by step, and so I decide to do it one room at a time.

Despite having already made a start on the kitchen by listing the pans and a brand-new china plate set on an auction site, I decide that I probably need to leave the kitchen until last. After all, I still need to make my meals for one for a little while longer. So, since the spare room is the place where we kept most of the junk, I decide this is the first room to start.

Debbie arrives and we both look at the wardrobe that is bursting at the seams. One of the reasons I can hardly close it is because my wedding dress still hangs there, taking up much of the space. Until now, it never occurred to me to part with it since we had such a beautiful wedding day surrounded by my family, who were all still alive and happy back then. But now I am finally ready to let it go. In fact, it feels empowering to make the decision and say goodbye to it. I don't need a huge wedding dress to remember that day. It is a memory that nobody can take away from me. Besides, the dress no longer fits and there is no way I'd have space for it on a house-boat. It's not like Hannah would ever wear it either. My meringue wedding dress puffs out like one of those toilet roll covers from the Eighties. In fact, Hannah always found my wedding photos hilariously dated; she would be more of a bohemian beach bride.

Together, Debbie and I pull the dress out with all our might. It is incredibly heavy, and I am surprised I managed to wear it comfortably all day, although with the excitement I probably didn't realise its weight.

'How on earth was I able to breathe in this thing?' I say, looking at the stiff boned bodice.

'We made some pretty stupid decisions back then. Look at me, I married Nigel.' Debbie laughs but I am not sure she is truly joking.

'Oh, he's not that bad.'

'Hmm, I have days when I do wonder if I had my time again whether I'd have bothered.'

'Really? I think I'd still have married Paul. Even if someone had told me what would end up happening. We had so many good years, and I wouldn't trade that for anything. Besides, Hannah wouldn't be the person she is if Paul and I had never met. No, it's all for the best. I have zero regrets,' I say as I throw the dress in the pile for the charity shop.

'Oh, look at this. I remember your mother wearing it. The colour really suited her,' says Debbie, distracted by a pink silk blouse she finds in the wardrobe. She pulls it out, and even after all this time we are overpowered by the heady scent of the Poison perfume Mam wore, despite being merged with the musty aroma of all the old clothes in here. The fragrance brings back every memory I associate with her. I immediately picture her putting her make-up on and how she used to sit at her dressing table squirting on her favourite scent. Then, finally, I think how the smell reminds me of the time I took a bottle into the hospital during her final days to see if it would help bring her round, as if it were some sort of smelling salts. As I remember how my plan didn't work, I realise just how ready I am for a new start. All of that is in the past and I have a new future to look forward to in a new country.

Then, as if it's some kind of sign, a photo flies out from underneath a jumper. I hold it in my hands, cherishing the memory as I look at the photo of Nicky and I standing in front of a windmill with tulips all around us. It was a wonderful springtime trip, and I forgot how everything was so colourful and in bloom. I press it to my heart, and it feels as though Nicky is giving me the nod of approval.

This is one item I won't be getting rid of, and I resolve to put the photo in a frame when I organise my new home.

With renewed determination, I continue with my purge of a lifetime of clutter, and by the end of the morning I have an empty pine wardrobe that I can sell to the house clearance people. The bedroom might look like a bomb has hit it, but I have to admire what we have achieved in a few hours. Debbie has to head back to drop Nigel off at the pub for a rugby lunch he's attending, but I am determined to carry on with my project for the rest of the day.

After a short break to have a couple of Jaffa Cakes for strength, I tackle Hannah's room. She was never planning on coming back and so, like Paul, she took everything she wanted with her, so this is probably one of the easiest rooms in the house. Already there isn't much left, except for a few posters on the wall of boy bands I have never heard of apart from when Hannah talked about them. Despite having grown into a woman in this room, she never took down those posters, something Paul and I used to tease her about. As I tear the first one down, I get another little niggle of hesitation. All these years, she fought with us to keep these up and here I am finally tearing them down as though she was never here. By the time I finish in Hannah's room, all that is left are bare walls and a few bin bags for the recycling on Monday. I place her pink dressing table stool in a corner so that it's easily accessible for the house clearance folk. Another room has been vacated. I smile as I look around. I have wonderful memories that will stay with me long after this house is gone. While the clear-out has been emotional, it feels good to take control. Instead of drifting along, I am doing something to enrich my life. How many people can say they do that? I feel empowered and in charge of my own destiny, instead of waiting for someone to save me.

With most of the upstairs done, it only leaves my bedroom. This is the hardest room, and I am already feeling daunted by the drawers that are straining with the weight of all my purchases. I daren't look at my cupboard doors that are almost hanging off. I worry that when I remove everything it may all come tumbling down and finally collapse under the strain it has put up with for so long.

Unlike the spare room, my wardrobe is full of brand-new clothes. Many still with the labels on. I get that feeling of embarrassment and self-loathing again as I look at the tags. It will be someone's lucky day to get these items for a bargain price. I place them all carefully in the bag for the charity shop and tell myself that I can't turn the clock back. I can do nothing about the past, it's too late for that, but I can turn over a new leaf.

Looking at all the money I have squandered, I can see that it was an addiction, just like the time I spent £50 on lottery tickets, thinking I would win. In that moment I had hope and excitement. When I was buying all this stuff, I felt the same. I had hope that I could wear that fancy new dress somewhere, until I realised that I had nowhere to go. I was addicted to that feeling of excitement and the promise that this stuff would make me someone I'm not. As it all lies discarded in bin bags around the floor, only now do I truly understand that none of it ever would have filled the hole in my world that my family left. Only I have the power to make that hole smaller by making my life more fulfilling.

Chapter Six

I can't get the brand-new clothes out of the house quickly enough. They hit a nerve, serving as a reminder of how irresponsibly I have behaved. I feel like an alcoholic waking up and looking at all the empty wine bottles that surround them, only I woke up and realised that I was surrounded by shopping. Just as 'wine o'clock' is deemed acceptable, so is 'shop until you drop'. It is practically a status symbol, a subject women joke about, but I am starting to realise that it can also be an indication that your life is spiralling out of control. That inside you are unhappy and doing anything to fill that void.

Of course, the charity shop is happy. When I hand over the bags, the woman eyes up some of the dresses I had previously bought because there was fifty per cent off – so they were a bargain. Or so I thought at the time.

'What beautiful clothes,' she says.

'Yes, they are.'

'Goodness, price tags on them too.'

I look at the woman suspiciously. Is she judging me, or am I being paranoid? 'Yeah, my mam died. Sadly, she never got a chance to wear them.' I am horrified at myself for lying.

'Oh, bless. Well, they look as though they might fit you. Are you sure you don't want to keep them?' says the woman, holding up a burgundy dress I thought would be ideal for a dinner party. It is a lovely dress, but I must be strong here. I close my eyes for a second and picture the houseboat and the small amount of space that I'll have available. I must not let my willpower wane.

'No, it's okay. I'd rather someone else enjoy them. Plus, I thought these might earn some money for your charity. I'm trying to do something good with them all.'

'Well, that's lovely. Thank you for choosing to donate them to us. I'm sure everything will be sold out in no time. They're beautiful. It reminds me of the time we had a designer bag come in. Women were practically fighting over it.'

The woman picks up a long pink taffeta ballgown that I was never going to wear. What on earth was I thinking? I'm not Cinderella!

'I might put this in the window.'

'Go for it,' I say, leaving her and a colleague rooting through the bag for the rest of the goodies they've inherited. I wouldn't be surprised if they have first dibs, judging by the expressions on their faces.

I walk out and immediately feel lighter. Not only because I have got rid of a couple of bin bags of clothes, but because I am satisfied that by purging my wardrobe, I am letting go of anything that doesn't serve me.

To celebrate I head to a cafe in town for breakfast. The smell of fried eggs, sausages and strong coffee hits me as soon as I open the door. It might be a bit of a greasy spoon, but it does the most gorgeous cooked breakfasts. After all that hard work, surely I deserve one.

As I sit down and tuck into a crispy hash brown, I notice that I have missed a call from Gerrit. I have a sudden panic that something has gone wrong with the sale. He was supposed to be giving me the details for a lawyer while he gets the rest of the paperwork drawn up. What if I have done all this clearing out for nothing? I tell myself to stay calm since, no matter what, I am still carrying out my plan for decluttering. Whatever happens, having a clear-out is a good thing.

I almost choke on my hash brown as I rush down my food. I desperately want to get out of the busyness of the cafe to call Gerrit. I finish my breakfast off as fast as I can and hurry outside into the autumn air. The trees on the high street have already turned golden autumnal shades. I was hoping I could be in Amsterdam by Halloween if we pushed things along a bit. My heart starts pounding and I get a fluttery feeling in the pit of my stomach as Gerrit's number rings out. When he answers I feel like I might not want to hear whatever it is he wants to tell me. But his reassuring voice doesn't sound like someone who is about to break bad news.

'Hey, Sandy. Thanks for returning my call. How've you been?'

'Yes, yes. Good. Do you have news on the barge? Is everything okay?'

'Yes, of course. Just wanted to let you know that the paperwork's all in order and I've emailed you the details of a lawyer you can use to check it over. Then, once you're happy, you can send over the final amount, and we can sign all the paperwork.'

'Wow, so it's all going through?'

'Yes, of course. Why wouldn't it?'

'No reason. I just have so much riding on this now. I'd be heartbroken if it fell through.'

'I shouldn't think it will. Unless there's a problem with the money, there are no issues from this side. The guy who owned it died so it's all very easy. It's not like there's an onward chain.'

'Okay. Umm, he didn't die on the barge, did he?'

'Oh, no! He lived a long life on there. He was away when it happened. He was very old.'

'Oh, right. Okay. Well, I can assure you that the money is safe as I've already given my bank notice to release it from the account.'

'Great, looks like we're all on track. You'll be able to move in once everything's completed.'

'Amazing!'

I am so excited on the phone that I don't notice I have stepped out in front of a car. The driver beeps at me and shouts obscenities. I hope Gerrit didn't hear. What would he think of the language around here?

'Are you okay?' he asks.

'Oh, yes, sorry. Almost got run over by a car but I'm okay.'

'That's good. We don't want that to be a reason you can't go through with the purchase. It wouldn't be the first time someone has died before we can complete a sale. Sorry, it's my Dutch sense of humour.'

'Oh, ha. Right, I promise to take more care of myself… I'm just really, really excited.'

'That's understandable. It's not every day someone moves country to live on a houseboat.'

He makes me sound like some sort of adventurous nomad and I love it.

Knowing that everything is going full steam ahead, I spend the next week throwing out broken Christmas decorations, spare buttons that don't match anything I remember owning and odd socks. I look at everything with a new-found clarity. Why did I keep all this rubbish?

I was always thinking 'just in case', but the truth is that it should all have been thrown out years ago. This life clearance thing is finally starting to feel cathartic. That is until the house clearance guys arrive and tell me how dreadful my stuff is. There is nothing cathartic about being insulted so that they can buy everything at rock-bottom prices.

'You can get those wardrobes brand new in Bargain Furniture up the retail park for under a hundred and fifty pounds,' says the guy who is doing all the negotiating.

'But this is solid pine. Those ones are made of that MDF stuff.'

I try to argue about the difference in quality, but he is adamant that my beautiful pine wardrobe is worthless. It is a choice of take it or leave it. Since I want the house emptied before the estate agent comes round to take photos, I regretfully agree. I want this place to be a blank canvas so that it sells quickly. I once read that viewers can be put off by houses full of clutter with too many personal touches, which I guess is understandable. Hopefully, any buyers can now imagine what their stuff will look like in here. I also don't want to leave the house with too much furniture when it's going to be empty – even if I do have a super-efficient neighbourhood watch team here. Perhaps I also secretly fear that I could back out at the last minute. This way, if there is nothing left here then there is no turning back, no matter what happens.

After the clearance guys drive off with my precious items of furniture, I turn my attention to all the little knick-knacks that I should have got rid of long ago. It takes ages to pack them all up ready for the car boot sale that Debbie and I are doing at the weekend.

By the time the car boot sale comes around I can't even remember what's in half the boxes.

'Are you sure people will buy this stuff?' I ask Debbie as we set up. There is a lot of tat among the boxes.

' 'Course they will. Everyone loves a bargain.'

When we get to the soggy field, I am not convinced that I'll sell anything. For the first hour, all the sellers talk about is how the awful weather has kept everyone away. As the heavens open above us, I wouldn't blame anyone for staying at home. However, by later in the morning, the clouds disperse a little and people finally start to appear.

I watch the crowds as they head in our direction. A young woman in her twenties is the first to explore our stall.

'What's this?' she asks.

'It's a Cabbage Patch doll,' I explain.

'It's very ugly,' she says, picking it up.

Her comment upsets me. I feel very protective of the doll I'd had since the Eighties, which I let Hannah play with as a little girl.

'Maybe it's best to say nothing rather than be impolite about someone's things,' I say.

'It's just a doll. I'm not exactly hurting anyone's feelings.'

'Well, you've hurt *my* feelings,' I say, snatching the doll back from her.

The young woman stares at me as though I have gone totally doolally and I am relieved when she walks over to the next stall. Thankfully, the next person who checks out my stuff is much more appreciative.

'Garfield! How much is that? Haven't seen one of those for years. Oh, I loved Garfield. Did you?'

'Oh, yes, everyone loved Garfield. Wasn't it lasagne he used to eat?' I say.

'That brings back memories. Yes, I'd never even tried a lasagne until I was introduced to it by Garfield.' The woman, who must be in her early sixties, laughs and chats with Debbie and me as she hands over the ten pounds for Garfield. I am so happy to have found someone who values the importance of things from the past.

It might be looking good for the Garfield teddy but the same can't be said for a Garfield lampshade. I look at it again; maybe I was a bit too enthusiastic to think that someone would actually want it in this day and age. I think that's one for the bin.

Fortunately, I start selling more items after the woman walks off. Perhaps she brought me some luck. Straight after her is a guy who buys my Walkman to show his daughter how we used to listen to music in the *olden days*. I am pleased with the sale, even if there was no need for him to emphasise over and over again how many years ago it was since he listened to one.

By the end of the afternoon, I have made £250 and I couldn't be more delighted.

'I guess that's it, Debs. May as well pack up.'

'Yeah, I don't think you did too badly.'

'No, it's only this lot we've got left.'

As I eye up the boot that is still half full of unwanted stuff, I offer Debbie the collection of *Coronation Street* videos.

'Are you sure you don't want these, Debbie?'

'No, you're alright.'

'There might be *Emmerdale*, too,' I say.

'I don't have a video recorder to play them on. I think that might be why they got left.'

'Good point. How about the Spanish donkey and the castanets?'

'No, you're alright.'

'Suit yourself then. If you're sure you won't regret it.'

'I'm sure.'

We drive back to our street giggling about all the characters we've met over the course of the day. It has certainly been a fun experience.

'We should have done this more often. I think you've inspired me to have my own clear-out. Nigel is a nightmare for buying golf jumpers that he never wears.'

'I didn't realise he was playing golf nowadays.'

'He isn't.'

We are still laughing by the time we pull up outside my house. Debs has kindly offered to dispose of everything that is left to save me emptying the car and bringing it all into the house again. She is such a good friend, and I hope she will visit me in Amsterdam as she has promised. I would love to show her around once I am there and pay her back for all her support.

I reach for the cash that I made at the car boot sale and count it again before putting it to one side to change into euros. I will keep it separately so that I can buy something special for the houseboat. It will be nice to make my mark on a new home. It might not be a family home, but it will be *my* home. If I want a bright pink sofa, I can buy one. This current house is quite muted with sensible colours, its magnolia walls long faded by the sun. Paul never liked garish colours, and wanted the house to be practical and easy to maintain. Unlike me, who has always loved bright things. You have to compromise when you're married, though, and I no longer have to do that. Now, as I look around with most of my belongings gone, the house feels bare and unloved. It no longer feels like the cosy home where my family ate, slept, laughed and occasionally bickered. This could be anyone's home, which it soon will be, as the next step is to put it on the market.

Chapter Seven

'Lovely place, Ms Davies,' says a friendly estate agent as he pokes around the different rooms. I'm glad he is so positive; that is usually a good start.

'Prices have gone up in the past year so it's a good time to sell. I think the market will bottom out by the beginning of next year.'

'Right. So, do you think it'll sell quite quickly then? The thing is, I've just been told the paperwork will be ready for my new home by the end of the month. I'm looking at leaving as soon as I can.'

'Yeah, that's not a problem. We can keep the keys in the office, and we'll notify you of any offers, don't worry. At least you won't have to come back and empty it all,' he says, looking around the practically empty living room. I notice how he eyes up the bean bag I removed from Hannah's room to use in place of the sofa that I let the clearance guys take.

'Yes, well, I'm eager to get over there.'

'I can see. Right, I'll put it on the market immediately and keep you updated.'

'Great. That simple, hey?'

'Yeah, very simple. Houses around here don't stay on the market for too long. I'll get the photos up on our website by the end of the day.'

It surprises me how calm I feel. I thought I might be nervous when this beautiful family home we all loved so much finally went up for sale. My younger self would have been horrified, but it feels like freedom. Downsizing isn't a bad thing in the slightest, and I don't know why anyone would be afraid of it. I certainly won't miss mowing the third-of-an-acre lawn every summer. This is all for the best.

However, while I am comfortable with my decision to sell, I have an urge to call Hannah. I need to hear her voice inside this house once again. I press on video call so that she can have a look around one final time.

'Hiya, love.'

'Hi, Mam. Everything okay?'

'Yes, absolutely wonderful. I just wanted to tell you that the estate agent has been around and the house is going on the market this week. I've already emptied it. You want to see it?'

'Yeah, I'd like that. I still can't believe my family home is going.'

I look at her in her t-shirt and shorts. Her mousy-brown hair has already gone a little more golden from the sun out there. Seeing her reminds me just how much I miss her. Is it selfish of me to secretly wish my baby girl could have stayed small forever and not grown up?

'I know, but you're so far away now.'

'Well, what if I fly back? Shall I come and see you?'

'Oh goodness, no. You enjoy yourself there. Don't even think about coming back. You've not been there that long. Besides, you know how long the flight is.'

'I know, but I'm worried you might be making a mistake. Once our home's gone, it's gone forever.'

'I get that, but I'm rattling around here. I don't use half the rooms. It's a waste of money paying council tax bills and keeping this just for myself.'

'Yeah, I guess.'

'Look, I've already worked out that if something goes wrong in Amsterdam, which I hope it doesn't, then I can always buy something small. There are always the retirement flats.' I laugh, hoping Hannah realises I am kidding.

'No, anything but those,' she jokes.

'You see, it could always be worse. Now, where's your sense of adventure? You're the first one to love a change of scenery.'

'Yeah, I guess you're right. So, go on then, show me the house one last time.'

I show Hannah around the kitchen first.

'I finally got rid of the cuckoo clock. It did nearly kill me though.'

'Oh, Mam, I never liked that thing. I'm quite sure I pulled the cuckoo out because he was freaking me out. I've always been a bit weird about birds because of that thing.' Hannah is laughing but I can't work out whether we genuinely scarred her for life and she needs therapy because of that silly cuckoo clock.

'Oh, he was only on a spring.'

'I know, but the way he shot out like that. Frightened the life out of me.'

'Bless. Well, he's finally gone in the bin now. You want to see your bedroom?' I head upstairs to show Hannah her old room, hoping she doesn't get upset seeing it empty.

'Oh, you took all the posters down.'

'Yes, sorry, love. I've had to be absolutely ruthless. Even Garfield's been sold.'

'Oh, it's fine. Don't worry. I'm sure the new owners won't want posters of McFly on their walls.'

'No, probably not.'

'Anyway, I don't even know why I made such a big deal about those posters. The walls would have looked better with some nice pictures on.'

'Wow, you are growing up.'

'Well, I'm thinking aesthetically. I was telling Dad I might go into interior design when I've eventually had enough of doing odd jobs. I'm loving my freedom too much at the moment. I think everyone needs to do what they want with their lives. There shouldn't be any constraints or expectations on anyone. So, I suppose I need to be happy for you instead of being so worried. I know you love the sun, but you always fancied the houseboat lifestyle, didn't you?'

'Yeah, I did, but with a family it's not so easy. Now it's my time for an adventure, just like you've had with moving to Oz.'

'I understand. I suppose it's for the best you're moving on. You know, Dad's moved on. He's met an Australian woman. Her name's Mary.'

'Oh. That's nice for him.'

'Yeah, she's from Melbourne. He went to a school reunion and met her there. They were at school together. I hope you're not hurt I've told you, Mam. It's just that I'd hate to think you weren't living your best life thinking about Dad.'

'No, it's fine. It's up to Dad, isn't it? I mean, it's just one of those things. Mary's a lucky woman to have such a genuine guy.'

'You'll have someone again one day too, Mam.'

'What if I don't want anyone? Being alone means I haven't got to answer to anyone. You know, today I thought I might buy a bright pink sofa for the houseboat. Wouldn't that be funky? In fact, now I've said it out loud, I'm going to order one I've seen online and get it sent directly to Amsterdam. Did you know houseboats have their own addresses and get post? It's weird but I hadn't thought about those things before.'

'Great. Well, I guess I have a cool mam. I'm proud of you, really. Wait until I tell Aaron.'

'Who's Aaron?'

'A guy I've been seeing. It's early days but he's nice.'

'I'm happy to hear that. You never really related to any of the boys around here, did you?'

'Nope. I always felt like a fish out of water with them. I always felt more Aussie.'

'I guess you and your dad have always been so close. It's not surprising.'

'Yeah, I definitely have more of the Aussie in me than the Welsh. So, anyway, I'd better go, Mam, because Aaron's coming over any minute.'

'Yes, of course. Well, I'm glad you don't mind about the posters!'

'Oh no, I don't mind at all. You know, sometimes we hang onto things when we should have let go of them a long time ago.'

'Aren't you wise, Hannah? And so, so, right.'

Listening to how Hannah is so matter-of-fact makes me even stronger. There was a bit of me that felt guilty for selling the old family home and getting rid of generational heirlooms. Every now and then it hits me that this is my final goodbye to my empty nest, where I sat up all night when Hannah was sick, or served meals in the dining room for Paul and Hannah when the wind howled outside our door. This house has kept us snug and protected for over twenty years. Now I feel as though I am being ungrateful for leaving it behind on a whim. But this is a house that needs to be filled. It needs children to run around the bedrooms; it should be full of noise and love and people, and I can no longer fulfil what it calls for.

I realise that the time has come for someone else to be resident here. After all, that is all we are for any home; merely custodians for the time we are there, and my custodianship here has come to an end.

Chapter Eight

Following a tearful farewell dinner with Debbie at our local pub, where our memories of each other flowed all night, and a fond goodbye to my lovely Abergavenny home, I take my one-way journey on the Eurostar to Amsterdam. I could have flown there in an hour but I wanted to relish every moment of my new adventure and watch the landscape go by as it changes from the UK to the Netherlands. Having managed to get all my belongings into one suitcase, I arrive at St Pancras to be told that I have been upgraded. I have never been upgraded for anything in my life, and am in shock as I am directed to the business lounge. Is this an omen for a wonderful new start?

Once on board, I toast my adventure with a complimentary glass of champagne. I sip as I listen to music on my phone and watch the scenery whizz past. It's mostly just greenery and houses, but still, I enjoy watching the difference as the homes change from typically British two-storeys to a more Dutch style with their sloping gambrel roofs. While watching the scenery, my head is full of questions. Will this be the wonderful adventure I hope it will? Or will I be faced with a leaky roof, floods and my worst nightmare? Doing something like this on a whim still feels surreal. I feel as though I am watching someone else. I start to wonder how I was even brave enough to make this big move, but then I realise that I haven't really stopped to think about what I am doing. This is probably the longest I have sat still since I made my decision. From the moment I saw the advert, it has been full speed ahead. I haven't processed any of this properly but now I have a slight fear of the unknown, which I try to quell as we pass the fields of Rotterdam until finally we reach Amsterdam Centraal station, our final stop. It's too late to back out now.

Having enjoyed three glasses of champagne, my head is slightly woozy as I walk through the station and the reality starts to hit me. I feel like Paddington Bear as I stand in the railway station far away from home and look around for where I need to go next. The fact is, I don't remember anything of this station from the time I was here before with Nicky. It sinks in that I actually don't know *Amsterdam* half as well as I thought I did.

Unlike some of the other passengers on the train, I have nobody waiting to greet me, and it also hits me that I don't know anyone here, apart from Gerrit. But then I cheerily remind myself that life is all about meeting new people. How difficult can it be to make new friends? So, with renewed courage, the handy invention of Google Maps and a smile on my face, I take the ten-minute walk to the cheap hotel I have booked for my stay before I pick up the keys and arrange the final formalities with Gerrit in the morning.

As I head towards the Red Light District, the cold sends shivers down my spine. I only hope the heating system on the barge is sufficient. I huddle into my jacket as a man in a hoodie skulks past me. I watch as he darts in through a door with a red light above it where a young woman with long dark hair wearing a black basque stands in the window. I look at my tired reflection in a nearby window as I walk towards it. At least there's no chance of anyone approaching me here and getting the wrong impression. I look far too worn out and exhausted for any of that!

The hotel isn't the most salubrious, but it's only for a couple of nights at most. After that, I am hoping I will be in my new home.

I walk up the steep, narrow stairs to my room on the top floor. My thigh muscles ache. It could certainly make me fitter living here with all the stairs in this city, although with the gorgeous waffle shops I passed on the way to the hotel, perhaps not.

My room is basic, but I guessed it wasn't going to be a palace by the cheap deal I got. With not much to look at inside the room, I go to the window where I watch the people walking along the streets below. You can see everything from here. Couples giggle together at the X-rated shops, and single guys leer at the windows with the red lights.

I begin to wonder if this is the right place for a single woman in her fifties to start over. Did I truly believe that one weekend trip with my late best friend would make this the right destination for a new start? It must have been sentiment getting to me again. I hear some shouting outside and have to hold onto the curtain to steady my legs as I feel a moment of panic set in. I was in my twenties the last time I was here, and I am beginning to realise how much I have changed since then. What if I hate it, and worse, it has become a city wracked with violence?

Thankfully, after a good night's sleep, my anxiety turns to curiosity, and I look forward to seeing my new home on the canal. As the sun shines down on a bright autumn morning, I feel ready to meet Gerrit and visit my house-boat for the first time.

Following what could be the easiest sale Gerrit has ever made, he is only too happy to collect me from the hotel. I saw a photo of him on the company website, so I recognise him when his teeny little car pulls up outside my accommodation. The car makes me smile as it looks like a little Lego car. There would be fewer problems parking if everyone drove something like this, though I do wonder if both of us can fit inside.

Gerrit is young, good-looking, tall and blond. He looks as though he should be featured on a Dutch tourist board advert, welcoming people with his friendly smile. He has a very firm handshake, leaving my knuckles feeling bruised. I realise that I'm going to have to toughen up if I am about to renovate a barge.

'It's so good to meet you,' says Gerrit with a warm smile.

'You too. I can't believe I'm actually here.'

'We definitely did it in record time. I don't think I've ever managed to get a sale put through quite this quickly before.'

'Well, once I put my mind to something, there's no going back. Even if I am getting a bit of anxiety now about whether I did the right thing in such a hurry.'

'Ah, there's nothing to worry about now that you're here. Sometimes it's best not to think too much about big things.'

'Yes, that's true.'

'So, I have to pass by the office first and then I'll take you to your new home. Does that sound okay?'

'Absolutely perfect.'

We weave our way through the Amsterdam streets, which are already busy at this time in the morning, until we reach Gerrit's office, which isn't too far away. He runs in to grab the key for the houseboat and jumps back in within minutes, putting down a key attached to what looks like a rubber ball for a key ring. I look at it, baffled, which Gerrit notices.

'It's buoyant. So if you drop your keys in the canal when you're trying to open the door, it'll float.'

'Wow, dropping my keys in the canal is something I hadn't even considered.'

'You'd be surprised. Especially if you've been out all night in some of these local bars.' Gerrit smiles at me, and I notice his beautiful white teeth. I feel like one of those annoying older ladies who says things like, 'If only I were ten years younger', as I look at him. Only I'd have to be around twenty years younger or more, and that would be weird.

Ten minutes later Gerrit's good teeth are the last thing I'm thinking about as he pulls his little automobile up right outside my new home. It is the one that I hoped wasn't mine as soon as I saw it lined up. Having driven past the grandest of houseboats of polished wood, eco-friendly sustainable barges and fancy modern glass designs, I can see why it was a lot cheaper than the others. Mine stands out for all the wrong reasons. It looks even more sorry for itself in real life with its flaky paint and rotting wood. The Dutch winters have obviously taken their toll.

'Yikes. I can see why it was a bargain compared to the others,' I say, gulping nervously.

'Ah, it's okay. I've seen worse,' says Gerrit.

Like, how much worse? I want to ask him. Any worse and it could possibly sink as much as my heart has. The video Gerrit sent me was certainly taken in a good light. There are so many things that require work, and I start to think the guy who did the survey was on the fiddle.

We step onto the deck and I look at the shabby front door in anticipation. The moment Gerrit opens this door, I will see my new home properly for the first time. Will it be even worse inside? I take deep breaths as Gerrit fumbles with the key. I look around me, as I try to calm myself down and spot a man on the houseboat next door, who smiles and waves over to us. I shout a hello across to him.

'As you can see, it's very friendly here,' says Gerrit.

'It certainly appears to be.'

I smile at the man on the houseboat who stands there, curious, probably wondering who his new neighbour is. Beside him is a beautiful creamy-coloured dog. The sight of his dog cheers me up.

'Oh, what a gorgeous dog,' I say to Gerrit.

'That's a Dutch Smoushond. They're good for getting rid of rats and mice.'

Rats? This is getting worse all the time.

'Oh, I guess with the canals you could get a lot of rats around here. I hadn't thought of that.' It occurs to me that I haven't thought about half the practicalities of my move. I mean, they never talked about things like that on *Rosie and Jim*, and thankfully the only rat I have ever come across was Roland Rat and his sidekick Kevin the Gerbil. I am trying to see the funny side here but inside I am being consumed by panic.

'Yeah, but they are pretty cool dogs too. Don't worry about rats, you'll be fine.'

'Umm, okay. I'll try.'

Finally, Gerrit opens the front door, which sticks a little as he pushes at it. Then he hands me the key ring with the weird buoyancy aid attached to it.

'Just needs a bit of love and attention, as I said,' says Gerrit, as a musty smell hits us. It makes me sneeze and I recall what Nigel said about the stinky man at his work. I don't want to smell musty, and am grateful I didn't throw out my nice perfume.

As I venture further inside and stand on what I thought was a secure hardwood floor, I trip up on a floorboard that is uneven, falling flat on my face with my head narrowly missing the edge of a kitchen cabinet that is hanging slightly awry.

'Are you okay?' says Gerrit, giving me a hand to get up.

'Yes, fine. Just a bruised ego. It's okay.'

'You must be careful. Some of the floor isn't so even.'

'Looks like I've learnt that,' I say as I brush myself down.

While it appears the interior floor is another part of the houseboat that needs replacing, I pathetically try to convince myself that things like this are superficial. I wasn't expecting it to be perfect. I have to be realistic, but I would have expected a decent floor at the very least.

Telling myself that everything is fixable and that I can do this, I move to the tiny bedrooms where the damp stench suddenly gets worse. That's the problem when you buy online; the video didn't give away the smell. I can certainly see why Gerrit wanted me to visit first, but I tell myself that it would have been snapped up regardless of the damp. This smell can be resolved. It simply needs a good clean, which is nothing I can't do. It might take some elbow grease, but I know in a week or so I will get it smelling fresh in here. I have a flash of regret that I sold the super-duper wet and dry vacuum that I bought from a shopping channel in my decluttering purge. Perhaps I should have hung onto some of my impulse purchases.

'So, here you go. This place is officially yours. Congratulations,' says Gerrit as we finish our tour of the inside. Well, perhaps it wasn't a tour as such since I only have a wheelhouse, a teeny boiler room, an open-plan living and kitchen area, two bedrooms and a small shower room. The master bedroom is far from glamorous with only a sheet that's been discarded and scrunched up in the corner; the bed it belonged to having been moved out. Without the luxury of fitted wardrobes, I appreciate the tiny storage area I spot, which is almost camouflaged into one of the walls, which looks like it has been stripped ready to paint. I leave the bedroom to check out the other areas again. I peek inside the small shower and toilet room. The first thing I'll do is tear down the old white mouldy shower curtain.

Fortunately, I am not much of a cook, as the kitchen area is tiny. My chunky kettle will probably take up half the worktop space. But it's worth it because, as the colours of a rainbow in the sky reflect down from the wheelhouse window, the beautiful view makes up for any lack of space.

I convince myself everything will be fine, but it dawns on me that there will be no more long hot baths on cold nights, and I am going to go around the city smelling of damp masked by strong perfume. I stand with my hands on my hips and glance around, astonished that I have impulsively bought a houseboat that I didn't even visit because I thought I was being fun and spontaneous.

As I hear a huge clunking noise coming from the boiler room, I ask myself: what on earth have I done?

Chapter Nine

Gerrit heads back to the office, leaving me at the house-boat alone. He told me to call him if there are any problems and said he is happy to show me a hardware store where I can find the materials I'm going to need to get this place into shape. I think it's going to take a whole construction team! I remind myself that Rome wasn't built in a day and that instead of looking at the big picture, I have to do one thing at a time. If I am to get myself out of this mess then I am going to have to take it step by step.

As I get a clearer view of the kitchen cupboard door that nearly hit my head, I can see that it is hanging off its hinges. My first purchase is going to have to be a set of power tools. To think, the last time I was in Amsterdam, I was rushing to the shops for cowboy boots. Now it's going to be paint stripper and planks of wood. I would never have imagined I'd be thinking about which power drill I would need over a fancy new dress, but this is the new me. 'I can do this,' I tell myself, something that I think might have to become my new mantra.

But when a piece of wood on the kitchen work surface comes off in my hand, I regret being even a tad positive. Everything I touch seems to fall apart. I tell myself once again that I knew what I was getting myself into and there is nothing that a handy screwdriver, or possibly a whole team of workers, can't fix.

Despite the risk of someone breaking in, I open the windows and let the fresh air blow through before I leave to return to the hotel and check out. I may as well spend my first night here, and there isn't anything much a burglar could take. The place can't get much worse: maybe they might even do me a favour and tidy up.

An hour later, I return to my new home with my suitcase and thankfully can see that nobody has been near here. Perhaps it looks a bit too haunted and unwelcoming and scares potential thieves away. As I grapple with my front door key to get back in, I notice my new neighbour rushing down from his houseboat.

'*Hallo! Wil je da ti je help?*' he says.

'Hi, sorry, I don't speak Dutch.'

'Ah, no worries. I was just asking, will you let me help you?'

'Oh, well, that would be great. Thank you. Everything I own is in this suitcase, so it's a bit heavy to wheel around.'

The neighbour grabs my suitcase as though it's only a feather.

'That's so helpful. Thank you so much.'

'You're welcome. I'm Abe, by the way.'

'Sandy. So pleased to meet you.'

As we both stand in the small doorway of the house-boat, I can't help noticing how handsome he is and how his blond hair is streaked with grey. Even though it's cold, he's wearing cargo shorts with wheat-coloured hiking boots. He reminds me of some of the Australians I met when I was in Melbourne. My first impression of him is that he looks like the type of person who wouldn't want to be constrained by a mortgage, a nine-to-five job or any sort of normal humdrum life. He looks quite nomadic and outdoorsy. As I look up at his bright green eyes, I feel something wet at my feet. I look down to see his beautiful Dutch water dog has followed him and is now greeting me with a big lick at my ankles.

'Hello, you're a happy little soul, aren't you,' I say.

'He likes you.'

'He's gorgeous. What's his name?'

'Ted.'

'Hello, Ted. It's so lovely to meet you.'

'Ted says it's lovely to meet you too,' says Abe with a big grin. I find myself blushing under his attention. I guess that is what happens when you've been around *things* more than humans.

'Well, anyway, I'd better head off. I guess you have a lot of work to do,' says Abe, gesturing around the room.

'Oh, yes. Not quite sure where I'll start. The first thing is to freshen this place up a bit, I guess.'

'It was empty for a while after the owner died. It got a bit stale in here. It was left in a bit of a mess before it was cleared out,' says Abe.

'Ah, right. That's okay. I'm sure I'll get it all sorted.'

'You look very capable of managing it yourself, but if you need anything then please give me a shout. I know the old guy here used to have trouble with some of the heating thermostats so I can try to help if you have a problem.'

'I did hear some funny noises coming from the boiler room earlier.'

As if there is the ghost of the previous owner on board, as I say it I hear a great big rumble once again.

'I think I might well be needing a plumber.'

'Sure, see how you get on. If there's anything else you need, just shout. I'm only next door.'

'Thank you. I appreciate it.'

Ted looks up at me for attention and I give him a big stroke before they leave me to my own devices. I close the door behind them and start to believe that I could be happy here eventually, even if the boiler, and everything else, is a bit dodgy. But then I see a shadow on the window of the wheelhouse. For a moment, I wonder if there is a strange man up there. How secure is it, living here? However, as I watch the window closely, I see a great big stork parading about. A stork! I have no idea whether they can be vicious, but I am so excited that I open the door to take a look. I quietly creep outside and sit down on a black-and-red striped deckchair that has been discarded, left by the previous owner. The stork spots me and glides away, leaving me alone.

Looking at my surroundings, I realise that the deck-chair directly faces Abe and Ted's houseboat. I move my chair slightly as I don't want Abe to think I'm watching them. Despite all the jobs I have to do indoors, I can't help but take time out to relish the scenery and watch as people pass me on the canal. At the moment, the thought of sitting out here is more appealing than being inside. A woman on a bike rides past with bright red tulips wrapped in paper in her basket. That's exactly what I need – tulips! That will brighten the houseboat up. A little voice in my head tells me that it will take more than flowers, and not to start my old habit of shopping again, but I drown it out and try to remember where the flower market is from my last visit. Once the barge is sorted, that's the first place I'll go. I am telling myself to imagine how rewarding it will be once all the work is done, when I hear the voice of my neighbour from his roof.

'Hey. Did you unpack that quickly?'

'Ha. No. I came out here because I saw a stork on the roof.'

'Ah, yes. It's a regular visitor around here.'

'How fabulous. I love storks.'

'Then you'll have to visit the house with the stork.'

'A stork lives in a house?'

'No, it's a landmark around here. Have you seen the movie *Ocean's Twelve*? It was in that.'

'Oh, no. I'm not much of a movie buff. I prefer...' I decide not to mention the felting hobby since he probably won't know what I mean. It might sound a bit strange trying to explain that I repeatedly stab needles into yarn, resulting in the creation of miniature animals.

'Even if you don't like movies, you should search for the house with the stork. It stands on the corner of a building. You should see if you can find it.'

'Oh, that's cute. I definitely will. Thanks.'

I watch as Abe turns his attention to a beautiful woman who opens the front door of his houseboat. I observe her closely as she takes her shopping bags inside. Ted is jumping all over her and I realise it wasn't only me he was pleased to see.

'Ah, Beatrix is here. See you again,' says Abe.

'Yes, have a great evening.'

We wave goodbye to each other, and I summon the courage to face the musty interior again. After I have scrubbed the barge from top to bottom, unpacked and put the photo of Nicky and I up along with one of Hannah, I can finally see the potential in this place becoming a home. By the time I stop for a coffee, the sun has gone down on Amsterdam and I pop outside the front door for some fresh air before it gets too chilly.

I watch as a couple snuggle up together as they walk down the street and feel a moment of loneliness. Everywhere I look people are with others. Abe is next door with Beatrix and Ted, while I am here with just an empty mug of coffee for company. Feeling slightly forlorn, I head back in. It's been a long, emotional day and I momentarily fall asleep on an old chair that's been left in the living room. But within minutes, I am woken up by a cacophony of unfamiliar noises. The wood creaks and crunches and the sound of groaning old pipes startles me as I wake up. In my dozy state, I begin to worry. What if I can't run from that hole in my life? All the other things I bought didn't make me feel any better about myself. What if the houseboat doesn't either?

Chapter Ten

By the next morning, I am much less emotional and convince myself there is no time to be lonely as I start to plan the restoration work. At Hannah's suggestion, I take some 'before' photos. The green Formica kitchen worktops will be one of the first things I rip out since they're practically hanging off already. For a moment, I consider starting some kind of blog, like the woman I read about in Brecon, although nowadays people would perhaps prefer Instagram or TikTok for the renovation updates. I then decide that it would be like inviting the whole world into my bedroom. Since I have always valued my privacy, I take photos of the progress to share only with Hannah and Debbie. It will be wonderful to look back at them when it's all done. Had I bought something shiny and new there would be no fun in it. What sense of achievement would it bring if this place was already perfect and ready to move into?

Gerrit has been most helpful and called to say that he is on his way to take me to the hardware store as well as a carpet store to check out some rugs. For someone who earned his commission so easily, his after-sales service is astonishing.

I hear the beep from his little black car and rush outside as he waits for me.

'Hi, I can't stay too long. I have to take my son to football practice. So, I'll take you to the carpet place first and then the hardware store.'

'Thank you. I'm so sorry for taking up your morning. This is so kind of you.'

'It's fine. I moved to London for a year when I was a student. I know how it feels to move somewhere and not know anyone.'

'Well, I really appreciate it.'

Gerrit knows the guy at the carpet store and is a regular customer. They chat in Dutch, and I wish I could understand them. What if he's telling him to rip me off? But Gerrit seems genuine enough so hopefully it's okay.

The sales assistant shows me some hard-wearing rugs that he says are ideal for a houseboat, but I am drawn to the most gorgeous red nomadic Shiraz rug with flecks of grey and black. It might be more Persian than Dutch, but it is so nomadic that it feels in keeping with my new life. This rug was made for me. I snap it up, paying for it with the car boot sale money, and the guy tells me it will be around two weeks for delivery since we won't be able to fit it in Gerrit's little car. Now the mission is on to paint and get the floors ready before my rug arrives. This is going to be the busiest few weeks of my life.

Next, we head to a hardware store where I find a great offer on power tools and, while I am there, I choose the wood that is needed for the flooring. Unbelievably, they have it in stock and they advise me that they can send a carpenter tomorrow morning to fit it. I can't quite believe my luck, and it almost feels as though the god of houseboats is looking down on me. I'd have had to wait months to find a carpenter who could fit me in back home. They tell me that he can also sort out my kitchen worktops. Thank goodness for carpenters who want to make a few extra euros on the weekend! Perhaps it isn't as difficult as I thought to renovate the houseboat – if you have a good team around you.

Armed with the equipment I need for the jobs I plan on doing, I arrive back home with power tools and some paint pots and brushes. I'm ready to give this houseboat the makeover it needs, but first it's time for a coffee. Since I haven't had time to stock up the fridge or the food cupboards yet, I put all the DIY stuff to one side in the kitchen and decide to treat myself to a hot drink along the canal and pick up a snack before I start.

I cross a bridge over the canal where a bicycle is decorated in pretty pink flowers. I look at the buildings around me wondering where the stork building is. I'll have to keep an eye out for it on my travels. It will always remind me of my first day on the houseboat and meeting Abe. I must try and meet Beatrix next. It would be nice to have some female friends here.

I walk past some coffee shops and look for somewhere I'd feel at home. A lot of the cafes have youngsters enjoying all sorts of things. But one place looks a little more grown up, with its Georgian windows and neutral-coloured squishy sofas.

The smell of pancakes as I open the door is simply gorgeous and I go to the counter where a huge blackboard advertises hot chocolates and lattes. Knowing the afternoon of hard work that I have ahead of me, I order their speciality hot chocolate with cream and marshmallows along with a Dutch pancake. The young girl at the counter tells me to sit down and that it will be with me shortly.

I can tell this is going to be one of my favourite places. With its Eighties music and black-and-white memorabilia decorating the walls, it has the coolest vibe. Customers quietly read and I spot a little library in the corner where people are encouraged to swap books. When my pancake comes out with whipped cream, Nutella and a Dutch flag, I know I'll be back. My hot chocolate is loaded up with cream and I am spooning a marshmallow into my mouth when I spot Abe walking in. I guess this is where most of the neighbourhood comes since it is so close to us.

I am tucked away in a corner and he doesn't notice me as he walks to the counter. To my surprise, he then lifts the counter flap up and walks straight into the kitchen area at the back. I wonder if he works here.

I carry on eating my pancake when I see Beatrix walk in with Ted. We haven't met yet and so she wouldn't know who I was if I tried to get her attention. The staff all seem to know her as they chat in Dutch and make a fuss of Ted. He seems to love everyone and equally, everyone loves him. Beatrix goes into the kitchen while Ted stays with one of the staff out front. Customers start making a fuss of him and then he wanders about until he sniffs around and spots me.

'Hello, Ted.'

He seems to want to jump up on my lap and so I help him up.

I'm stroking his head, telling him what a good boy he is when I hear Abe's voice.

'Hey, my new neighbour. Great to see you here.'

'You too.'

I look at the chocolate feast I have on the table and feel like I have to explain myself.

'I'm having a treat since I'll be doing a lot of work on the houseboat later.'

'I'm not one to judge – enjoy. And anyway, we always love the custom. Thank you.'

'Oh. Do you and Beatrix own this place?'

Ted jumps down and brushes against Abe.

'Yeah… and Ted, too.'

'Ah, of course. Well, I'll definitely be a regular. This hot chocolate is amazing!'

'We aim to please. I only use the best Belgian hot chocolate. It's my secret ingredient.'

'Great decision. I don't think I've ever tasted a hot chocolate like it.'

A group of cyclists walk in, and the coffee shop fills up.

'I'd better go. I need to give them some help behind the counter,' says Abe.

'Yes, me too. I need to get cracking with the painting.'

'Well, good luck. I'll be seeing you.'

'Thanks. Yeah. See you soon.'

I leave the cafe on a high, thanks to the sugar fix coupled with the happiness of making new friends already. What a lovely person Abe seems to be, and I hope I'll make a friend of Beatrix soon too.

As I walk along the canal with a big smile, I wrap my scarf around me tightly to protect me from the cold air. I'd love to think the houseboat will give me a warm welcome but it's still a little cold in there. The heating will be one of the next jobs in store. For now, though I want to start the painting, which should keep me warm.

I change into an old tracksuit that I purposely kept as I knew it would come in handy for working on the houseboat, and start with a base coat in the master bedroom. The previous owner must have already planned on painting this room since it is already sanded, which saves me a huge job. The sooner I get my room sorted, the sooner I can sleep in there. My new bed should also be arriving any day, so I need to get moving.

I am about to finish the first bright blue coat when I think there is a shadow blocking the natural light from the skylight window. At first, I think the stork might be back and obstructing the light, but then I realise it's Abe, who is standing beside me and trying to get my attention.

'Abe. Oh my god, you gave me a fright.'

'I'm so sorry. It wasn't my intention. Your front door was open. I did shout but I guess you couldn't hear me from in here.'

'Oh no, I can't have closed it properly. I guess that door will have to be another priority to look at.'

'It just needs filing down a little. Make sure you pull it tight after you. There's a knack to it. Anyway, I just wanted to pop in with a *broodje gezond* I had left over. I knew you were going to be busy at work here so I thought perhaps you wouldn't have time to eat tonight.'

'Is it that time already?'

'Yup. I already closed the shop.'

I look down at the baguette with lettuce, tomato, ham and egg. I didn't think I would need any food after that pancake earlier, but I have worked up quite the appetite after a couple of hours of painting.

'That's so kind of you, thank you. It looks delicious.'

'It's not a problem. You'll see that we all look after each other around here. It's hard work, renovating one of these. I did mine a few years ago and the neighbours made sure I ate and drank. Sometimes you forget to look after yourself when you've been painting for five hours straight.'

'I can see how that happens. That's interesting. So, any tips on restoring these things?'

'Nope, except be careful of your knees. You may want to wear some kneepads before you start on the floors,' says Abe, gesturing to the pots of antique pine varnish that are stacked up in the corner ready for the next step of the renovations.

'That sounds like great advice.'

'Anyway, I don't want to keep you. You've made a great start, by the way,' says Abe, eyeing the bedroom walls.

'Thanks, I appreciate it, and thanks again for the sandwich.'

'Anytime.'

Abe heads back to his boat and I wash the brushes and tidy everything up. I'm happy with the progress I've made. Not bad for my first day on the job. I am so enthralled by my progress that I decide to get the power drill out and fix the kitchen cupboard door. Looking at the results of my paint job, I convince myself I am capable of anything. I unravel the lead and plug the drill into the wall. But as soon as I place the drill onto the latch that needs fixing, my hand slips off and I look in horror at the perfectly round hole I have made in the kitchen cabinet. Any bigger and I'd be able to poke my finger though it. How on earth do they make it look so easy on those home makeover shows? I might have known things were going too smoothly and quit before I do any further damage. I'll have to add it to the list of jobs for the carpenter.

I would have thought by bedtime that I would be so exhausted I'd have collapsed into a deep sleep. Unfortunately, though, with the groaning of the pipes, the creaking of the wood and someone shouting something random outside, I find it hard to nod off. When I eventually do, I have a dream that Abe is standing right over me. But unlike what happened today, he doesn't have a sandwich in his hand but a bunch of tulips. He hands them to me and then kisses me on the lips. He then moves down to kiss my neck, unbuttons my shirt and slips his hand down as he removes it from me.

Oh my god. I wake up with a start. He is only a kind neighbour. Why on earth am I having weird dreams about the Dutchman who lives next door? I am never going to be able to look him in the eye again, let alone poor Beatrix!

Chapter Eleven

It's a strange feeling when you dream of someone and then can't get them out of your head. I don't think I will be able to speak to Abe ever again without going bright scarlet. It's not like he knows about my dream, but I still feel so terribly guilt-ridden. His poor partner Beatrix, what would she think if she knew I was having strange dreams about her man?

To take my mind off the dream, I keep myself busy for the rest of the morning until the carpenter arrives as promised. He introduces himself as Erik and has helpfully brought the sander and floor polisher with him that I hired from the store. Even though he is here for the floor, he looks at the kitchen cabinet I managed to destroy as he passes.

'You have woodworm?' he says, pointing.

'Oh, no. That was me. I, umm, drilled.'

'No, you have woodworm,' he says, taking a closer inspection.

'Look at this.' Erik points to a tiny two-millimetre hole in a cabinet that I didn't go anywhere near with a power tool. My stomach lurches. Woodworm on a boat? The survey didn't mention that.

'I'll have to treat it. This isn't good.'

'Oh, no. How much will that cost?' I say, trying to avoid sounding panicked.

'I'll have to check it for you back at the store, but you don't have much choice unless you want things to get worse.'

He then proceeds to inform me that I will have to change the cabinets, which I was hoping I wouldn't have to do, but I can see that he is right. He says I can order new ones, which he should be able to fit in a few weeks' time. I am just about to browse the hardware store's selection of kitchen units online when there is a knock on the door.

'Hey! Sorry to bother you. We're just going to the Sunday market. We wondered if you wanted to check it out?' says Abe, standing at the door with Beatrix. I try to forget the dream as I see Beatrix smiling at me.

'That's so kind of you but I have the carpenter here and it's a bit stressful.'

'Ah, is it Erik?'

'Oh, yeah. I think that's his name.'

'Then he'll be fine. You can trust him here on his own if you want to join us. He works on all the boats around here.'

'Oh, I don't know. I shouldn't really leave him. We have some drama with woodworm.' Although as I say that the drilling noise becomes unbearable in such a small space and I realise I would quite like to get out of here for a bit.

'Oh, no. Sorry to hear that, but Erik will see it right. He's great at all this kind of stuff. You're in capable hands.'

'That makes me feel better.'

'Yes, don't worry, and forgive me, I don't think you and Beatrix have met properly, have you?'

'No, we haven't. I've seen you around and in the coffee shop. It's great to meet you, Beatrix.' I smile but still can't look her in the eye.

'You too, it's good to have someone new living here. It was dark and so empty before,' she says with a genuine smile.

'Thanks, it's going to take time to get it into shape, but I hope I'll make the neighbourhood proud by the end.'

'Yup, I'm sure you will. It just needs a new breath of life and maybe some woodworm treatment here and there,' says Abe with a smile.

'Anyhow, we wondered if you wanted to join us at the flea market. It's a Sunday market, so it will be another week before you can check it out. But, if you really don't want to leave Erik here alone, I understand,' says Abe, as I notice him looking at some masking tape that Erik must have used somewhere that has now attached itself to my trousers. Why did I not feel that latching onto me? I quickly pull it off and with the racket that Erik is continuing to make, decide that perhaps I should go along after all.

'You know, that sounds like an offer too good to refuse right now. I'd love to check out the market. I'll just need to get changed.'

'Sure, take your time. Just give us a knock when you're ready,' says Abe.

I hurry to get changed, popping on a polo neck jumper to ensure I don't have any further weird thoughts of Abe unbuttoning anything. Then I rush over to their house-boat. It's good to have a closer look at the barge. Like mine, it's not as modern as some of the others around here but you can see by the shiny, fresh red paint that it has been lovingly restored to look as good as new. There is a gorgeous seating area outside with upcycled pallets that have been painted white and made into sofas and a matching table. As a bouncy egg chair swings in the breeze, I can just imagine Abe, Beatrix and Ted enjoying sitting out there.

Ted happily greets me when Abe opens the door. He is already wearing his red bandana, ready for his shopping trip.

'You look cute,' I say.

'Oh, thanks. I'm glad you like my new coat,' says Abe.

'Oh, no. I meant Ted… Oh…' I blush so badly that my face turns the colour of Ted's bandana.

'Just teasing you. Sorry, Beatrix always says I have a silly sense of humour.'

'Oh, ha. Um, yeah. Anyway, where is Beatrix?'

'She'll meet us there. She had to go and grab something first. I'm afraid it's just me and Ted for now. Is that okay? I hope you don't mind.'

'Um, no. It's okay. Very okay.' *Very okay?*

As we walk along the canal in the direction of the flea market, Abe points out shops and places I must visit around here. He shows me a great place to buy chocolate, which is much appreciated, and there are a couple of bars he recommends.

'So, do you like markets?' he asks.

'Oh, yes, I love them. Although the good thing is that when you live on a houseboat you don't have the space to get too carried away.' I should probably stay away from them completely since I am recovering from a shopping problem, but I don't admit that to Abe.

'That's true. We can't accumulate too much. It's a shame because there are so many markets around here. You can find almost anything. I love buying vintage books and clothes,' says Abe.

'Ah, I thought you had good style.'

'Do I? Thank you.'

As I gaze at Abe in the shaggy full-length coat he's wearing, he suddenly grabs my arm.

'Hey, careful.' It is only then that I spot the bicycle whizzing past me.

'Wow, you saved me. Thank you.'

'It's okay. You have to be careful of bikes around here. Remember two things… Always use kneepads when working on the houseboat floors, and look out for bikes. Those are my two tips. You have to look after your knees and, well, nobody wants to be run over by a bicycle.'

'Now that definitely sounds like good advice.'

'I'll try to think about what else you'll need to learn to survive life on a houseboat in Amsterdam.' Abe laughs, which is infectious, and I grin from ear to ear as we walk along until we finally reach *Westergasfabriek*, which sells everything you can imagine. Stallholders stand around selling Spanish ham, organic food and drinks, crafts and paintings, and there are even vintage stalls selling gorgeous fake fur coats. I suspect this is where Abe bought his long coat.

'Oh wow, I love this place already,' I say.

'It's great, isn't it?'

The smell of spicy salami wafts over as we walk past a food stall. I remember that I still haven't done a proper supermarket shop since I arrived here as I have been so preoccupied with getting the barge comfortable enough to stay in. So, I pick up some cold meats to take home with me. They smell spicy and delicious. Then we make our way towards some of the crafts and I admire some pretty handmade crocheted teddies. It gives me the idea that I could maybe have a stall here selling my felted animals one day.

We wander around the stalls until we bump into Beatrix, who waves as she spots us. Then the three of us stroll around the market with the sound of traders vying for attention and the smell of onions sizzling on food stalls.

'Hey, I have to show you my favourite stall,' says Beatrix, pulling us all in another direction. She leads us to a stall selling home-made wines, where the owner allows us to sample some.

'This is delicious,' I say. It is made of elderflower and nothing like the wine you buy from the supermarket.

'There are no sulphites, so you don't get a bad head with it,' says Beatrix.

'It's totally organic,' says the stall owner.

'Wow, now I can see why this is your favourite stall,' I say to Beatrix. I take a bottle of the wine to try at home and then move on to a stall selling art. The most beautiful pastel painting of a canal in Amsterdam with bikes and people dotted around attracts my eye. I can't leave without having it to hang on the wall of the barge and I promise myself that I won't spend a penny more. This market might be just my kind of place, but I am determined I'm not going to slip back into my old shopping habit.

By the time we head for home, Abe is carrying the painting and I am laden with food and drink. As always, I ended up going overboard but I did need a painting for the wall and, well, who can say no to a bottle of wine that promises it won't give you a headache? Maybe having a stall in a flea market like this wouldn't be such a good idea. I'd end up spending more than I could make on buying stuff. I try to tell myself that I don't need *stuff* any longer, buying a houseboat is fulfilling enough. But today was different. This is about organising my new home.

When we reach our canal, Abe brings my new painting inside the houseboat, and I thank him for giving me such a lovely time.

Erik is finishing off for the day and gathering his tools when we arrive back, and Abe and Erik say something in Dutch to each other. Abe looks disappointed and they both shake their heads. I spot the half-completed floor, which looks worse than when he started.

'I'll have to come back next Sunday,' says Erik.

'What? Are you going to leave it like this?'

'I'll put something over it. I'll see what I can find in the van, but I'm full until next weekend. There is more rotten wood than you said. I should have come here first to check before starting. I thought it was a small job, but now I've started…'

'Oh, I thought at least we could finish the floor. I've got the floor sander ready and everything now. I've only rented it for a week.'

'I'll explain to the store what happened. These things take time. You can't expect a big job like this to be finished so quickly. There's been no work done here for a long time. I'm sorry. Look, I noticed your front door was sticking. At least I can do this on the way out so it's secure for you. Would you like me to take a look at it?'

'If you could. Thank you.'

I try to weigh up the positives – at least I won't have to fight with the door each time I open it, but I am disappointed that I can't get down to polishing the new floors tomorrow as planned. I am also a little freaked out that I have been sharing this place with little critters unknowingly, although Erik assures me before he leaves that the woodworm damage is limited to the kitchen cabinets and we have caught it early enough.

We say goodbye to Erik, and as Abe and I stand there looking at the carnage that Erik has left behind with practically no floorboards or cupboard doors, I could burst into tears. There were bound to be hiccups, and with Abe standing here in the middle of it all, I desperately try to hide my disappointment. I thank him for introducing me to the market and to Beatrix, and we part ways politely as our day together comes to an end. I have enjoyed his company, and after the setbacks with the houseboat I open my new bottle of wine and devour some cold meats and cheese, trying not to dwell on the negatives and instead thinking about how I could have spent so much longer with Abe and Beatrix. In fact, I wish they were here now sharing this bottle with me but that would be terribly pushy of me. We have only just met. They have their own lives and other friends. Just because Abe is particularly caring and helping me settle in doesn't mean that he wants to spend an evening with me too. No, he is a helpful neighbour and there is nothing more to it than that. In fact, this super-cool handsome guy and his lovely wife probably feel sorry for their new neighbour and that is why they are so kind.

Chapter Twelve

Over the next few weeks, I live in a building site. Every now and then Erik drops more materials off with me and the houseboat feels increasingly smaller. It seems his estimation that he could do most of the work in one week was far too optimistic. It is like a huge can of worms, and as one thing is done, another problem seems to appear. Then the inevitable finally happens when he tells me that I must move out so that he can arrange for the fumigating of my home to make sure there is no chance of the woodworm returning. It was the last thing I wanted to do, but I don't fancy being fumigated, so I happily oblige.

Finally, once it is safe to return and I have checked out of the seedy hotel I stayed in when I first arrived, I return home to find Erik already at work as I weave my way through new kitchen units and yet more planks of wood.

'Today I'll be done,' says Erik with a big smile.

'That's great news. What a headache it's been.'

'Ah, this is how it is when you start. But you'll have a brand-new kitchen by the end of the day. You'll be happy.'

'Thank you, so everyone keeps telling me.'

He is right, and by the end of the day, the pale blue worktop and co-ordinating kitchen cabinets look wonderful. The wooden flooring is also finally perfectly level.

'It looks amazing. Thank you, Erik. What a difference.'

'You see, it's worth doing the job right. No point taking short cuts, it needs to be done properly.'

'You're so right. I will bear that in mind tomorrow when I start on the sanding.'

By the next morning, I am eager to start work, and as instructed by a YouTube video, I start with brushing the floor. Then I don my goggles, ear defenders and mask and press the start button on the sander. Even with the ear defenders, the noise is deafening. I brace myself for the pull of the drum sander, but it almost takes me flying across the room as it kicks off. A harsh scrape appears along one of the boards where I have viciously sanded the area while being preoccupied with keeping my balance. I am horrified that I have managed to mark a brand-new floorboard in seconds. It seems I am not as cut out for this as much as I thought I was. How does YouTube make it look so easy? The woman I watched glided across the floor like a gracious ballerina, while I was more like a bull in a china shop.

I take a breather and switch off the machine to try and compose myself. Eventually, I tell myself I can do this and refuse to admit defeat. I start again and, knowing how much force to expect this time, I grip on harder and make sure my feet are properly balanced so I don't cause the floor any further damage. This time, I manage to glide it along and instantly see that it is making a difference, even if there is dust and grit all over the living area and it ends up surrounding me like a smog. Thank goodness I have only painted the bedroom walls so far. Despite the mask, I cough and splutter and stop for a moment, waiting for the air to settle. It's a win.

Once I finish brushing up all the debris, I start varnishing the floor. I want to get started on it as it's going to take an age to dry. I've no doubt it will feel like one of those dodgy nightclubs with a sticky floor for ages if I don't do it properly. I remind myself that patience is needed and feel content as I paint on the first strokes of varnish, revealing a glossy dark-wood floor. Ten minutes later, my body forces me to remember Abe's advice about the kneepads. Now I see what he meant. My knees are killing me. In desperation, I find two tea towels and wrap one around each knee using some masking tape. Thank goodness nobody can see me now.

I sing to myself as I varnish the floor and start to see the rewards of my hard work. Two coats and the floor will look like new. But then, as I am screeching out a song, I think I hear a knock on the door.

I groan as I stand up, since I can't seem to move nowadays without groaning. Then I look down at the tea towels on my knees as I head to the door. Oh no. I have no choice but to open the door like this. It's Abe, and the first thing he does is look down at my knees.

I try pulling at the masking tape but practically manage to strangle the circulation around my legs and end up plopping backwards as I stumble.

'Are you okay?'

'No, not really. Would you mind coming in and helping me cut this tape off, please? I think I'm stuck.'

I manage to limp my way to the kitchen drawer where I keep the scissors, and pass them to Abe as I plonk myself down on the old chair. He proceeds to patiently cut off my home-made kneepads.

'Never again. I don't know what I was thinking.'

'Well, it's just as well I came over to give you these. I was off to work but wanted to see if you needed them before I went. I guess you did,' he says, handing me a pair of proper kneepads.

'Thank you. You're amazing. And my knees thank you very much…'

'No problem. It's looking so much better in here already.'

'I'm glad you think so. I guess I'm lucky that Erik is such a great carpenter. He's made a huge difference.'

'Well, that and what you've done so far. You've done a lot of the work, too. You should be proud of it.'

'Thank you. I guess you can buy anything, but putting the work in yourself feels so much more worthwhile.' He doesn't need to know about all the mishaps I have had.

'For sure, and talking of hard work, I'd better get over to the cafe. Good luck with the rest of the varnishing.'

'Thanks again for the kneepads, and good luck at work!'

Good luck at work? Shouldn't I have said, *have a nice day,* or something else?

As Abe heads off into the distance, I return to finishing the floor with the help of his kneepads. The sooner this boat is sorted, the sooner I can get out and explore the wonderful sights of Amsterdam and maybe meet more new people. If everyone is as lovely as Abe and Beatrix, then I can't wait to make new friends.

By mid-afternoon, I have finished the varnishing and stand back to look at my work. I am delighted with the result. It almost looks like new in here. The damp odour has been replaced by the fresher smells of polish and varnish. My final job of the day is to bang some nails into the wall of the living area and hang the painting of Amsterdam that I picked up at the flea market. I only need my Persian rug to be delivered once the floors are dry and the interior decorating will be complete, which will then leave the job of the outside renovations – but one step at a time. In the meantime, I will be hobbling around on tiptoes trying to avoid walking on the wet patches of varnish, which feels a bit like playing hopscotch as I pray I don't lose my balance.

As I contemplate going outside to get a quick snack, I see that Debbie has messaged me. I had let Hannah and Debbie know that I was safely in Amsterdam when I arrived but, apart from that, I haven't spoken much to either of them since I've been so busy.

> How's it going there? Send pics of the work you've done. I can't wait to see it. I bet it's gorgeous. Nigel is driving me up the wall here and I've never been so jealous. I know I've said it before, but I really wish I could flit off to live on a houseboat.

It might sound idyllic but I'm not sure Debbie would have enjoyed all the grafting and stress there has been. I also haven't told her about the woodworm incident. Nobody sees that side of things, and it's still very cold in here. It's only the hard graft that is keeping me warm.

> You know you're welcome anytime. Whenever you want to escape, come over and stay.

I might take you up on that. I need a break. If Nigel moans about us not having a new lawnmower once more then I might not be responsible for my actions!

I think of my life back home and the competition between the neighbours to have the best garden, the best cars and the newest kitchen on the street. No wonder I was getting caught up in a retail frenzy there. As far as I've seen, it seems much more relaxed here, and nobody cares what anyone owns. Walking around that flea market with people buying gorgeous pre-loved vintage clothes made me realise that having the latest of everything is a waste of time. It's much better to have quirky, interesting pieces rather than the same as everyone else.

As I lock up the houseboat to venture out for lunch, I think of Abe. He's quirky. He's not your Mr Darcy type at all, but I think that is what makes him so attractive. Beatrix is a lucky lady. I would much prefer someone laid back and cool with a greying ponytail than a dashing man in a suit who could potentially tread on anyone to get what he wants. I couldn't imagine being with a snobby, stuck-up man who irons his socks or his underpants and wants everything perfect. Give me stubble and a dirty laugh any day!

Like men, I like my food casual and so I search for a place that sells fast food through a hole in the wall. I love the food from the automatiek that is almost like a vending machine with hot food; it's so different. Where else can you open a sliding window and remove a warm ham and cheese croquette for two euros? I always wonder what goes on behind the sliding window. There are no staff around, and it is as if there is some robot behind the sliding window making fresh croquettes and burgers. I wonder why anyone needs fancy food when you can munch on one of these mouthwatering masterpieces!

Heading back home with a full tummy, I realise how happy I am starting to feel here. The loneliness I felt back home has been replaced by a sense of satisfaction. For the first time in years, I feel content with myself and am not afraid of the future and what it may or may not bring.

I arrive home to the houseboat to see a delivery man knocking at the door. He has my huge nomad rug all wrapped up in plastic.

'So sorry, I didn't realise you were delivering today,' I say, as I rush up to him.

'We were told we could only delay your delivery until today. We were in the area, so we thought we'd drop it off.'

'Umm, it's still a bit soon, but that's okay.' The floorboards are going to take forever to dry but I suppose I can leave it in the plastic in a corner for the time being. At least it's here ready for when the floor does dry.

I squeeze past my glorious rug as the delivery guy leaves it with me. I can already see that it is going to fit perfectly once I can put it down. While part one of my superficial houseboat makeover is practically done, I won't send photos to Hannah and Debbie until I've been to the market for my tulips. I want it just right before I send them the final 'after' photos.

Forty-eight hours later, when the floor is dry and I can put my nomad rug out, it couldn't look better. Since I want to get some tulips for the finishing touch, I decide to head to the *Bloemenmarkt* early. As I walk along, I begin to think how I may need to get a bike with a basket, just like that woman I saw on my first day here. That might have to be my one last investment. I probably can't consider myself a true Amsterdam canal dweller until I own a bike and leave it propped up on the side of my houseboat. As I envisage myself riding along the endless cycle lanes, I become excited at the idea. The funny thing is though, despite all the bikes around, I haven't noticed a cycle shop yet.

The floating flower market was one of my favourite places the last time I was in Amsterdam with Nicky. Here, flower shops lined up in barges along one of the many canals sell every kind of tulip imaginable, along with exotic orchids, geraniums and narcissus depending on the time of year. I might be starting a new life in a new country, but if I could have imagined myself alone in my fifties, this is just what I would have dreamed of. Living the life of a nomad and walking around a flower market is not a bad way to live at all.

The scent of red roses wafts over me as I admire a bucket full of flowers in bloom. Tall, bright sunflowers sit alongside them, making the stall a colourful sight. I admire all the vibrant shades of the different flowers, despite the autumn season. I have to force myself to remember that I am here for tulips and not to fill the houseboat until it looks like someone's greenhouse.

With a big smile on my face, I try and barter over a colourful bunch of everlasting tulips displayed at a stall. The selection is too pretty to narrow down a choice of colours, so I've gone for them all. The stallholder wraps the mix of pink, red, purple, yellow and white tulips together as they are all merged into one.

In no hurry to get back, I take a walk along the market with my bouquet. There must be around twenty stalls on the barges, and I stop at one of them to look at the harvest collection of ghostly white pumpkins sat among the most glorious orange ones. One juicy pumpkin catches my eye, but as much as I would love to take it home with me to decorate the outside of the houseboat, it would be far too heavy to carry all the way home. So, I make myself move on and window-shop at some of the stores on the other side of the street. I heard the market has been open since around 1862, but I can't help wondering whether the neighbouring shops were selling the cannabis-patterned socks that are on display back then. I presume not. Nowadays, they seem to have everything here, including tacky boxer shorts and ceramic tulips, but I avoid all the souvenirs of Amsterdam and instead plump for a small coffee shop on a corner to rest my feet. I order a hot chocolate, wondering if it's anywhere near as good as one of Abe's.

I wish I could stop thinking of his hot chocolate – or anything else about him, for that matter. I tell myself that Abe isn't the only hot chocolate maker in Amsterdam and this one will be just as lovely. But it's not. It's nowhere near as creamy and gorgeous. Nothing compares to anything Abe does because he is so lovely, and I am beginning to realise that I have a hugely embarrassing midlife crush on my next-door neighbour, who also has a very lovely wife. The further I stay away from him the better.

Chapter Thirteen

Back home, I settle my tulips into a vase and stand and admire my revamped and improved living room with its beautiful rug, Amsterdam portrait and the soft lighting that gives off a warm glow. I can't believe how much I have transformed this little houseboat already. It is still a work-in-progress, but at least the living area is more enjoyable to relax in now and I don't fall flat on my face when I walk in here, which is a huge bonus.

This evening, the wind is beating against the windows, and I am so thankful for how cosy it feels inside. But before I can settle down for the night in my dressing gown and huddle up, I remember that I have left the deckchair at the side of the barge. One gust of wind and it could end up in the canal. I rush outside to fasten everything down, and see that Abe is doing the same thing. I guess securing the barge will need to become second nature if I don't want to lose anything overboard in a storm. As I fight with the wind and my deckchair, Abe waves. I try to shout hello and tell him that I have finished the last of the work inside, but he can't hear me over the storm, so he comes rushing over asking if I need any help.

'No, I was just trying to say that I finished the living room.'

'Oh, I'd love to see how it looks. Let me go and secure everything back home and I'll come over.' So much for staying clear of Abe. Why does he have to be so friendly?

When he returns, I am surprised to see him standing at the door with a bottle of prosecco. I look around hoping Beatrix is close by, but she is nowhere to be seen.

'It's a housewarming present for you, now that you've finished some of the hard work.'

'That's so sweet of you. Still plenty of things to do but at least it's habitable now. Thank you for the bottle. Please thank Beatrix for me too.'

'You're very welcome. We both agree that it's tradition. You have to christen your houseboat.' I am not sure whether the tradition is to open the bottle, or if you're supposed to smash it against the side. I don't want to waste prosecco and leave it to run into the canal, no matter what the tradition dictates.

'Christening sounds good. Umm, would you like some?'

'Ah, are you not doing anything?'

'No, not really. I'm just sat here listening to the wind outside. No exciting plans. Where's Beatrix and Ted? Do they want to celebrate with us too?'

'Ah, Beatrix is at her book club tonight. But I'm sure Ted will join us. I'll go and get him. I'll be right back – don't go anywhere!'

While Abe goes to pick up Ted, I search for wine glasses and then straighten down my jumper. I'd be happier if Beatrix was here as I would hate for her to get the wrong impression and think I am trying to lure her husband away but at least Ted is coming. When Abe and Ted arrive, I pour out the prosecco and pop a cushion down on the floor for Ted. I sit down on my new pink sofa, which has finally been delivered, and perch myself as far into the corner as possible.

'It's looking great. You did such a good job. I love the rug.'

'Thanks. I felt the nomad look suited this place.'

'For sure. Have you always been a nomad?' asks Abe.

'Oh, no. I was married, paid my taxes, worked in the same job since I left school, had a home on a street where everyone kept up with the Joneses and...'

'So, it's true everyone's called Jones in Wales?' interrupts Abe.

'Ha, no. I mean, it's a saying. When everyone competes with each other.'

'Oh, okay. So, what made you move to Amsterdam and leave the Joneses behind?'

'Well, a lot of reasons. I needed a new start. To be honest, I had a bit of an addiction to buying things. I am getting better. But I suppose you could say I was verging on becoming a shopaholic. Then, as I was selling loads of stuff, an advert popped up for a houseboat – not this one. But it started me thinking how wonderful it would be to move here, plus I'd always dreamed of living on a houseboat. My daughter had been telling me for ages I needed to do something. I've loved Amsterdam since I came here with a friend, many years ago. I thought it sounded like fun, and this was my ideal chance.'

'Well, I'm glad you did. It's so good to meet someone different. Like Beatrix said, it's good to have a new neighbour here.'

'Yeah, it's always nice to meet new people. So, anyhow, what about you? Have you always lived on a houseboat?'

'No. You could say I was similar to you. You said you were a what? Shopaholic? So, I was a workaholic. I worked seven days a week. My ex-wife had had enough of it and couldn't take any more. Looking back, I see I was absent all the time. We didn't even have children because I would always promise after the next big deal, I'd have more time to be a father. I was more worried about my boss getting rid of me in the competitive finance industry than I was about my wife finally having enough and leaving me.'

'Oh, I'm sorry to hear that.'

'It's okay. It was a big life lesson. As I got older it made me reconsider what I wanted in life. In the divorce, we sold the big house that the salary paid for, I got rid of my nice car and got a new home on the water. Thankfully Beatrix helped me get through it all.'

'That's good. Beatrix is a lovely woman.'

'She is,' says Abe, looking down at Ted. 'So, yeah, then Ted's owner died six months ago and I took him in. He actually used to live here. Did you know this was Ted's old home?'

'Oh, poor Ted. I had no idea. No wonder he feels so at home here. Well, he's welcome here anytime. How old is he?'

I look at Ted, who seems so content. I hope he doesn't mind that I have made some changes to his old home.

'He's around nine.'

'Such a sweetie. Well, I'm so glad he has a fabulous new home.'

'Me too. He's a good boy.'

I lift my glass and hold it out to Abe.

'Well, cheers to the brilliant company of dogs.'

'To brilliant company.'

Abe and I look at each other for so long that I eventually have to turn my head.

'So, what's next on the agenda for the home improvements?' he asks finally.

'I'm pleased you mentioned that. I wanted to ask if you have that number for the plumber to look at my boiler. I can't seem to warm this place up.'

'Ah, yeah. I'm so sorry. You did ask me. I'll find it for you because you definitely need it. Wait until winter really kicks in. You need lots of layers here and something to cuddle up to.'

I avoid Abe's gaze as he says this and jabber on about my hot-water bottle nervously. Why I am telling Abe about my hot-water bottle, I don't know.

'So, where is your husband to keep you warm? Or is that rude of me to ask?'

'No, it's fine. He's in Australia.'

'He's in Australia and you're in the Netherlands. How does that work?'

'It doesn't. He's moved back permanently. We're no longer together.'

'Okay, is that so? I'm sorry. Breaking up is hard.'

'Yeah, it is, but I also see my best friend who is quite unhappy in her marriage right now and she keeps telling me how envious she is. Paul and I weren't unhappy. We just wanted different things in life as we got older. We never argued. It just came to a natural end.'

'Well, that's good. There's nothing worse than arguing. My house was full of it, which is perhaps another reason I worked so hard, to stay out of the way. To be honest, my relationship was harder work than my career at times.'

'Yeah, I know what you mean. It can be if you don't get along. It's not the best way to live. Perhaps, when we hurt subconsciously, or feel lonely, we do things that are unhealthy. We binge on food, alcohol, work too much, or, if you're like me, shop too much. I'm glad you're in a better place now though. So, how did you and Beatrix come to set the coffee shop up?'

'Everything is about coincidence. The guy who owned this boat, Henrik, he was the previous owner of the cafe. He wanted to retire and asked me if I'd like to take over. I was still thinking about what I wanted to do with my life as I'd not long quit my job in finance when he approached me. It seemed like it was the ideal time to run my own business, on my own terms.'

'Isn't it funny how sometimes things present themselves to you at the right time? Like this place did with me.'

'Absolutely. Sometimes you're wondering what to do with your future and then something you never dreamed of comes along,' says Abe.

'So true.'

'Here's to new opportunities,' says Abe, refilling our glasses. 'So, once you finish the renovations, what then? Do you work?'

'I was thinking how I'd love a stall in the market we went to the other day. I make things – like crafts – so it would be great to sell them there.'

'If you're serious, I'll ask Beatrix. She knows everyone down there. I'm sure she can help.'

'Yeah, I am serious. I think. Give me a few weeks and I'd love to talk to her about it. I can't believe how kind you've been to me since I turned up. You've helped me with everything. From kneepads to work.'

'We couldn't have you wearing those fake kneepads, could we?' Abe laughs and my face flushes with embarrassment. How could I have been caught in such a state?

'Well, thank you. You've really helped me settle in… both you and Beatrix.'

'It's not a problem. Maybe I'm trying to make amends for being a little self-centred before. I worked in a business surrounded by greed. I learnt the hard way what is not important and what is. Kindness, compassion and being helpful are much more important than material things.'

'Oh, I can relate to that. I guess shopping and buying far too much to try and fill an empty space in my life was a bit like that.'

'It looks like we really get each other then,' says Abe.

His ponytail flips to one side as he looks at me for a moment. His lopsided smile sends a tingle down my spine.

'Yes, indeed,' I say with a big grin.

But then I quickly kneel down to play with Ted and change the subject. Abe and Beatrix are the only friends I have here, and I don't want anything to spoil that.

Chapter Fourteen

Ambling along the canals of Amsterdam, I smile to myself as I think how nice it was to share the evening with Abe. It would have been even nicer if Beatrix had been there too, but I do enjoy being with him and it makes me remember how nice male company is. It's good to have male friends. They give you a different perspective on things and, with a Dutch guy like Abe, there is no beating around the bush, which I like. Why have small talk and dance around a subject, when you can get straight to the point? It was interesting to learn more about him and his suggestions for what I must see around Amsterdam. Last night he told me that there is something like 165 canals here, and they form a ring of canals which they call Grachtengordel. I wonder how long it would take me to get around all 165? I think I'll stick to the main ones for now.

Some days it's nice not to have to be anywhere and have no commitments. Today, I can finally take my time since I don't need to do any jobs on the barge. With no rush to get anywhere, I admire a row of crooked seventeenth- and eighteenth-century gable properties that line the canal with their thin structures standing tall and proud. Then I turn to study the houseboats beneath them. I enjoy looking at the different styles with modern and old juxtaposed along the canals. One has practically got a whole garden on the roof, while another looks well insulated and is all white and pristine. I think of the occupiers and wonder if the houseboats reflect their personalities. One has a painted red door with big yucca plants framing it. The houseboat looks like an Instagrammer's dream.

Eventually, I get lost down the backstreets of Amsterdam and then I am overcome by a feeling of déjà vu. I remember this street from when I came with Nicky. As I look up at the building beside me, I realise that I am standing in front of the museum known as 'Our Lord in the Attic'. I seem to remember it is a seventeenth-century church that looked like an ordinary canal house, which was once used for clandestine church meetings. I consider going inside but decide I will save the museums for when Debbie decides to visit. I can't wait to show her around, even though I am only just getting my bearings myself. Next, I walk all the way to Dam Square, passing a man feeding the pigeons. The birds flock around him – he must be the famous birdman of Amsterdam. Tourists gather round to take photos and videos as the birds ignore the attention and focus on their food.

I don't remember seeing him when we came here in the early Nineties, but I suppose as young women in our twenties we were more fascinated by the shops. The cowboy boots we bought were so different to what was available in Dolcis or Stead and Simpson back home; the shoe shops of the day then. I would love to find the shoe shop we splurged in again, but I can't seem to retrace my steps. Perhaps I will never find it; maybe it's long gone, just like my beautiful friend. Life has moved on since I came here last, and I don't remember the shops that I pass selling leather coats and touristy jumpers with 'AmsterDAM' emblazoned across them.

I do remember the fabulous cheese shops, although I can't help thinking the artisan cheeses for sale at the Sunday market are perhaps more authentic. The good thing is that, despite the fabulous shops here, I don't find myself tempted to buy anything. It is only when I have walked around the shops for most of the afternoon that I realise this, and I am proud of myself for not spending. Perhaps it's because I know there won't be the space for it; or maybe it's because I am out and about and finally enjoying my life. It's a new environment to explore, a place where everything is still exciting and ripe for adventure. Even when I see the sparkly clothes on mannequins that have already arrived in the stores to tempt the forthcoming Christmas revellers, I show restraint. Living on a houseboat, I am more likely to need a thick fleece than a twinkly black dress.

I watch as three women head inside the shop excitedly, pointing to the dresses on the rails and looking at themselves in the mirror. I feel like an outsider as I realise that I am happier getting my hands dirty, and find myself surprised by how content I am with this new leaf I have turned over. All I care about is my houseboat and enjoying each day as it comes as I establish myself in this beautiful city.

It's a lovely autumn day, and as the sun beats down on my face and I start having to unravel my layers, I decide to stop at a pub selling Dutch craft beers. The seats outside are right on the canal and Frank Sinatra blasts out from inside the pub. Sometimes, there are moments in life when you sit back and are grateful for all that you have. This is one of those moments where I am thankful for everything.

As I hold the pint of craft beer in my hand and taste the golden ale, its bitterness biting at my tongue, I acknowledge to myself that coming here was the best thing I could ever have done. Bogged down with everyday life and societal expectations, I didn't realise quite how much I needed a change of scenery and a new start. I am enjoying myself so much that I order another beer and then another.

By the time I am on my third beer, the bar gets busier, and some English tourists ask if they can share my table. I am only too pleased to have the company.

'That's fab. My feet are killing me,' says the woman.

'You certainly do a lot of walking around here.'

'Yeah. That's the problem when you only come for a weekend break. So much to see in such a short time.'

'I'm lucky as I live here.'

'You live here? How fabulous.'

'Thanks. I love it here so far.'

'If you're a local, perhaps you can tell us all the best things to see.'

I try to remember the places Abe mentioned, but I feel too insecure to pronounce the names.

'I'd love to, but I've only been here a couple of weeks. I'm not that familiar with things yet. I mean, I know all the main museums and stuff.'

'Ah, right. Do you live near here?'

'Yeah, not too far away. I live on a houseboat on one of the canals.' I'm still so proud of my new home that I love telling random people that fact.

'No way? That's so cool. I've always wanted to live on a houseboat, haven't I, Barry?' she says looking at her partner.

'Oh, yes, she loves them. You've started her off now. I'll never get her to stop talking about them. I've promised Tracy we'll try the Norfolk Broads one day.'

'That's definitely our next holiday after meeting you. We must do it,' she says enthusiastically.

They both start asking me all sorts of questions about the houseboat and as I answer them, I feel like pinching myself. For the first time in my life, I am not Hannah's mother, or the accounts assistant at the council, but an interesting woman who owns a houseboat on the canals of Amsterdam. My next mission is to learn Dutch; after all, I can't live in a country and not attempt to speak the native language.

'So, what made you move to a houseboat? It's quite a big thing to do.'

'It was one of my wilder moments, I suppose. I saw an advert on the internet and bought it. I hadn't even visited it and just bought it from what I saw online. I truly don't recommend you do that, but it paid off. I'm very lucky that it was a risk worth taking. We've got to take risks sometimes, don't you think?'

'I always say that, don't I, Barry? You've got to grab life with both hands. Make the most of every moment. You're so inspirational and brave. You should do TED Talks about giving it all up and moving here.'

'That's very kind of you. I'm neither inspirational nor brave, to be honest. I just realised that I didn't have much to lose and took a chance.'

'Well, I really admire you,' she says.

'Thanks.' I drain the last of my beer, which is quickly going to my head. That beer was stronger than I thought. Then I bid the couple goodbye and head off in what I hope is the direction of home. Now I understand why Gerrit gave me the floating key ring.

The sun is already starting to go down as I head towards home. The temperature has dropped since I was sat outside, and the thought of a nice hot cup of coffee is spurring me on as I walk. As I pass some of the buildings, I count the windows as I go by, remembering a story about how people used to be taxed by the number of panes. Some of the buildings I pass have so many windows that I wonder how the owners could ever have afforded to pay the taxes. Maybe they were showing off their wealth. I would have probably chosen to put up wooden boards in front of the windows, like some of them have, to avoid such a hefty penalty. Then, as I am looking at the next set of windows, I reach a house on the corner where I see a large stork built into the architecture. For a moment I wonder quite how many beers I have had, until I recall what Abe told me about the stork house. I take a photo of it on my phone and excitedly hurry back to tell Abe I found it. I feel like I have been on a treasure hunt.

I have a spring in my step as I rush home to tell Abe and Beatrix about the stork, but as I approach, I notice that something has been moved on my doorstep. It looks different, and then I realise that something near my front door is slightly off. There is something different about the location of the reclaimed rocking chair I picked up in a flea market. I hold my hand up to the wind. Has there been some kind of huge breeze that is strong enough to shift a rocking chair? It's been the most beautiful day, so that wouldn't make sense. As I get closer, I can see something orange either side of my door. How strange. Someone has been here. At first, I feel afraid. What if someone has burgled my houseboat? I have heard of things like this happening when I did my research back home. I even heard of someone stealing a houseboat and sailing off with everything inside; fortunately, this one can't move. It's bad enough having someone break in, so imagine having your whole home stolen.

Nervously, I approach my front door, wondering if I have anything heavy in my bag to knock someone out if I have to. But, as I get a closer view of my door, I notice the orange objects I saw from afar are two beautifully round, large pumpkins. Surely a burglar wouldn't leave a calling card, unless there is some kind of Pinching Pumpkin Thief of Amsterdam that I am blissfully unaware of. How strange.

Chapter Fifteen

Although I am surprised by the arrival of two pumpkins on deck, I must admit they suit the place. They are just what I would have picked had I been able to carry them. They are perfectly plump, and if there was a pumpkin contest, I've no doubt they would win. I look around for signs of who could have been here, but I don't see anything, and I notice that my lock hasn't been tampered with, so I gingerly open the door. Despite everything looking exactly as I left it, I still call out in case I have missed something. Fortunately, it is silent and there is nobody in sight, so I can breathe a sigh of relief.

Since the only people I know around here are Abe and Beatrix, I pop over to thank them for dropping the perfect pumpkins off. I wanted to tell them about the stork house anyway, so it gives me the perfect excuse.

Ted greets me on deck and lets out a friendly bark as he spots me.

'Hello, Ted. Are your mam and dad in?' I ask.

A guy in a long black coat walking past the barge overhears me and gives me a strange look. Then I notice Abe, who is pottering about on the other side of the roof. I should have guessed he wouldn't be too far away if Ted is around. Abe must be doing some work on board as he's wearing navy dungaree overalls splashed in paint. His ponytail is tied back as always, and he looks like he could be one of the famous Dutch painters at work. How can someone look so good in overalls?

'Hey, how's your day?' he says.

'Great. I came to tell you that I saw the stork house. I came across it on my walk.'

'That means you're practically a native now.'

'Well, I'm still finding my way around, but… Anyway, I also came round to say thanks for the pumpkins. They're so gorgeous. So perfect, and they look amazing.'

'Pumpkins? What pumpkins?'

'The two you dropped off outside the front door.'

'You know, I should have thought of doing something like that for you, but I'm afraid that wasn't me.'

'It wasn't you? Maybe Beatrix?'

'No. It wouldn't have been her either. Not guilty, sorry.'

'Oh. Did you see anyone near the boat today?'

'I haven't long come back in from work. I was just trying to get some painting done before it's completely dark.'

'Oh.'

'I'm sorry if I can't help with the mystery but, since you're here, do you want to come in for a coffee? I'm done for the night. It's getting too dark.'

Although I have knocked on the houseboat door a few times, I have never been inside. In fact, I haven't been inside anybody's houseboat yet and I'm intrigued to know what they're like, so I gladly accept his offer. Besides, it isn't like I have anything planned for this evening except felting and, after three strong beers, stabbing a needle into a piece of foam is probably not the wisest idea. I don't even know where the nearest A&E is yet.

Abe and Ted lead me inside the houseboat, where the delicious aroma of a hearty stew hits me right away.

'Something smells very nice.'

'I'm making *Draadjesvlees*. My gran's special recipe for beef and onion stew. It comes with a serving of boiled potatoes and red cabbage. You fancy some?'

'Oh, no, I couldn't. You keep it for you and Beatrix.'

'No, I'm happy to share. Beatrix isn't here tonight. There's plenty. Please, be my guest.'

If the smell is anything to go by it is far too tasty to decline. I also realise I should eat something after spending the afternoon at the canal-side bar.

'Okay. That would be lovely, thank you.'

'Great. I'll set the table for two.'

As Abe goes into the kitchen drawer to get the cutlery out, I scan the living area and open kitchen. It has a similar layout to my place, and I sit on the comfortable sofa with its grey throw and take in the small oakwood dining table with its two black stools. It's no-frills, but it's homely and cosy. A mahogany bookcase beside the sofa looks as though it is straining with the heavy books it holds. While much of the furniture is simple, the walls show Abe's casual style. A photo of Abe and Beatrix, who look as though they are dressed for a special occasion, sits on a small side table. An eclectic collection of black-and-white photographs of famous people decorates the walls. A Jimi Hendrix portrait hangs beside a print of Dean Martin and a Marilyn Monroe print sits beside Joaquin Phoenix. It's an interesting collection.

'So, you like famous people?' I ask, indicating the walls.

'I like classics. They're all classics from the past. These prints are stories of a bygone era. I mean, I don't live in the past, but it was a cool time in music and the arts in those days. Now everything seems like it's all the same. Industries are so regimented – in those days everything seemed free. I feel like now we are being told what to listen to and how to live and I don't like that.'

'Yeah, I get that. Who wants to conform, hey?'

'Exactly. I told you we got each other.' Abe smiles and I play with my hair self-consciously. Fortunately, dinner is ready, so I don't have to look into those piercing, playful eyes for too long.

'Would you like some wine with your meal?'

'Oh, no, thank you. I've had enough for one day. I found a fabulous craft beer place. It was quite strong stuff.'

'Yeah, you need to be careful of those craft beers. How about a glass of home-made lemonade?'

'You make your own lemonade?'

'It's just stuff I make for the coffee shop. I bring home what I have left. You want to try it?'

'I'd love to.' Seriously? Abe is a man who not only looks cool in his painting dungarees but cooks beautiful hearty dinners and even makes his own lemonade. Beatrix has truly struck gold! But then it occurs to me that nobody is this fantastic, and I wonder if he has secrets to hide.

Still, as I tuck into the stew with little Ted at my feet, I feel so at home. Why are houseboats so cosy and blissful? Anything in the world could be happening on the outside, but inside here with Abe and Ted, it's so peaceful and calm. It's just glorious.

Over dinner, Abe tells me about his day at work and how he made ten Dutch waffles before nine thirty a.m. I somehow can't imagine him in his previous career in finance. The waffle-making lifestyle suits him much better.

'It's amazing how you used to be in finance but are happier now around *stroopwafels* and home-made lemonade. I love what you've done, but I'm intrigued as to what you were like before.'

'I suppose I was more driven then. I guess we change as we get older. We learn what's important in life and what we truly want. It's not the same as when you're younger and have big dreams.'

'You're so right. That's exactly what happened with my ex-husband, Paul. He wanted to go back to Australia and live a different life. One without me.' I am starting to wonder if all these men are going through the manopause or something.

'I don't know why he'd want to live it without you.'

'Oh, thanks.' Why does it feel as though he is flirting with me when he has a beautiful partner? Do Dutch guys flirt, or do they just come out with what they want to say? I desperately try to think of something else to talk about.

'So, umm, do you have any photos of the younger version of yourself? Did you always have the ponytail?'

'No way. I'd never have got away with my ponytail at work. That's why I'll never cut my hair. It's a statement. I'll get you a photo. You can see if you recognise me.'

Abe clears away the plates and enters his bedroom. A few moments later he returns with some photographs. We sit on the sofa together to go through them.

'Here, this is me in my suit.'

I look at the man in an expensive suit. His skin is less lined than it is today, his hair is short and neat, but his eyes look dead. They don't have the beautiful sparkle that they have now. He is a smart man but looks beaten down and it doesn't suit him.

Then he shows me photos of his fast car and his big house. They are all impressive, but I much prefer the houseboat.

'I prefer the person you are today. You look so much more relaxed and chilled,' I say.

'Me too. I was taking tablets for blood pressure. I was super stressed. I wasn't sleeping. I had the wrong priorities. As I said before, I'm not sorry for anything I did, but my ex-wife leaving me like that woke me up. I knew that I didn't want to live the rest of my life in that way. I was an easy-going Dutchman, who deep down loved long weekends, but once I got into that career, it kind of took over.'

'I guess sometimes a career sucks you in. You fit in with those around you and become like them. So, did your ex-wife ever see you now you're like this?'

'No. She was with my boss six months later. So much for not liking career men.'

'Oh, I'm sorry.'

'To be honest, I'm not sorry about anything. I'm glad now. I think part of me was only doing the job because I wanted to keep her happy. She wanted the best of everything, and the pressure was on to be like some kind of power couple. She had friends who would compare their husbands, and I kept not wanting to let her down.'

'Well, I'm glad you found your true self. You look a lot more at ease now than in those photos.'

'I am. A year after I quit the job, I grew my hair like I wanted and became the real me again. I no longer needed the blood pressure medication either. I'll never force myself to be someone I'm not again.'

'That's wonderful. You're so right. Sometimes we lose our own identity in a relationship, and that's not good for anyone. I think Paul may have done that a bit to try and keep me happy, but in the long run he was making himself miserable and he wanted to be back in Australia. I'd have preferred him to be honest and confide in me.'

'Some advice… Often guys don't feel like they can say what they really want to. They don't come out with it.'

Abe stares into my eyes and I feel my face flush. It is time I went home.

'Um, anyway. I don't mean to rush off, but I realised I forgot I left something on at home. I have to go. Thanks for a lovely evening. It's been amazing. You're a fabulous host, but it's getting late. It's time I went home. Please say hi to Beatrix for me.'

I jump up to my feet and hurry out of the door.

Chapter Sixteen

I wake up with a banging headache, a dry throat and the memory of running out of next door's houseboat last night. I sit bolt upright as I remember the evening and decide that it might be best if I keep a low profile for the next few days. My kettle whistles loudly, bringing me back down to earth, and I hear a knock on the door at the same time. What if it's Abe? I hesitate about answering it. Then I see a shadow outside and I can tell by the build that it isn't Abe but the postman.

'Good morning, you need to sign for this,' he says.

I peek my head outside, towards Abe's boat. There is no sign of Ted on deck, so I guess they are already at the coffee shop. I decide it might be for the best not to pop in for those lovely hot chocolates anytime soon. I would hate for Abe or Beatrix to think I am always hanging around. The only consolation is that my mail will keep me busy for a while. I look at the books that have come in the post – *Dutch in Four Months*. Since I managed to find a beginner's Dutch class in Amsterdam that starts next week, I wanted to be prepared. There's nothing worse than walking into a class with no experience, so I thought this should help me feel a little more confident. With nothing planned for today, I sit with a coffee and start reading right away.

'Dank je,' I repeat. At least I can say thank you for my coffees now.

'Goedemorgen,' I say out loud to myself. I'll practise this the next time I see the postman.

This is going to be so easy. Then I look up the words 'I am sorry', since I always seem to be apologising for myself, although I am trying to stop that terrible habit.

'Het spijt me.' Is that right? It sounds like *spit on me* or something. I hope I don't say that wrong. This then leads me down a rabbit hole of new vocabulary. By the time I have learnt a few basic words, my head is thumping. A mixture of yesterday's beer and it being a long time since I had to concentrate on learning something new, I can feel the fatigue setting in. Knowing that Abe is safely nowhere near home, I decide to go for a walk to clear my head.

The autumn air is exactly what I need, and I feel better for getting outside. I have no idea where I am heading but it feels good to take my time and look around the streets. As I am walking past a shop, the smell of caramel and fresh dough wafts over me. Since I skipped breakfast, my stomach rumbles, reminding me to eat something. The caramel smell is too tempting, and I quickly find myself ordering a *stroopwafel*. An enthusiastic Dutch guy tells me the extortionate price of the waffle and I hand over my credit card. The cost of waffles seems to have risen hugely since my last visit here, but then again this is a European city. However, instead of being handed a takeaway, the guy hands me an apron. At first, I am confused. I suppose eating waffles can get messy if you heap it up with maple syrup, but then he takes me into a room at the back where five happy faces smile at me. For a moment, I wonder if they are still drunk from partying the night before.

'Have you ever made *stroopwafels* before?' asks the super-excitable host.

'Um, nope.'

'It's very easy,' he tells me.

He then presents me with a waffle maker and puts it in front of me. I've heard of self-service but making your own waffles isn't something I had expected, particularly for the price they charge. I look around, bewildered and finally summon up the courage to ask someone what is going on. An American tourist kindly informs me that I have walked in on a waffle-making workshop. No wonder it was more expensive! At first, I feel like asking for my money back and explaining that there has been a terrible mistake. I was only feeling peckish! However, while it isn't quite how I saw my day panning out, looking at all the happy faces, I decide that it isn't the worst way to spend it and so I gleefully muck in and knead the dough without complaint. As I do so, a young guy next to me manages to drop his dough on the floor.

'Ah, it's okay. Start again,' says the patient host, Jan. We all give the guy a sympathetic look.

'So, if you take your waffles and use your cutter. There are all different shapes you can use.'

We all scramble for our nearest cookie cutter. Mine is in the shape of a star.

When I am finally happy with the shape, I pop it into a waffle maker and, like magic, I manage to make the perfect hot waffle. Having made our waffles, Jan instructs us on the next step, which means it is time for the topping. My mouth is watering as I look at the choices of maple syrup, whipped cream, Nutella, honey and hot fudge sauce to choose from. There are healthier options too, like fresh fruit, but I'd have to be a maniac to choose that.

'Oh, I don't know which toppings to choose,' I say to the American tourist.

'I'm going all out. Nutella, whipped cream and hot fudge,' she says.

Jan brings around coffee and tea for us all to enjoy with the waffles and we sit back and relax. I take a bite of the delicious *stroopwafel*, which is truly divine.

'How have I been here so long and not tried a fresh *stroopwafel*?' I say out loud.

Everyone is too busy making 'mmm' and 'ahh' noises to answer. The look on everyone's face tells anyone who might be looking into the room that this is a truly orgasmic experience.

By the end of it, I feel as though I have made five new friends, and I even have a certificate proving that I attended the workshop and that this wonderful experience wasn't some kind of fever dream. I may even frame it since I don't have many certificates that I've earned through life. We all say our goodbyes and I head off with the extra waffle I made, which is wrapped in tissue and tucked in my bag. I consider whether I will eat it later. Then I think how Abe and Beatrix have always been so kind, sharing food with me and lending me equipment for the renovations, so I decide to give them my extra waffle. More importantly, it might also help break the ice after I ran out on him last night, and act as a sort of peace offering to show that I am as interested in Beatrix as I am in Abe.

Even though they are probably sick of *stroopwafels* by the time they leave the coffee shop, I decide to drop the extra one on the doorstep.

When I get back to mine, I am surprised to find a handwritten note has been posted through my letterbox. The writing is in Dutch, and I realise it can't be from next door because they would know I couldn't understand it, so

I quickly try to read it. Is it from the mysterious pumpkin picker? I still have no idea who that is.

I attempt to read the torn piece of paper, but I can't understand a word of it. So, I reach for my language books for help. Word by word, I do my utmost to translate it all.

The first part says, 'You're invited.'

Okay. What am I invited to?

It takes me ages to translate each word but finally I get the gist of it.

> Halloween houseboat plate party on Dutch Schooner. 30 October. Bring your own drinks and one dish. 7 p.m. RSVP

A Halloween houseboat plate party sounds so much fun. Abe, Beatrix and Gerrit have told me how sociable it is around here, but I have been so busy settling in that I haven't had a chance to enjoy the community. I still haven't met many people. This party sounds just what I need. I might even find out who left the pumpkins. Maybe it was someone on one of the other houseboats? Was it a housewarming gift, perhaps?

I don't know which boat *Dutch Schooner* is, but I immediately write a note to say how much I would love to attend and apologise for my lack of Dutch. Having the note to deliver will give me an excuse to check out the neighbours' houseboats. I decide to drop the note off right away, before I forget to RSVP.

I pop my coat back on and pass next door's boat first. I look at *Aquaholic*, which is such a fun name for a houseboat. Now that I know about Abe's past, I guess the name also seems appropriate given his previous life as a workaholic. I consider what mine should be called. At the moment, it has a Dutch name, which is quite a mouthful, and I am ashamed to admit I can't even pronounce it. So, I try not to mention its name and merely call it 'my houseboat'. Looking at these fascinating names that tell me something about the personalities of those who live on board, I really think I should register mine with a new name. I remember Gerrit mentioning that this isn't too difficult to arrange. I think about what I should call it. I study the other houseboat names that I pass, some of which make me smile. There is *Liquid Asset*, *Ship Happens*, *For Cod's Sake* and *Bullshipper*, while other boats have Dutch names that I don't yet know the meaning of. I remember a doctor who had a houseboat on the canals of Brecon called *Knot On Call*, which I guess was appropriate. It's further proof that people's personalities shine through via the name of their boat.

Finally, I find the barge I'm looking for. *Dutch Schooner* is an older houseboat, which is similar to mine since it needs some TLC. I try to work out who lives there. Who invited me to this party? There is no sign of anyone around and a simple solitary blue wooden deckchair sits on the deck. Pots with the remnants of perennial plants are scattered around and moss grows on the roof. Whoever lives here doesn't have time to pamper their boat. Perhaps they would rather party.

The scruffy wooden door has paint chipping off it and I post my note carefully in case I accidentally remove any further paint. The boards creak as I try to scarper before anyone comes out. Although I received a friendly party invite from here, it looks like one of those places where someone might come out and threaten you with a shotgun for trespassing. There is something a little creepy about it, and an awful thought occurs to me that I could be the only person invited to the Halloween party. Now that would be incredibly scary. Surely the person who owns this place isn't that weird?

Chapter Seventeen

Five days later I find myself standing outside the *Dutch Schooner* with a plate of Welsh cakes in one hand and a bottle of Chardonnay in the other. I thought if I had to bring a plate, then I may as well bring a traditional Welsh delicacy as my first introduction into the community. It doesn't get better than Welsh cakes. They're freshly cooked and still warm; I hope whoever is about to eat them finds them as tasty as the nation's *stroopwafels*.

All day I have been filled with trepidation. The thought of meeting others in the community is exciting, but I'm also a teeny bit nervous that the invite might be from some strange person luring me here under the pretext of a party. Although, by the noise of the music and the people I can see hanging around outside, it seems there is nothing to fear; the party is real and I haven't been invited here on some false pretext.

I fiddle with the devil horns I am wearing before making my entrance. The invite didn't mention anything about the dress code, but since it's a Halloween party I thought I should make some kind of effort. If nobody else has dressed up then I figure I can quickly whip them off. It's a win either way. Although when I look around, I can see some people have made a much bigger effort than me. There are ghouls and witches; someone is even dressed as a pumpkin, which reminds me to ask if anyone here knows about my mysterious pumpkins.

I say hello to a witch with a big green wart on her nose. She waves her drink at me, and I carry on walking to try and find out who the host is. Inside people are crammed together and it makes me wonder how many people can legally fit on a houseboat. I am sure it can't be this many. I hope it is strong enough to withstand the weight and we don't all sink. It seems I am the only outsider here, as when I stand around inside everyone seems to know each other and is chatting away. I put the Welsh cakes down on a long table filled with Dutch snacks and pour myself a glass of wine. I didn't realise quite how awkward I would feel as the only person here who doesn't know anyone. Instinctively, I search for Beatrix and Abe. I'm sure if they are here then they will be kind enough to introduce me to some people. I just need one friendly face, but it is hard to see who anyone is between the costumes and the way everyone is squashed together. I manoeuvre my way into a little corner in the kitchen where I hope to feel a little less intimidated. Fortunately, I hear a female voice shout my name.

'Sandy, hi.'

I look around to see Beatrix dressed up as a gothic princess. She looks amazing in her long purple and black dress with her hair pulled back into tight braids.

'Beatrix, how lovely to see a friendly face. I don't know a soul here.'

'We can't have that. Let me introduce you to some people.'

I almost feel like a child on her first day in a new school as Beatrix takes my arm and leads me towards a woman dressed as a gory nurse covered in blood.

'This is Annelise, who invited you. It's her place.'

The woman, who must be in her early thirties, holds out her hand to greet me.

'I heard a British woman bought old Henrik's houseboat. Welcome, it's good to finally meet you. Sorry, I should have written your invite in English. I just wrote them all out and posted them. I didn't think.'

'Oh, no. It's fine. I'm supposed to be learning Dutch anyhow. *Stroopwafels*! You see? That was the first word I learnt.'

'Ha. Well, that's an important one, for sure.' Annelise laughs and then tells me that I must meet Pieter, who spent a while in the UK.

'Pieter, I want you to meet Sandy. She's bought Henrik's boat.'

Pieter is a friendly, jolly guy, with red cheeks and a smile that beams from ear to ear. He juggles his pint as he stretches his hand out to greet me.

'It will be good to speak English again. It's been getting rusty since I left as an exchange student.'

'Great, well, I'm happy for you to keep up your English if I can practise my Dutch on you. I'm trying to learn. I start my lessons next week.'

'Anytime. You'll find me on *Ship Happens*, it's just on the other side from here.'

'Ah, yes, I remember seeing that one.'

'It's not the finest houseboat here, but I love it. It's named after my divorce.'

I can't help but laugh and tell him how fabulous the name is. We chat about things he misses in England, such as the fish and chips he enjoyed on his school exchange in Barnsley.

Pieter insists I meet his girlfriend, who has moved in with him on board *Ship Happens*, and so we head over towards the bathroom where she is standing. Lotte is as friendly as her boyfriend and welcomes me to the community. Beatrix joins us and says Abe is on his way but has been delayed at the cafe.

I don't know much about Beatrix, and I am about to ask her about herself when a tall, handsome Dracula walks in.

'Ah, my brother finally got here,' she says.

'Your brother?'

I look in the direction of where she is looking and the only person that I can see is Abe.

Pieter waves him over.

'I haven't seen Abe for a while. It's good to catch up.'

'Sorry,' I interrupt. 'Is Abe your brother, Beatrix? You're brother and sister?'

'Yes, what did you think?'

'I don't really know. I thought perhaps you were together.'

Beatrix laughs so hard she makes a funny snorting sound.

'Hi, what's so funny?' says Abe, joining us.

'Did you know that Sandy thought we were dating?'

'Well, I didn't know. I mean, you seem to get on well and… umm.' I think of how Abe talked about how Beatrix helped him when he was getting divorced. How could I get it so wrong? She helped as his sister!

'Ha. I must be spending too much time with you,' says Beatrix to Abe.

Abe looks at me and smiles, then he shakes his head.

'You got it all wrong, but I'm very glad it's been cleared up now,' he says, giving me one of his bewitching smiles. Does this mean he is free and single?

I take a sip of my wine to compose myself as he stares at me.

Pieter and Lotte interrupt the silence by telling us they need to go over and speak to someone and Beatrix goes with them. I am about to turn to Abe again when a woman called Camilla comes over and makes a fuss of him, putting a halt to any conversation. Abe introduces us but she isn't as friendly as the others. She seems hostile towards me. She simply says hi and starts whispering in his ear, making me feel like a spare part.

I turn to watch some of the revellers dancing in their crowded space as they start to get merry. As much as I want to mingle, I don't have the confidence to approach strangers and introduce myself. I am certainly not as confident as Camilla, so I am grateful when a young lad named Dirk comes up and says he likes my devil horns. He then gets whisked off to dance by a girl in her twenties, and I am left with Camilla who still won't leave Abe alone. Eventually, I decide it's time to leave. At least I have shown my face and will now hopefully recognise more people around here. While everyone I have spoken to has been lovely, apart from Camilla, I can't help feeling like the outsider. I find Annelise and thank her for having me before leaving, grabbing a beef *bitterballen* from the buffet table on the way out.

As I have this big ball of beef in my mouth, I come face to face with Abe, who must have somehow managed to tear himself away from Camilla.

'Hi, I was hoping I'd catch you before you left,' he says.

I try to swallow as quickly as I can so that I am able to respond. I curse myself for being so greedy and not taking a delicate bite out of it instead of shovelling it all in. That will teach me!

It seems like forever that he watches me chewing like some kind of goat, and then finally I swallow and reply.

'Yeah, I wasn't sure who'd be here but, yes, it's good to see you.' I look at him, trying not to acknowledge that I got him and Beatrix completely wrong, and a part of me is secretly ecstatic but also incredibly nervous about doing anything about it.

'You too. How have you been?' he asks.

'Good. I learnt how to make *stroopwafels* the other day.' I eye him nervously, waiting for some recognition; some sign of gratitude for the one I left him and Beatrix. Will he thank me for it when he realises it was me who dropped it off for him?

'That's great. You're really settling in well.'

I feel a twinge of disappointment that he doesn't offer even a flicker of recognition or gratitude.

'Umm, yeah, I am. I'm starting to learn Dutch, too.'

'You'll have to let me teach you the best words. They're not in the books. Only a local can teach you those words.' Abe winks and then stares intently at me, with the collar of his Dracula costume touching his ponytail, the red face paint bleeding down from his lip. By the naughty look in his eyes, I don't think he means he wants to teach me polite Dutch words for *please* and *thank you*. I am so attracted to him, but I still have to remember that he is my next-door neighbour and I am not looking for a relationship.

'*Ik wil je kussen.* I mean, did anyone teach you that?'

'Um, no, but it's early days. I've only read the first few pages of a book.'

'Ah, well, I hope you can study it quickly and then you can answer me if it's okay or not. Although, why wait? I asked if I can kiss you. Is that rude of me?'

'Oh, umm. No, it's not.' I feel my cheeks flush and despite all my fears and reservations, I lean over to him and give Abe the quickest peck on the lips. It feels so functional and unromantic and I curse myself for being so clumsy. However, Abe gently pulls me back to him and kisses me. My body feels as though it wants to explode, and a warm tingle runs right through me. The houseboat might be full to the brim with partygoers but, as Abe kisses me, I am oblivious to everyone around us.

When Abe insists on walking me home, I don't argue that I am a grown, independent woman who doesn't need a chaperone. Instead, I take his hand and walk along the canal with him. We walk past the nearby houseboats, most of which are in darkness, since their owners are still at the party. You can tell which are the barges that are rented out to tourists as they are still lit up with twinkling lights.

We walk hand in hand beneath the street lights that shine down on us, creating ghostly shadows that complete the eerie Halloween feeling in the air. As we hold hands it strikes me quite how tall Abe is compared to my five foot five stature. He must be at least six foot three.

While we walk, I make small talk by asking Abe outright if he received the *stroopwafel*, but he seems genuinely baffled.

'No, I never found anything on my doorstep.'

'You didn't see anything wrapped up in a red tissue?'

'A red tissue?'

'Yes.'

'Ah. Okay. Now it makes sense. I came home the other night and Ted was ahead of me. When I reached him, he had shredded tissue everywhere. He must have eaten it!'

'Oh, naughty Ted. How funny. Thank goodness I hadn't put any chocolate topping on. I should have thought. I'm so sorry.'

'No, it's fine. Thank you, I am pretty sure Ted appreciated it.'

We have just stopped laughing about Ted and how naughty he can be when we reach my houseboat. I am nervous of what Abe will expect. I hope he doesn't want to come in.

'Umm, so I guess I'd better get to bed,' I say. I hope he doesn't think I mean with him joining me!

'Yes, of course. It's late and I'm in the cafe early tomorrow.'

'Well then, thank you for walking me home.'

'Thank you for allowing me to.'

Abe reaches towards me and kisses me goodnight. It is all very polite and, thankfully, he is the perfect gentleman. I practically skip inside and lean against the door as I think about how lovely he is. As I grin to myself, I know exactly what name I am going to call my lovely houseboat. It is going to be called *New Beginnings* and I couldn't think of anything more appropriate.

Chapter Eighteen

It's not exactly a beautiful new beginning when I wake up bleary-eyed the next morning, but I still have a smile on my face and nothing is going to take that away, despite the fact that I could stay in bed and *cwtch* in all morning. I force myself to get up and put the kettle on in case I am tempted to stay in bed. I switch on my phone as I wait for the kettle to boil and am surprised that it starts ringing immediately. My first concern is that something has happened to Hannah. Is it an emergency? I calm myself down by reminding myself that Paul is there with her in Melbourne, but still, the anxiety is unbearable until I realise that it is Debbie.

'Hi, everything okay? It's early.'

'You must have slept in. It's nine thirty a.m. here already.'

'Oh, gosh, yes. I have. Had a bit of a wild night last night. Who'd have thought I'd be having wild nights out in Amsterdam at this stage in my life, hey?'

'I'm so glad for you, but…' Debbie starts crying.

'Oh, Debbie. I'm sorry. I'm going on about myself. Are you okay?'

'No, I'm not. I've had the biggest row with Nigel. Can I come and stay?' Debbie sobs down the phone and I wonder what can be so bad between them that has got her into such a state.

I can't bear to hear her so sad. The one thing I don't miss about being married is an upsetting argument with your other half.

'What on earth's happened?'

'He's being a jerk. You know what he can be like. He's giving me the silent treatment and the atmosphere is awful. He's slamming things down and being horrible. I can't live with him any longer, honestly. I know you've only just moved there, but please can I come and stay for a week or two? I need some time to think.'

'Of course you can. I told you that you're always welcome here. Tell Nigel to stop being so childish. Do you want me to sort him out? Shall I speak to him?'

'Ha, no. It's okay, I think we need a bit of a break away from each other. We're around each other too much and getting on each other's nerves. A break will do me the world of good. Thank you, Sandy. You're the best friend ever.'

'Don't be silly. Look at the times I was upset when Hannah moved over to Australia. I was always bursting into tears because I missed her so much. That's what friends are for. Through thick and thin, we are. So, when did you want to come over?'

'Tomorrow? Is that okay? There's a flight leaving Cardiff around five and there were a couple of seats left when I last checked. Is it okay if I get that one?'

'Yes, of course it is. It'll be amazing to see you. Goodness, tomorrow. I can't wait to show you around.' I should be starting my Dutch lessons tomorrow, but I guess it can wait a week.

'I know. It'll be brilliant. I get to see my best friend and escape Nigel's bad mood. You truly are a superstar, thank you. All being well, I'll be in Schiphol early evening and will get a train into Amsterdam. I already looked it up and it seems quite easy.'

'Yeah, it's very easy. I'd pick you up if I had a car, but the only thing I plan on getting here is a bicycle and I don't think you'd want a lift on my handlebars.'

'Now that would be hilarious, going along the canals of Amsterdam with me riding shotgun. But no, it's more than enough that I can stay with you. You've already cheered me up no end. Please, don't think about organising anything special. I'll get a taxi to your place. I've got the address.'

'I'm happy to meet you at the station. It's not that far, just a twenty-minute walk.'

'No, it's fine. You know how much luggage I travel with. I always overpack. I'll grab a taxi and be with you by evening. Can't wait to see you. Oh, and do you need any creature comforts from here? Anything you miss from home?'

'Ooh, what have I missed since I've been here? Let me think.' I've been enjoying the Dutch food so much that there isn't anything I have missed particularly.

'Perhaps custard creams. I've not seen any in the supermarket yet. Although maybe I haven't looked hard enough, but a packet of custard creams and some of those fancy sea salt crisps I like would be amazing, thank you.'

'Brilliant. I shall see you tomorrow then, with your goodies.'

'I can't wait.'

By the time Debbie has put the phone down she is sounding a lot happier. It will be so nice to see her, although, as I look around, I realise I have a few things to sort out first. The spare room, for a start. Until now, I've used it to dump my suitcase and anything that didn't quite fit in my bedroom. It's going to be a busy time getting everything ready for Debbie's arrival. I panic as I realise there's not even a bed in there.

I haven't had much to do with Gerrit recently, but I pick the phone up to ask him where he thinks I could find a camp bed at such short notice.

'Hey, how are you settling in?'

'Oh, brilliant. Everything's perfect.'

'I'm so happy to hear that. It's a different way of life living on a houseboat. I guess it's not for everyone, but if you can be chilled and okay dealing with the occasional leak, then you'll be fine.'

'Leak?' He never mentioned anything about those when he sold me this place.

'I guess it's been quite dry this year, so you've been lucky there's no leaks so far.'

'Okay, let's hope there aren't any in the future. Anyhow, do you know where I can find a folding bed?'

'Yes, of course. IKEA. There's a big one here. Have you been there to look?'

'Nope, but that's a great idea. I'll go online now and check it out. Thank you, Gerrit. Don't know why I didn't think of that – you're always so helpful.'

'No problem. Oh, and while you're on the phone, did you get the surprise I left for you?'

'Surprise?'

'The pumpkins?'

'It was you who left them for me? Ah, thank you so much. They add a splash of colour to my front door here. I wondered where they had appeared from.'

'Sorry, I should have sent you a message. I hope it didn't alarm you.'

'No, not at all. I wasn't alarmed, only curious.'

'It's just my wife and I took the kids to a pumpkin patch, and they got a little carried away. They couldn't decide which pumpkins they wanted, so we took far more than we needed. The kids carved the ones they wanted, and we had two left over, so I thought, since you're such a great customer, that I'd drop them over to you. Call it a housewarming present.'

'Well, that's very kind, and thank you for finally solving the mystery.'

As soon as I finish chatting to Gerrit, I order some bits from IKEA, including a camp bed, sheets and a single duvet, along with a print of a sailing boat for the room. It's not quite a houseboat, but hopefully it will make Debbie feel at home. Although as I look at the room in its current state, I can see that it is going to be a big job to sort things out in time for tomorrow.

I sigh as I look at all the mess. Why did I think it would be a good idea to use the spare room as a storage area? There's some cupboard space still left in the wheelhouse, and I find myself stuffing books and photographs inside. By early afternoon, I have made enough space for the bed to go in. By the end of the afternoon, the room is practically empty, although if Debbie opens the cupboard in the wheelhouse, everything is going to come flying out. Perhaps I should have been even more conservative with all the stuff I brought over. I dust and polish and wonder if I have enough time to run to the flower market for some fresh tulips. It would be nice for Debbie to arrive to tulips in her room to make it even more authentic.

Since I don't want to risk missing the IKEA delivery tomorrow, I pop my coat on and head over to the flower market before it closes. As I am passing *Aquaholic*, I see Abe outside.

'Hey.' He waves over to me as Ted comes running down off his houseboat to greet me.

'Hello, Ted.'

'Sandy, I was hoping I'd see you today. How's the head?'

'Yeah, it's not too bad. It was a lovely evening. Hope you didn't have a sore head this morning.'

'No, I didn't have too much last night.'

'Me neither.'

'That's good, I'm glad. Hey, you know, I was wondering if you wanted to get a bite to eat tomorrow night? I know a great cosy traditional place I think you'd love.'

'Ah, I can't do tomorrow night. My friend is arriving. In fact, I'm just on my way to the flower market to get some tulips to brighten up the place for her.'

'That's a shame. Maybe after she's gone, perhaps we could go then?'

'Yes, that would be lovely. In the meantime, I'm sure you'll get to meet her while she's here. In fact, I was thinking of having a party, if she's up to it. I'm officially renaming the boat *New Beginnings*, and I was thinking I might have a naming ceremony party. Although I won't be smashing anything against the deck, of course.'

'That's a great idea. I love the name. It suits you and the boat.'

'Yeah, I guess it does.'

'Anyway, I'd better catch the flower market. I'm going to have to run.'

'Of course. I'll look forward to seeing you soon.'

'Yeah, me too.'

As I walk away from Abe and Ted, I smile to myself. In fact, I am still grinning by the time I reach the flower market and choose two bunches of perky-looking tulips.

The colourful market is so vibrant, and I realise that life can't possibly get any better than this. I am in a city I love, my best friend is arriving tomorrow, and my next-door neighbour is utterly gorgeous and we kissed last night. There is nothing more I could possibly ask for.

Chapter Nineteen

The hours fly by before Debbie's arrival, and I finish getting everything ready for her with only half an hour to spare before the taxi is due. There is no time to even think about Abe and what is going on between us, as I can't wait to see my best friend, who is my priority for as long as she is staying.

Even though I've not stopped organising things and ensuring everything is perfect, I double-check I have a chilled bottle of wine in the fridge, along with some lovely local cheese. I'm going to make sure Debbie has the best holiday ever. I can't wait to give her a big hug and make everything better for her. How I have missed her being able to pop round on a Saturday morning.

I am so excited for her arrival that I can't sit down, and find myself fiddling around with the kettle, then the sink drainer. I must play around with them four times before I am happy that everything is lined up straight.

At the time Debbie is due, I put my jacket on and pop outside to see if I can spot any taxis, but there is no sign of her. I sit down on my deckchair to look out for her. It's getting chillier every day now that the nights are drawing in. I wrap my fleece jacket around me tightly to ward off the cold air. I can see the lights of *Aquaholic* and wonder what Abe and Ted are doing. I picture Ted curled up beside Abe as he reads one of the literary books from his disorganised bookcase.

Finally, I take my eyes off Abe's cosy houseboat as I see the lights of a taxi approaching. I spot Debbie in the back, waving and smiling. It is so good to see a smile on her face again. I run down to the roadside and give her the biggest hug while the taxi driver struggles with her suitcase. She was right about not travelling light, and for a moment I wonder if she is considering moving in.

'Oh, Debbie, it's so lovely to see you.'

'I'm so happy to be here. I honestly couldn't do another night with that man. Anyway, I'll tell you more of that later but, wow, look at this! What a place you've got. This is just so cute. What a beautiful spot you're in.'

'Yeah, that's part of the reason I had to move so fast. Finding something like this is hard. I had no choice but to take the risk and snap it up.'

'Looks like it was worth it. Look at you. You look so relaxed and rested. I'm sure it's taken years off you.'

'Oh, I don't know about that after all the hard graft I had to put in turning this place into some sort of home, but now I can take a bit more time off and enjoy the place. Anyway, come on in. It's so cold out here.'

'It is. I'm sure it's colder than back home.'

'Yeah, it's definitely a few degrees lower. You soon get used to the Dutch climate though, believe it or not.'

Debbie is full of enthusiasm as I show her around the houseboat. I am so proud of my work as she admires what I have done.

'Look at the wheelhouse, and all the lights from the street shining through. Oh, Sandy, this place is just magical. No wonder you're so happy.'

'I am. You know, sometimes a stork lands on there and blocks the sunlight. It's amazing the things you see on the canal.'

'I can imagine. Oh, it's so lovely to be here. I am so chuffed for what you've achieved.'

'I've missed you, Debbie. Come on, I'll show you your room and then we'll open a bottle of wine.'

After offering my room to Debbie, who politely insists the camp bed is fine, we settle down with the wine along with some cheese and biscuits.

'So, tell me. What's happening with Nigel?'

'I've been sleeping in the spare room for the past week. Joanne and Michael, the new neighbours three doors up, have got a new conservatory and now Nigel thinks we need an even bigger one. He wants one of those with a retractable roof. Have you seen the price on them? I said we need to save for retirement next year. We're not getting any younger. Nigel's dad had a stroke before he was sixty. Who cares about a fancy conservatory when that happens? I'd rather open a bloody ISA than the roof of a conservatory. Anyway, he's going ballistic. He's telling me that it is his money, and he'll do what the heck he wants with it, and now he's in a sulk and the atmosphere at home is just awful.'

'Aww, I'm sorry. I suppose it's a lot of peer pressure. That's what I love about it here. Nobody cares what anyone's got. They just want to enjoy their lives. I went to a party the other night with the other houseboat owners and, okay, I may not have spoken Dutch, and felt a little out of place, but what I noticed was how carefree everyone was. It was all about having fun and not who had the best houseboat.'

'I think I need a houseboat, sounds bliss.'

'It is. Well, so far. Although Gerrit, you know, the agent who sold me this place, said something about leaks in the winter, so I'm a bit concerned. Everything seems far too – pardon the pun – smooth sailing so far.'

'No, I'm sure it'll be fine. I guess there's a reason people downsize and live out the rest of their days as they want. It doesn't get better than this. It's perfect for you,' says Debbie, looking around.

'Yeah. I made the right decision. I hadn't even been into half the rooms back at the cottage for months before I did the clear-out. Such a waste of space. Hopefully someone will come along soon and enjoy it there as much as we did.'

'Oh, that reminds me. Someone was there with the estate agent the other day. Fancy car, they had. Some electric vehicle, Nigel said. They seemed all smiles when they came out, and then Nigel said he spotted the car coming back in the evening. I think they were the type that want to check what it's like in the evening, in case there's any antisocial behaviour and stuff.'

'Well, the good thing about *Maes Clos* is that everyone behaves themselves.'

'In front of people's faces, perhaps. You know that Adrian got five years for swindling the cricket club. That's the end of them both on the street. No sign of either of them. Well, I suppose there wouldn't be any sign of Adrian when he's been banged up. But the house is for sale now. Although, don't worry, it won't be any competition to yours. You've a much nicer back garden.'

'I must admit, I do hope it sells soon. It'll feel like closure. I really don't think I'll ever be going back to the UK. I want to stay here for the rest of my life.'

'I hate to hear that, but I'm glad you're so settled. It's good to see you like this. So independent and happy. It's like you've got a new lease of life. I'm still so jealous. Not in a mean way – I just wish I could have your life. It's amazing,' says Debbie as she finishes off the rest of the wine. 'Thank you again for having me to stay, I feel so much better already. Just getting out from under the same roof as Nigel is a relief.'

'Oh, I'm sure you'll both make it up soon. You know what you two are like.'

'I don't know this time. I really don't.'

'Well, how about we do the sights of Amsterdam tomorrow to take your mind off him? I was thinking we could check out a couple of the museums, art galleries, shops and stuff.'

'That's brilliant. I'd love to do that. See, I told Nigel there was so much more to Amsterdam than the Red Light District and cannabis. You tried to tell him, and I did. He's so set in his ways.'

'Forget about Nigel for a bit. It's time for us to enjoy ourselves. Who needs guys, hey?'

'Definitely. We're so much better off without them,' says Debbie.

I decide that perhaps now isn't the best time to bring up the subject of my gorgeous next-door neighbour.

However, nobody does a hot chocolate or a *stroopwafel* quite like Abe, and so the next morning I decide we should start the day off with breakfast in his coffee shop. I wonder what Debbie's opinion of him will be. Will she think he is as charming as I do? She is quite a good judge of character, and I always value her opinion.

Abe is behind the counter when we walk in and gives us a huge welcoming smile.

'Hey, Sandy. So, is this your friend who's visiting?'

'Yes, Abe, meet Debbie. She's my best friend from home.'

'How lovely to meet you, Debbie. It must be great to catch up. What can I get you both? It's on the house.'

'Thanks, Abe. That's so kind of you.'

'Ah, just being neighbourly.'

I smile at Abe and Debbie eyes me suspiciously.

'Um, is there something you want to tell me?' she whispers as we sit down.

'No, not at all.'

'Go on, I'm not that daft. I can see there's a spark between the two of you. Look at that chemistry.'

'Really? You think?'

'You can see it a mile off. It's like bonfire night looking at all the sparks between you two. I don't blame you, though – he is utterly gorgeous.'

I look over at Abe, who is putting the drinks on a tray to bring over to us.

'Yeah, he is. He's so nice, as well.'

'He certainly is, but if I were you, I wouldn't rush into anything. Have fun and enjoy a bit of a fling perhaps. You're literally living your best life right now. You have no idea how lucky you are to have nobody to answer to, and do what you want when you wake up. I mean, you can do your felting, go shopping… Forget that, maybe try and stay away from the shops, but you know what I mean, you can do anything you please. You don't have anyone to rush home for. Quite honestly, that sounds like bliss.'

I know Debbie has sworn off men and marriage right now but she does have a point. Under no circumstances do I want to give up any of my independence.

'You're right.' Maybe I shouldn't get too involved with Abe. We're good friends who have a bit of a thing going and that is where it needs to end. It would be incredibly awkward if anything went wrong between us with him living next door.

Luckily, we have just stopped talking about Abe as he places our hot chocolates and waffles down in front of us.

'Oh, a man who makes the best hot chocolate and waffles. Perhaps your independence is overrated,' says Debbie, laughing.

'What's that about independence?' says Abe.

'Oh, nothing. We were just talking about something. Thanks for these, Abe,' I say.

'He does seem to tick all the boxes,' says Debbie, once Abe is out of earshot.

By the time she has finished her *stroopwafel* she thinks even more highly of Abe.

'On second thoughts, I think I'd marry someone this good. That was divine,' teases Debbie.

'The one thing I'll never do is marry again. No matter how fabulous they are. I've been there and done that. I don't think you have to marry someone to be committed.'

'Look at you. You really have changed. Nobody is ever going to get you to settle down again, are they? Not even gorgeous Abe. You're free as a bird. Oh, no, talking of freedom, or lack of it, Nigel's texting. "When you coming back?" he says. When I'm bloody ready, Nigel. When I'm bloody ready. On second thoughts, I was right the first time. Never give in to a man. It's a slippery slope. They start by wooing you with hot chocolate and end up driving you up the wall.'

'You two really aren't getting on, are you?'

'No, not at all. Maybe we've been together for so long we've forgotten what we liked about each other in the first place. It'll be forty years next January. Forty years! I suppose it's to be expected that we drive each other insane at times. I was sixteen when I met him. He used to be fun then. Spontaneous and bonkers. He'd make me laugh. Now all he does is irritate me. You know, I nearly bought a book the other day. It was called *Is It a Divorce You Need or a HRT Patch?* Right now, I think I need both.'

We burst out laughing and are so loud that Abe looks over from the counter and smiles at us.

We are giggling as we bid Abe goodbye and leave the coffee shop, walking arm in arm to our first tourist spot – the Rijksmuseum.

'Oh, it's good to have someone to share the sights with. I'm so glad you're here.'

'Me too. It's not the same without my bestie next door. But now I can have fabulous holidays visiting you. It's not all bad.'

'That is true.'

At the Rijksmuseum we immediately head to the second floor so we can see the Great Hall. The headsets that we picked up feed us with information about the museum, telling us how the stained-glass windows, which depict the most important of Dutch artists, are dedicated to the art of sculpture and other mediums.

'Can you imagine Nigel coming here? He'd want one of these stained-glass windows next to the front door if he had his way. That'd get the neighbours talking.'

Poor Debbie, she can't get Nigel out of her mind. If I didn't know better, I would think she is starting to miss him. Every other word seems to be about him.

Next, we head to The Gallery of Honour to see the Rembrandt and Johannes Vermeer paintings. Debbie is excited about seeing a Rembrandt so close for the first time. We are both thrilled to find the famous *Night Watch* painting. We try and count the number of characters in the painting but there are so many. The recorded guide tells us that there are thirty-four, which we can't see clearly as the painting is under renovation. Although we don't mind as it feels as if we are part of an important historic event as we witness restorers working on the piece of art.

'Shall we head to the still life next?' says Debbie.

'Oh yes, I'm looking forward to this bit.'

The still life paintings are incredible. If we hadn't had such a satisfying breakfast, they would make me hungry with the depictions of cheese, oysters and leftover dishes.

Time escapes us as we wander around and then realise our slot is almost up.

'Time to let someone else enjoy it,' I say.

'Yeah. Thank you for bringing me here. I love museums but I never get a chance because Nigel hates them. I'm having the best time.'

'Good, I'm so happy you are.'

'Oh, talk of the devil and he's sure to appear. It's Nigel. I've told him I'm at the museum with you. He's asked if it's the sex museum.'

Debbie rolls her eyes and even though she is still furious with him, she can't help but laugh.

'Ha, well, that might be a museum you could entice him to. Maybe you should bring him out with you next time.'

'No, thanks. I'm relishing my bestie time and besides, I wouldn't want him getting ideas. God forbid, he might want… sex!'

Once again, we giggle through the streets before we decide to stop for a glass of wine at a canal-side cafe. One of the many things I love about this city is that there are so many places to choose from.

Over our wine we talk about how Hannah is settling in in Australia and if I hear anything much of Paul.

'You know, I don't really. We're leading such different lives now with him back home in Oz and me here, there's not much to say. At least things aren't awkward between us. I'd hate to be one of those couples who would have to sit miles apart at their daughter's wedding one day. No matter what has happened, we had a beautiful daughter together. We just drifted apart as we got older. Nothing is going to change the good times we had.'

'Sounds like a sensible outlook. Life's too short to bear grudges, except when it comes to me and Nigel, of course. But seriously, it's not nice when the kids get caught in the middle of two adults separating. I know she's grown up, but you've done Hannah proud the way you both behaved.'

'That means a lot, thank you. So, yeah, it's fine. We're all friends, but there just isn't much to say to each other. That part of our lives is over. I know if he was concerned about Hannah, he'd let me know, and she seems happy over there. I have to leave them to it, really. I miss Hannah though.'

'I bet you do. Maybe she can come over and visit you here?'

'One day, perhaps. For now, she's too busy settling into Melbourne life, living the dream. I'm glad she's found her feet. She always felt like an outsider. By the way, Hannah told me Paul's met someone. It was inevitable, I guess.'

'Really? I wonder what she's like?'

'Well, Hannah seems to get on well with her; I guess that's the main thing.'

'So, you're okay with that?'

'Yeah. I suppose I never expected him to stay single for the rest of his life.'

'I would. If Nigel and I got divorced I'd want him single forever. Ha! But I wouldn't bother again, I'm pretty sure of it.'

'Yeah, I absolutely get the bit about not bothering again. It's different when you're young and want children, marriage, the whole nine yards. I feel as though I've had my family. I'm too long in the tooth for nonsense from anyone now. Besides, I don't want the pain and having to find my feet after a break-up ever again, even though I know it was probably for the best for Paul and I.'

'Totally. That's why it's much better to stay single. You're so lucky,' says Debbie.

I think of Abe and how tempting he is. Am I lucky? I guess I am. I don't even know that I could live with someone again now that I've become so used to my own space.

'Anyway, we'd better drink up. We're not far from the Anne Frank House.'

I lead Debbie through the narrow streets and past the beautiful buildings of the Jordaan District, where we pass antiques shops and art galleries.

When we finally reach the house, I get that déjà vu moment as we stand outside the black doors. This is where Nicky and I came on our weekend trip. I will always remember coming here the first time round. How could you ever forget this place? It will always be emotional, eerie and utterly devastating.

'Are you sure you want to go in? It's quite upsetting,' I warn Debbie.

'Yeah. I want to pay my respects. Such a terribly sad story. She was just fifteen or so when she was killed, wasn't she? Why do people have to go to war?'

'I don't know. As a complete pacifist, I absolutely can't bear it.'

'So sad. It makes you think, doesn't it? Here I am, moaning about Nigel. He's moaning about wanting to spend money and it puts everything into perspective. I think I'm going to give him a ring once we're out of here.'

By the time we have finished our tour of the museum we are both in tears. What awful things this home has witnessed.

'Oh, Sandy. I'm going to give Nigel a ring now. I need to speak to him.'

'Yeah, of course. I'll leave you to sort things out. I'll just pop into a shop around the corner.'

'I won't be long. Just give me two minutes,' says Debbie.

I walk around the corner to a vintage store that I'd heard about. However, as I look at all the beautiful old clothes, it feels so superficial after where we have just been. I am not sure there is much that can lift my mood right now. No beautiful silk scarf is going to make what we have just seen any less horrific.

Chapter Twenty

By the time Debbie finds me, it is obvious from her face that she has finally made up with Nigel.

'Oh, we are a pair. As bad as each other. We're friends again now. Life's just too short for all this nonsense, and I've told him we need to put things into perspective.'

'Too right. I'm glad you've both finally seen sense.'

'Yeah, sometimes you need a huge fight and a reality check to make things better. It was a long time brewing, and now I am actually looking forward to seeing him again. Never thought I'd find myself saying that!'

'Well, that's great. So now that you and Nigel are all sorted, do you want a quick snack? All this walking's made me peckish, even though we had a humungous breakfast.'

'Oh, yeah. Now you mention it, I could do with a little something.'

'Right then, I'll take you somewhere really special.'

I noticed that we passed a hole in the wall selling croquettes earlier and I can't wait to introduce Debbie to one of my favourite snacks.

At first, she looks a little dubious as I put the euros into the vending machine.

'Umm, I thought you said you were taking me somewhere special?'

'I am. You haven't tried it. Reserve judgement for after you've tasted it, please.'

'Are you sure I won't get food poisoning?' she asks jokingly.

'Nope. You won't.'

I hand over her hot ham and cheese croquette and she bites into it nervously.

'Oh my god, this is delicious.'

'Told you, didn't I? Looks can be deceiving!'

Debbie enjoys it so much that she finds a couple of coins in her pocket and buys another.

'I knew you'd love it once you'd tried one,' I tease.

'Better than a lunchtime pasty any day.'

'That's the problem, the food is just too good here. You could eat everything. Which reminds me, where do you fancy going this evening?'

'After being so greedy I'm not sure I'll eat, but I wouldn't mind trying somewhere authentic. I'll be back on the pie and chips in a few days; I want to make the most of the experience.'

'Okay, I'll ask Abe. He was on about a restaurant he wanted to take me to that he said was authentic.'

'Ah, I knew there was more to it than you'd let on. He asked you out for dinner?'

'Well, kind of, but obviously I was busy with you arriving and… We'll see. As you said, I don't want my situation to change here. I'm happy as I am.'

'Yeah, I know. Maybe you're better off as friends. You really don't want to fall out with any of the neighbours. You know what it's like at home. It gets so awkward. I'm still not talking to Dilys at number nine, and every time I go to hang the washing out it's uncomfortable.'

'She still won't forgive you for the car alarm going off then?'

'Nope. I can't help it there's an electrical problem. It's an electric car, sometimes it goes a bit bonkers, it's the way it is. The manufacturer doesn't know what to do with it, so it's not my fault it has a mind of its own and goes off at three a.m. on the dot. I'm mortified, and it disturbs us too. I just wish she'd move, but it doesn't look likely. She's been there forty years and has been awkward since the day we moved in.'

'Well, at least Abe has been helpful since I moved in. He's been a great friend that I wouldn't want to fall out with.'

As we return home, I am more adamant than ever that I'm going to make it clear to Abe that nothing more can come of our friendship. Although as I see him throwing a ball for Ted from the roof of his barge when we get home, I realise it's not going to be easy.

'By the way, I was thinking of throwing a party while you're here. I decided to rename the boat. I'm calling it *New Beginnings*, so we could have a naming party. Do you fancy meeting some of the neighbours? They're quite hospitable around here, and I should probably invite some people over to see the renovations I've done. They might like to see it.'

'What a perfect name. Oh, that would be so much fun. I'd love that.'

'Great stuff. I guess it would be a bit last-minute, but I could invite them. They can only say no. We could drop off the invites before we go for dinner.'

Talking of dinner reminds me that I still haven't asked Abe about the restaurant for this evening, but perhaps I am better off googling it for myself and minimising our contact. I don't want him thinking I'm looking for an excuse to speak to him.

'Do you have invites we can use, Sandy?'

'No, they're pretty cool around here. Paper's fine.'

'Great, well, I'll help you write them up.'

Between the two of us, we handwrite thirty notes and the first one I drop off is at Abe's, where I see him from the window reading by a lamp. I tiptoe quietly off the deck so I don't disturb him, although I hear Ted barking as I leave. As we make our way to a restaurant I've found on Trip Advisor, we post the rest of the invites through the various houseboat letterboxes. I wonder if many will want to come.

When we finally arrive at the restaurant it is small, cosy and like being in someone's living room. It is so quaint, and has even more photos on the walls than at Abe's.

As we sit down, the aroma of hearty Dutch food reminds me of the night Abe cooked. Why does everything have to make me think of him? When I look at the menu, I see a similar beef stew, so it is not surprising that he came to mind. I wonder if this is where he wanted to bring me?

I try to put Abe out of my mind and focus on the exhaustive and delicious menu. Since we have eaten quite a lot today, we can't manage any of the large dishes that we watch the waiters bringing out from the kitchen. Instead, we share a dish between us of mashed potatoes with sausage, bacon and red cabbage, making sure we leave room for a Dutch beer to accompany it.

'I've never eaten so much in one day,' says Debbie.

'No, me neither. Maybe it's the cold weather and all the walking we've done.'

'Or the delicious choices,' says Debbie.

'Yup, you definitely get spoilt for choice here.'

'The silly thing is Nigel would love all this food, if only he were more worldly and would stop refusing to eat anything that isn't egg and chips. Oh, and, of course, he does enjoy his fried spam too,' says Debbie, tucking in.

'Perhaps he'll fancy a trip out here once he sees all the fabulous things you've done in Amsterdam. In fact, he'll probably be jealous when he finds out all that you've been up to. Which reminds me. I know you're staying on a houseboat, so you may not want to do this, but I thought a trip down the canal might be nice for you tomorrow. Do some proper sightseeing from the water.'

'On your boat?'

'No, it's fixed. It doesn't go anywhere, but I thought we could take one of the little boats down the canal – with a proper guide. I've seen lots of people going past on them, I wouldn't mind trying it for myself.'

'That sounds fabulous. I'd love to.'

'Great, we'll do that tomorrow. I can't believe we only have all day tomorrow and then we'll have to prepare for the party on your final night. Time's going far too fast, and you've only just arrived.'

'I know. It'll be horrid saying goodbye to you, but I promise I'll be back again soon.'

'That'll be something to look forward to. In the meantime, I shall read, knit and get on with my felting.'

'Sounds bliss. How's the felting going? Still making dogs?'

'Yeah, the labradoodle club loved them, so I've joined a cockapoo group on Facebook. I may casually drop in a line about how I can make replicas of their little pooches. Although I am prioritising making one of Ted next.'

'Ted?'

'Abe's dog. He used to live on my houseboat. His owner was the person who had the boat before me. He died, and Abe took Ted. He's such a cutie. You'd love him.'

'That's kind of Abe.'

'Yeah, he's a lovely guy, or so he seems to be, as far as I know. Do we truly know anyone, though? Look at Adrian. He was a pillar of the community until he got caught, and everyone thought he was a good neighbour.'

'You do have a point. I hope I can trust my Nigel. I wonder what he's up to right now?'

'Oh, I'm sure he's sat there watching a shark documentary or something. You've nothing to worry about with Nigel.'

'True. He doesn't move from that blasted telly. Now you've really put me off going back,' says Debbie, laughing at the thought.

As we laugh and joke and I enjoy Debbie's company, it hits me how quiet it is going to be again when she leaves. No matter how independent I am, I realise that I like being around people. I enjoy the company of others but then I also don't want to be committed to anyone. Whenever you're in a relationship, it seems there is usually one person who is more serious about it than the other. Is it truly possible to find that balance between having company and not committing? In the longer term, I don't know that it is and so there really is no point starting a relationship with anyone, not even lovely Abe.

Chapter Twenty-One

I knew exactly which cruise I would take Debbie on for our last day of exploring. I have seen it passing the houseboat enough times to know that it looks great fun. I can't wait to see Debbie's face when she sees the boat. We make our way down the canal and, sure enough, when Debbie spots the boat we are going on, she is delighted.

'Am I hallucinating or does that seriously say unlimited pancakes and prosecco?' asks Debbie, pointing to a sign on the side of the boat.

'Yup, I'm taking you on the pancake and prosecco cruise!'

'I think I've died and gone to heaven. Did I tell you how much I love this place?'

'Now you can see why I moved here at the drop of a hat.'

'I must say, I've never seen anything so perfect for us two,' says Debbie, grinning.

I am also chuffed that I can finally go on the boat as Debbie being here gives me the perfect excuse. It is a little awkward to go on something like this on your own when you are a resident. I love having the excuse to be a proper tourist while showing Debbie the hot spots. Normally, when I have seen the boat pass by, it has been full of holidaymakers, but today it seems a large group have cancelled at the last minute, which means we can have our own private tour. The super-friendly Dutch host takes our money, and we set off down the canal as she pours us a welcome glass of prosecco before starting to cook us fresh Dutch pancakes. The cold wind bites at our cheeks as we set off, and we are both grateful for the cosy blankets that are provided as we wrap them tightly around us. It's yet another reminder that my first Dutch winter will soon be upon me, and that will be the real test of my endurance on board the houseboat.

'Did you want fresh fruit, cheese or Nutella on your pancakes?' asks the host. Of course, there is only one answer to that, and both Debbie and I reply at the same time.

'Nutella!'

As we bite into our steamy-hot pancakes, the host turns into a knowledgeable tourist guide. She starts by telling us all about the old-fashioned window tax that I knew about, and then tells us why the Dutch often leave their curtains open. Something that I have been most curious about.

'So, it dates back to the war when families of soldiers could keep an eye on each other. If they left their curtains open, neighbours would know if the people inside the home were okay or not. There are some stories about it being because the Dutch are open and have nothing to hide, but that is the true history of it. Nowadays, people don't really expect you to stare in, as it's not good manners.'

'That's so good they looked after their neighbours like that. Almost sounds like home,' I say.

'Yup, it does. People trying to have a nosy inside your home. Sounds just like our street,' says Debbie, giggling.

As we cruise further along the canal, we reach my houseboat. It is exciting to see it from this angle. Although it still stands out next to the other homes for all the wrong reasons. It is easy to spot the one that looks worn and shabby. I promise myself that the minute Debbie has left I will sort out the exterior paintwork. The paperwork will hopefully have gone through for the name change and the exterior modifications soon, then I can paint the new name on it too. I look up at my place and realise there are so many jobs that need doing when I compare it to others. But who cares? I am not in a competition with anyone any longer. Although it doesn't look quite as loved and homely on the outside as I would like, I try not to be too hard on myself by remembering that it's still early days. In the short time I have been here, it has come on in leaps and bounds. While it is missing the pots of flowers that the neighbouring houseboats have, with the winter incoming, that will be a job better saved for spring.

We soon drift past my home and move next door to Abe's. As we run alongside it, I can see into his bedroom, a room I have obviously never seen before. I find myself staring in, suddenly oblivious to what the guide is saying about the district. No matter how much I try not to look, my eyes are fixed on the man inside who is removing his top. His body is well-built and firm, just as I expected, as I've seen it in my imagination when I can't sleep at night. I am horrified with myself for not averting my eyes. What has become of me? I have stooped to becoming a Peeping Tom! I am about to turn away when Abe looks out the window and catches me. He looks directly at me, surprised. I am mortified but, then again, if he keeps his curtains open with all the canal cruises going past, what does he expect? Perhaps he thinks people will be polite enough not to be nosy and look inside.

I wave and then quickly look away. I have been caught gawping and there is nothing I can do about it.

'You alright?' asks Debbie who, fortunately, seems not to have noticed what has just happened since she was looking at the other side of the canal and listening to our guide, like I should have been.

'Yeah, where were we? What was she saying?'

'Oh, were you daydreaming? She was just telling us that the buildings here are narrow because the government wanted to fit in as many properties as possible. So, they're narrow but tall.'

'Ah, that explains all those steep and scary stairs in the buildings then.'

'Yeah, I wouldn't fancy going down those to use the bathroom in the middle of the night when you're half asleep.'

'No, indeed.'

'She was also saying how no more houseboats are allowed on this stretch, but I remember you telling me that too.'

'Yeah, that's why I was so impulsive, but I have zero regrets.'

The host asks if we'd like more pancakes, and Debbie and I look at each other knowing that we really shouldn't but we can't possibly refuse. After all, I didn't choose a cruise that offers unlimited goodies for nothing.

'Oh, go on then. I'll just have the squirty cream and the chocolate drops this time,' says Debbie.

'I'll have the Nutella again, please.'

The hour-long cruise flies by and soon we are full of pancakes and prosecco. The cruise was worth every penny.

'So, where do you fancy going next? Would you like to visit the Van Gogh Museum?' I ask.

'I'd love to. What a treat of a day I'm having.'

As usual, we walk arm in arm as we find our way to the museum. It's not somewhere I have been to before, not even the last time I was here. So, today's experiences are new for me too.

The museum building is more modern than the older parts of town that we perused around the canal. Its large glass structure at the entrance is part of a new wing that has been added on in recent years. Inside, however, is an immersive experience that is full of history. Both Debbie and I gasp at the beauty of the bright yellow *Sunflowers* painting, while the blue and pink 1890 *Almond Blossom* is incredibly beautiful. *The Potato Eaters*, with their bony hands, has the most amazing detail. Every painting has its own merits, and we are both mesmerised by their beauty.

'We've been truly spoilt. I mean, Rembrandt, Van Gogh – I just can't believe the culture here,' says Debbie.

Yet again I feel immensely proud that this is the city I live in. Surely there aren't many places that has everything Amsterdam offers and comes with such a great lifestyle. It doesn't even feel like city life here. I haven't seen anyone stressed out since I've arrived, for a start.

When we finish at the museum, I ask Debbie what she would like to do next. We could go to an Eighties roller-skating place, a walk in the park, shopping; I don't know where to start with the choices we have.

'Right then, it's up to you where you fancy going next. Is there anything else you'd like to do before we spend tomorrow planning the party?' I ask Debbie.

'I wouldn't mind doing a bit of shopping. I might even pop into one of the lovely lingerie shops we passed now that Nigel is behaving. I'll miss being with you, but it'll be nice to get back to him now.'

How Debbie has changed her tune. I am so relieved things have calmed down for them.

As we head back to the main shops of Dam Square, we pass a flea market. Debbie is fascinated by the juxtaposition of the antiques with the newer items. She roots around the stalls excitedly, although she only manages to find a couple of bits to take home.

'You know, there's this fabulous Sunday market here. I went when I first arrived. There were stalls selling all sorts of crafts. Once my Dutch gets a little better, I was thinking of enquiring about a stall.'

'That's a fabulous idea. I still wear that gorgeous jumper you knitted for me last Christmas, and the felting is going so well for you too. You should get your crafts out there. I'm so proud of you. You know, I almost feel as though this was your destiny. Does that sound weird? If things had stayed the same, you'd still be at home. Look at the adventure you're having. It's brilliant. You seem more alive than I ever remember you being before.'

'Thanks. Yeah, you're right. Maybe that's why I married an Aussie. I was never going to settle with one of the boys from school who'd not left the village. I was always drawn to adventure and travel. Hannah is a chip off the old block.'

'Well, you made the right choice, even if you both went your separate ways.'

'Yeah. I did. I have no regrets. I know it meant that Hannah moved to the other side of the world, but I'm glad for her. We all need to live the life that's best for us. She has found hers, and I think I have found mine.'

Debbie gives me a hug before we head into a lingerie store where the conversation lightens.

'Oh, my goodness, can you imagine Nigel's face if I bought that?' says Debbie, looking at a mannequin wearing a black corset and carrying a riding whip. 'I think he'd probably have a heart attack. Or let me have my own way about the conservatory.'

'Well, you never know. It might be worth buying if that's the case.'

As always when we are together, we laugh and chat while we browse around the shop. After a good look round, it surprises me that Debbie leaves with only a pair of French knickers.

'Don't want him getting too excited.' She laughs.

It's already getting dark by the time we leave the store and stop for a drink at a bar in the Red Light District before heading home. This is the only chance we will get since tomorrow we will be entertaining. I still have no idea who will be joining us, so I'm hoping I will have enough food and drink.

The atmosphere in the Red Light District in the evening is different to when I have passed the area in the day. The red lights above some of the windows are like a beacon in the darkness. As ever, it is bustling with people from tourists to locals, men on their own and couples holding hands. I glance over at the guys who stare into the windows, curious but afraid to go in. When you're in De Wallen, sitting outside a bar under a patio heater is like an interesting social experiment. There are all walks of life down here.

A stag night with the average age of twenty brushes past our chairs as they rush off to the next pub, already merry. I look at them and think how I don't miss my youth. I wouldn't change anything. I certainly wouldn't want to be young now with camera phones recording everything.

I'm glad I spent most of my partying time in the Eighties. I mean, the music was a lot better then, for a start.

We stay at the bar for an hour or two when a rowdy band starts to play, and Debbie and I both agree we should finish the night back home. Something else that has changed as I have got older is the fact that I can't bear too much noise. Thankfully neither can Debbie.

Reaching home, I sneak a peek over at Abe's houseboat as I open the front door. His lights are on. Perhaps, just like me, he prefers to be at home in the evenings.

Debbie is only too happy to head to bed as soon as we get in and, since we have a party tomorrow, it is probably for the best. Besides, I'm more than happy to have an early night. After all, it means I can lie in bed and think about Abe and the bird's eye view I had from the canal cruise today. Now that will most certainly give me sweet dreams tonight.

Chapter Twenty-Two

Debbie has always loved entertaining. She is forever doing a Macmillan coffee morning and when her son, Ollie, was younger, she would be in her element having the school mums over and arranging bake sales. So, I am not surprised to see that she is up at the crack of dawn the next morning and, by the time I get up, she already has the oven on ready to bake for our party. I hope she realises that my teeny oven is going to be nowhere near as effective as her top-of-the-range Rayburn at home.

'I popped out early to the supermarket. I hope you don't mind. Thought I'd bake one of my Victoria sponges. We can show your Dutch friends that we have good food in the UK too.'

'Fantastic… And if nobody comes then I can eat it all myself.'

'Silly, of course people will come. I bet they're looking forward to seeing you again.'

'I don't know. I really should have put an RSVP on the invites. At least then I'd have some idea. I just didn't want to stress everyone out since it was so last-minute that I decided to throw this thing.'

I haven't spoken to Abe about it and he hasn't popped over to say he is coming either. I am still so embarrassed by the fact that he caught me ogling him on the canal. Why do I always make such a buffoon of myself when it comes to him? I have never felt so clumsy and silly around a man. I always seem to be mortified about something I have done.

'I was thinking I could make some cucumber sandwiches, what do you reckon?' asks Debbie.

'Do the Dutch like cucumber sandwiches?'

'I've no idea, but I thought we could put on a British night. Of course, it's your party. But how about jugs of Pimm's and cans of apple cider?'

'Sounds great, although they might think they're at Wimbledon and not at an autumn houseboat-naming celebration.'

'You've a good point. Okay, let's rethink this. How about pumpkin soup, apple and blackberry crumble, as well as my speciality Victoria sponge, pumpkin spice lattes and mulled cider?'

'Now that sounds amazing. Shall I give you a hand with the cooking?'

'No, you know what I'm like. I'm in my element. Leave it to me. You organise the decorations and I'll carry on with what I do best.'

'Fabulous. I'll pop to the shops in that case, and pick up what I can to decorate.'

I rush out, not having brushed my hair properly as I am in such a hurry to get organised with the decorations. As soon as I leave my front door, I see Abe locking up. *Oh no, do we have to exit our homes at the exact same time?* I quickly pull my hood up and try to pass incognito, even though I realise I look like one of the guys down the Red Light District. I don't manage my disguise though, and Abe shouts over to me.

'Hey, Sandy.'

'Oh, hello, Abe. Didn't see you there.'

'You all set for your party later?'

'Yeah. I'm just off to get some bits to brighten the place up. Are you coming over tonight?'

'Absolutely. I wouldn't miss it. I'm really looking forward to it.'

My heart skips a beat at the thought of him joining us.

'Ah, good. I wasn't sure if you'd be able to make it.'

'Oh, I wouldn't miss my favourite neighbour's party.'

I giggle nervously and consider his words. Did he really say *favourite neighbour*? Mind you, I still don't know who Abe has living on the other side of him, so perhaps that is someone totally miserable, and anyone would be an improvement.

'Anyway, I'd better get going. I've left Debbie in charge of the oven, and it can be a bit temperamental. I don't want to leave her for too long.'

'Yeah, I heard terrible things about that oven from Henrik. You must be careful not to let it overheat.'

Oh. I guess a new oven should be next on my never-ending list of home improvements then. I think of Nigel's words about the cost of boats. I am beginning to think he wasn't just being a killjoy.

I bid goodbye to Abe and set off to the shops. I want to get back as soon as possible so that I can make sure everything is absolutely perfect for tonight; especially now I know that Abe will be coming.

By seven p.m. I have tied Dutch and Welsh flags all around the houseboat and we are ready to expect the unexpected. I might have no idea who will show up tonight, but at least I know Abe will be here, and Gerrit is coming along with his wife.

Debbie has arranged a mouthwatering display of autumn dishes and the smell of pumpkin soup is wafting through the air. With the mulled cider simmering away, you could almost bottle the smell in here and sell it as an autumn cologne down the market.

We put on some Nat King Cole in the background and wait for everyone to arrive. The one thing I have learnt about people here is that everyone is quite casual and, while back home I would have probably put on a nice dress whenever I was throwing a party, tonight I am wearing jeans and a jewel-coloured plum jumper that sweeps down at the neck, revealing a thin silver chain. I take one last look in the mirror and get ready to welcome Abe and the rest of my neighbours.

The first people to arrive are Pieter and Lotte, whom I met at the Halloween party.

'Hey, you made it. Good to see you.'

'We never miss a party. Smells gorgeous in here. Like cinnamon and spices,' says Lotte.

'Ah, that's all down to my friend Debbie here, she's amazing at catering for parties. Please do try one of her mulled ciders,' I say, handing her and Pieter a cup each.

I leave them chatting to Debbie as I open the door to more arrivals. Six strangers, who I don't remember from the party, turn up and introduce themselves as neighbours from further down on my side of the canal. They say their names quickly, but I am unable to remember or pronounce them, so I point to Debbie and tell them she will get them drinks. Let's hope Debbie doesn't ask me to introduce them to her. Next, Gerrit appears with his wife, who I have heard so much about. Annika is just as he described. Gerrit told me that she plays a lot of basketball and it's clear by her athletic build. I feel quite unfit just looking at her. She is every bit as friendly and pleasant as Gerrit, and I excitedly introduce Debbie to them, leaving them chatting as I have to welcome another couple who I think I recognise from the previous party. They tell me how much they love what I've done with the houseboat. I thank them and then lead them over to Debbie, Gerrit and Annika for their choice of cider or pumpkin latte and rush back to the door to open it to yet more neighbours. As I am about to close the door, I spot Camilla making her way towards me. Ah, I wonder which houseboat she lives in. I bet it is the perfect one with the cutesy pink roses all around the door. I smile at her as she walks towards me.

'Hi.' I try to welcome her, but she still seems a little hostile.

'Hello. Is Abe here yet?'

I am taken aback by her forthrightness.

'Um, no, I'm sure he won't be long though.'

'Good.' She walks in, almost barging past me. I look over to Debbie, trying to warn her that Camilla is more foe than friend. Other than Camilla, it is wonderful seeing how many strangers have turned up to my party. I never expected so many to show up, although there is one guest that I have been anticipating all evening, and so has Camilla. Eventually, I open the door to Abe and Beatrix, who are holding gifts. Beatrix has a single orchid in a pot for me and Abe has a bottle of the wine we picked up that day at the flea market.

'Oh, you two. This is so thoughtful. Thank you.' I lead them inside and put the plant pot in one of the windows so that people will see it when they walk past. It is far too pretty to be hidden away.

'Can I interest you in the wine you brought, or would you like some of Debbie's speciality cider?' I ask them.

'Cider would be nice, smells lovely. Thank you. The wine is for you, anyhow. You don't need to share it. I remember how you liked it. Please save it for yourself,' says Abe. He smiles kindly at me, sending my pulse racing.

'Great, well, I think that must be everyone here. Let me get you those drinks.' I watch Camilla make a beeline for Abe as they move in to mingle with the crowds. I hand Abe and Beatrix their drinks as Camilla approaches them and head over to speak with Pieter and Lotte. At least they are friendly faces.

Once the final guests arrive, an older couple called Danique and Eddie that I haven't met before, I get everyone's attention and start my speech.

'I haven't met everyone here yet, but to those I have, I wanted to say thank you. You've all been so kind to me. You have made this Welsh woman feel so at home and welcome in your country, and I appreciate that so much. I've also got to make a special mention to Gerrit for finding me my dream home and not trying to dissuade me from buying a houseboat that I had never seen. He must have thought I was really dotty!'

'Ach, you're welcome. I knew you'd love it in the end,' shouts Gerrit.

Then I tell them all how I am renaming the houseboat and that it will now be called *New Beginnings*. We raise a toast to the new name, which all the neighbours seem to agree is the perfect fit, except for Camilla, who stares at me emotionless. Once I finish the speech, I notice her make her way out the door, without even a goodbye. I don't know what her problem is, but the atmosphere feels much nicer once she has left.

From then on, the evening continues with the guests chatting politely and talking about life on their houseboats to Debbie. I think she has heard a whole new language this evening between all the talk of bilges, clogged sump pumps and the way they use the Dutch term *woonboot* for houseboats here. But I think they might be putting her off the idea of wanting to live on one, as they share some of the dramas they have experienced on board. I must admit, since I am still a complete novice myself, some of the stories also take me by surprise, especially the one about the previous *Dutch Schooner* having sunk and the neighbourhood trying to save all the stuff on board. I had tried not to believe that could happen, and it makes me glad that I was ruthless with my clear-out and there is no longer anything of great value, or anything particularly sentimental, in here. I have insurance, but still, it would be devastating to lose everything in the canal like that. Apparently, the incident on *Dutch Schooner* happened all because of a water hose that leaked into the boat caused by frozen pipes. As the temperature gets lower, I will keep that in mind.

By the end of the evening, I forget my concerns about sinking houseboats and frozen pipes, as we are all merry and dancing. The subdued Nat King Cole music has been swapped for a dance CD that one of the new neighbours, who I now know is called Koenraad, has dashed home to get. My little houseboat has been transformed from a cosy home into a social hub full of lovely new people. The evening couldn't be any better.

Abe finds me among the neighbours and asks me to dance with him to David Guetta. We laugh and smile as we come closer together and I feel that electricity between us again. Eventually, we sit down on the sofa, where I ask about Ted and anything else I can think of to make sure he doesn't bring up the fact that I was caught gawping at him. He still hasn't mentioned it and I pray he doesn't. When I tell him about all the things that Debbie and I have done over the past few days, I make sure to omit the bit about the canal cruise even though he seems okay with me, and I begin to wonder if he really did see me. Let's hope he has bad eyesight and needs a pair of varifocals.

'I was thinking. Would you like to come to the market on Sunday with us?' he asks.

'I'd love to, but I have some catching up on the felting to do. I've an order back in the UK and I'm way behind after taking a few days off with Debbie. I wish I could come, but...'

'No, it's fine. I understand. We all have our jobs. Maybe next time.'

I hope he doesn't think I'm making an excuse.

'I so wish I could go, but definitely next time. It's just been so busy with Debbie over.'

'I understand, it's okay.'

Abe moves closer to me on the sofa as we chat but, with a houseboat full of people, I hesitate to get any nearer. I pull myself back and once again wonder to myself what I am trying to prove. Why am I fighting this so hard? I am aware that everyone here is enjoying themselves too much to even notice what I am doing with Abe. I am the problem and nobody else. While I haven't felt an attraction like this since I met Paul all those years back, I have way too many insecurities nowadays. What if I fall in love, even though I don't mean to? I already have strong feelings for the man, and it's early days! I don't want to put myself on the line like that and let my heart rule my head. I am a woman in her fifties who is expected to know better.

As the evening closes in, the neighbours start leaving and Abe and Beatrix are the last to head home as the four of us chat late into the night. It's almost one a.m. by the time they eventually head home, and Debbie and I are left with flags that are starting to fall down and the leftovers of a successful party. With everyone gone, the houseboat looks like a dumping ground of used plates and cups. Looking at the mess, it feels as though we had hundreds in here, not less than thirty. Debbie looks at it all and gives out a big yawn.

'I'll sort it out in the morning. You head to bed,' I say.

'No way. I'm not leaving you to sort this out. And besides, we need to dissect the evening. It was a great success, wasn't it?'

'It was. What a great bunch of people they are. Everyone loved your food, and those pumpkin lattes were the perfect touch.'

'Oh, I loved it, and yes, your neighbours are gorgeous people, except for that one miserable woman.'

'They are. Hmm, Camilla, I reckon she's got a bit of a thing for Abe and doesn't like me being so friendly with him.'

'You could be right. Anyone can see how well you two get on. I noticed you on the sofa there. Are you sure there isn't something you want to talk about?'

'Oh, goodness. No. Honestly. He's lovely, gorgeous and so nice. I admit, I do have a bit of a stupid crush on him, but my life here is about me. I'm not sure I want to get involved with anyone.'

'Well, I understand that. It's obvious there's something between you, but I also get why you'd want to be careful. I'd be the same. You've got everything you need here. Do you really need a man to share it with?'

I don't answer Debbie because I am not sure I know the answer. I don't know what I want. I never intended to meet anyone; it simply wasn't on my list of priorities.

But with Abe living so close by, my feelings for him grow each day. I have never been so confused about anything.

Chapter Twenty-Three

Saying goodbye to Debbie is harder than I imagined and almost as painful as when I left her in Wales. As we promise to see each other again very soon and her taxi pulls away, I close the door to an eerie quietness. It's gone from being party central to total silence overnight. For a while, I find myself walking from room to room until I decide to remove Debbie's bedsheets and fold the camp bed back up. Anything is a distraction from the sudden quietness in here.

With all the mundane jobs complete, I take out my felting for company. I have ten cavapoos to make by Monday morning and desperately need to finish them instead of procrastinating around the place.

Soon, my arm is hurting from jabbing the needle into the foam base so many times. Right now, it feels as though it will be impossible to get these done in time without developing some sort of repetitive strain injury. I consider that I may have bitten off more than I can chew with this latest order, and it makes my confidence crumble. What was I thinking? I am not a felting superwoman; it is a hobby that is getting too big. If I can't handle a Facebook order, I'd never manage a market stall. I don't know what is wrong with me. Suddenly, I have gone from thinking I can take on the world of felting to feeling down about myself. I feel like a silly woman who has moved to a country where I don't know anyone and am trying to fit in with a whole new crowd that listens to dance music. The more I think about it, it is starting to sound like a midlife crisis. I begin to doubt all my decisions, despite being so deliriously happy since I've been here. Debbie leaving has obviously affected me more than I thought it would. I pick up the phone and ring Hannah for a much-needed chat. We hardly ever speak anymore, and I miss her so much, even though I know she is out enjoying herself too much to call.

'Hey, Mother.'

'Hannah, nice to hear your voice. I miss you.'

'I miss you too, and I've got so much to tell you. So, I went to the Great Barrier Reef last week. That's why I haven't called. I only just got back, like. I walked through the rainforest. I went swimming on the reef. You should have seen the colours. It was so magical. I've never seen anything like it.'

'I can imagine. How wonderful for you.'

'Oh, it was. I could easily move over to that side of the country. Who knows, one day? You'd have to come and visit if I do.'

'That would be lovely.' Although whether she's in Melbourne or Cairns, we couldn't be further apart. Listening to her excitement, I realise how selfish I am for wishing we were closer. I tell her how lucky she is and put my worries aside. She doesn't want to know her mam is feeling a bit down when she is having so much fun. If she is worrying about me, she might feel she has to fly over to check on me, and I don't want that. I want her to be free to live her own life.

'So, how's the houseboat?'

'Yeah, great. Had a party on here last night. Invited all the neighbours. You'd love them. Someone brought a dance CD over.'

'No way. Were you up dancing?'

'Yeah, of course.'

'Good on ya. That's my mother. Oh, gee. I'm going to have to dash. Dad's here, and I promised we'd head to the mall. He really needs some new clothes, and I need to save him from buying something he may regret. You know what Dad's like – he'll buy the first thing to get out of the stores.'

'Ha, yeah. He never changes. Oh, great. Well, say hello to him.'

'Yeah, will do. Take care.'

As Hannah puts the phone down, I imagine them laughing together as she tries to get Paul to wear something she thinks would suit him. Paul's such a great dad, but still, I can't help feeling a little envious of the fun they are having together while I am here alone.

I begin to wonder about my house back home. Would I be happier going back to Wales? I tell myself that I am simply missing Debbie. That's all that's wrong, but next I call the estate agent for some reassurance that I've done the right thing.

'Hello. This is somewhat spooky, as I was just about to call you,' he says.

'Really? Do you have an update for me?'

'As it happens, I do indeed. I've a young family who adore your house. I took them around on Wednesday and they've just this second called to say they want to make an offer.'

'Well, that's good.'

'It certainly is. They've made quite a reasonable offer.'

Before I can listen to what they want to pay, I need to know what they are like. How many children do they have? Are they a young, happy family, just like Paul and I were when we bought the house with a daughter on the way? If I am going to hand over the house to new custodians, I want to make sure they are the right ones.

'Oh, they're a lovely family. Husband is an accountant, wife works for the Post Office. Two lovely little girls. Around seven and ten, I'd say. The kids loved the tree-house out the back. You should have seen their faces. Comical, they were.'

This memory of Hannah's beloved treehouse leaves me with a mixture of emotions. She would have lived in there when she was young, had we allowed it.

'They loved the treehouse, hey?'

'Oh, yes. I think that was the moment the parents were sold.'

'Okay, they sound lovely. So what sort of offer were they willing to give?'

'Five thousand off the asking price. They said they need to put new windows in around the back, so wondered if you'd accept that.'

Those windows in the back do need replacing. They have for years; we just never got around to it and then Paul left. The family's offer may have caught me by surprise, but how can I refuse? Winter is on the way, and while I don't want the pipes freezing here, I don't want them to freeze there either. My beautiful home deserves to be lived in.

'Yeah, that's fine. I'll accept the offer.'

'Oh, that's brilliant. I don't think there'll be any hitches, but I'll go back to them now and confirm.'

I sit on my bright pink sofa, looking at the felting that remains to be done and still waiting for me. I sigh loudly, knowing that nobody can hear me. I feel so sad, yet I have everything I dreamed of. I couldn't ask for more when I have a beautiful houseboat, a hobby that keeps me busy, a gorgeous next-door neighbour, and I can decorate my home the way I want without answering to anyone. I have complete freedom to do as I please.

It has been a long time since I cried but, once I start, I can't seem to stop. I may have convinced myself that my life has turned a very exciting corner, but the fact is I also never thought I would be alone at this age. When I was younger, I assumed I would be married, surrounded by my adult children and grandchildren. Then, if we had enough money, my husband and I would go off on a cruise somewhere in the sun to escape the coldest months. Instead, I am living on a houseboat, all alone, on the other side of the world to everyone I know. Would I have been better staying next door to Debbie? I am beginning to wonder. Today somehow feels like a day of closure. My best friend has gone home. I am reminded again that Hannah and my ex-husband have made lives for themselves without me. Finally, I am told that my house is going to be sold, and I will never be able to go back there. I remind myself that it was me who chose this new life. It's just that when everything changes and there is no chance of turning back, there is that moment when you get cold feet. What if I've made a mistake? As I sit here alone with my felting, I need some convincing that selling up was the right thing to do.

Chapter Twenty-Four

Sometimes, when you're feeling low, someone comes along and cheers you up. It can be a stranger on social media, or it can be a random conversation in a corner store, but as I hear a knock on the door the following day, I am grateful to whoever it is. I could really do with seeing a friendly face right now, and when I find Abe on the doorstep, I couldn't be happier.

'Hey, sorry to disturb you. I know how busy you are, but I wanted to check you have lunch? I'm off to the market, can I get you a takeaway?'

'That's so kind of you to offer, thank you. I need to finish another two dogs before lunch although I could do with a bit of a break, to be honest...' I shake out my arm to release the tension.

'It's okay. Don't worry about getting me anything. I could probably do with some fresh air, so I might go out myself and grab something.'

'Well, why don't you come along with me? I'll get you back here as soon as I can, I promise.'

It takes me all of two seconds to agree.

'Oh, go on then. That's a great idea. I'll grab my coat.'

The fresh air instantly does wonders for the soul, and I realise how much I need to stretch my legs as we walk that familiar route along the canal towards the market.

'Thanks for a great party, by the way,' says Abe.

'Thanks for the great wine. Once I get all these felt dogs off, I'm going to sit back and enjoy it.'

'Sounds good. The perfect night in, hey.' Abe gives me one of his glowing smiles that light his face up and walks closer to me. I smile but then look down as I think how it would be nice if he joined me, yet I also don't want that, because then I might get sucked in by his charm.

'Is everything okay? You seem a bit... off? I don't know if *off* is the right word. I suppose it's not. But you seem like you don't want to be too close to me. Are you upset that we kissed the other night? Sorry if I'm being too direct.'

'Oh, no. I'm happy we kissed, it was absolutely wonderful. I'm just a bit, well, confused right now. I'm settling into a new country and still finding my feet. I mean, you've been fantastic in helping me settle here. It's just that I suppose I am used to being by myself. Don't get me wrong, I love your company. I don't particularly even like being alone, but that doesn't mean I want a relationship at this stage of my life. To be truthful, I don't know what I want. I'm feeling a bit of a mess right now.'

'No, I get that. I didn't mean for you to get the wrong impression. You know that I'm not asking you to be my steady girlfriend, right?'

Abe's bluntness takes me aback. It also feels like a stab in the heart. I was scared of getting close to him, or having a steady relationship, and now he makes it sound like all he wanted was a casual affair. That is something that is definitely off the cards. What is he trying to say?

'Um, no, I didn't think you were asking me anything of the sort. I hope you don't think that.'

'Relax. It's okay. Maybe we should leave things as they are, hey? Maybe that's the best thing to do. No pressure for anyone.'

'Okay, that sounds like a good idea.' I smile but my emotions are mixed. I like Abe so much, but I am so terribly afraid that all of this is not a good idea.

'Now, come on, let's find that stall with the organic wine. I need to stock up,' says Abe.

As we walk towards our favourite wine stall, I pass the woman I saw last time who is back again selling her crocheted teddy bears. She seems to be popular with a family who are standing in front of her buying two teddies. Her cheeks are red from the cold, but as she chats with her customers, you can see how much pride she takes in her stall and how she enjoys being there meeting new customers. I watch her, just as I did the last time, and decide that's how I want to be. Looking at her gives me back the motivation and confidence that I seemed to have lost yesterday. I remind myself that this is exactly what I dreamed of. I just need to stick with my dream and work a little harder. I am in touching distance of this. Why can't I have a stall? I don't know why on earth I was feeling so overwhelmed. This is exactly what I want to do. I am a bit stressed about the orders I have right now, but if I was to make lots of stock in advance then I could keep on top of it. Of course, I need to also improve on my Dutch so that I can chat with customers, but now that Debbie has left, I can go back to learning and start the class.

I look back at the woman once again and promise myself that I will get there one day. I want a stall here more than anything and, as I think about it, I realise that my shopaholic days are far behind me; now I'd rather earn money than spend it. I even manage to resist the next stall along with the eye-catching sparkly shawls and pashminas. I came here for lunch, not accessories that I don't need.

Finally, we reach a food truck selling pizzas with Dutch salami toppings. We sit down with our pizzas, the cheese melting away as I take my first bite. I wipe at my mouth.

'Oh, my word. How have I never tried Dutch cheese and salami on a pizza before?'

'You have definitely missed out for all these years.'

'For sure. I think I have a new favourite food place.'

We wash the pizzas down with a cup of mulled wine and any homesickness I was struggling with after Debbie left is once again replaced by the love I have for this country. Everything is going to be absolutely fine. I was being totally overdramatic. Amazing what a bit of fresh air can do.

Taking a final bite of pizza, I watch the crowds of people walking through the market as they examine the wares, munching on snacks as they mill around and generally soaking in the atmosphere. Music plays through speakers in a corner where some of the visitors enjoy a beer. It is the perfect way to spend a Sunday. It's so typical of Amsterdam with nobody rushing around but instead enjoying their leisure time and making the most of good food and drink.

Even though we are both thoroughly immersed in the market, as promised Abe reminds me that I have a few more felt dogs to finish before tomorrow, so we should head back. Sensibly, I agree and we walk home.

Just as we are approaching my place, Abe stops and looks at me.

'I want you to know that I'm so glad you moved in next door. I enjoy hanging out with you.'

'Thank you. That's nice of you to say. You've been amazing since I moved in.'

I stop and look into Abe's beautiful eyes. He is so difficult to resist.

'You know, you were straight with me earlier so I guess I should say something to you now. One of the reasons I am so afraid of what could happen between us is partly because you're my only friend here and I love our friendship. What if it went wrong?' I say.

'I agree with every word. Although I think we're both attracted to each other, or am I wrong?'

Once again, I think of that glance I had of him when I was on the canal boat. I certainly can't argue with what he is saying.

'You're right. That's exactly why I am so scared. I'm not ready to fall head over heels for someone.'

'Nobody is asking you to do that. Why don't we take things slowly? We don't need to think about the future, or worry that we will have some big falling-out one day. If we are both attracted to each other then let's just live for today.'

I scratch my head, knowing what I want to say but hesitating to say it. I think of Debbie telling me to be careful. I have always been spontaneous, but this needs some consideration.

'You are gorgeous, you know that? I'm very attracted to you,' I say, touching his cheek.

'Then how about we try going on a date? We can see how it goes.' Abe smiles as he awaits my reply.

'A proper date?'

'Yeah, we can go for dinner to that place I told you about. We still didn't go there. I'm not the most romantic man, so don't expect candles and flowers, but I promise you good company and even better food. Why don't you give it some thought?'

'Okay. I'll do that. I'll pop round tomorrow and let you know.'

'Promise?'

'I promise.'

'Okay, now go and finish that order and I'll look forward to your answer.'

Abe kisses me on the cheek, and I walk inside with that spring in my step I often have here. Despite the workload that is still waiting for me on the table, I sit down with a big smile and get to work. I'm going to get through this and tomorrow, I'm going to give Abe my response.

I'm going to go on my first real date since my divorce. This really is a new beginning.

Chapter Twenty-Five

After I have been to Dam Square in the morning and dropped off the parcels with the miniature felt cavapoos bound for the UK, I head back home to finish off one last felt dog. This one is the most special of all.

I have been working on it for a few weeks, making sure that it is as perfect as it can be and that it is identical to the real thing. I glue the eyes on and tweak the mouth, pushing more felt in around the face until I am completely happy with it.

By late afternoon, it is just right. Even I am astonished at the likeness. I carefully place the dog to one side. Then, I get myself ready to pop round to Abe's with my answer about that date. I already have butterflies in my tummy as I imagine his response to me finally agreeing to go out. I wait until I know he will be home from work and, as the darkness descends, I walk the few steps to Abe's, with the dog carefully encased in my hand. I knock on the door, taking care not to drop the little felt dog, and smile at the thought of Abe seeing what I have made for him. I'm sure he'll agree that it looks exactly like Ted. As I walked over here, I pictured Abe's face when he opens the door. However, when the door springs open, Camilla is standing there!

'Yes, hello,' she says, giving me one of her steely glares.

'Oh, um, I was looking for Abe. Did I come at a bad time?'

I hear Abe's voice behind her, and he comes to the door.

'Sorry, I was in the bathroom.'

'No problem. I, umm, just came to give you this.'

I hand over the dog and Abe strokes it in his hand.

'Wow, this is amazing. Is this Ted? It looks just like him.'

Camilla is still standing beside Abe, and it doesn't look as though she is going to let me talk to him alone.

'Well, I'll, um, leave you to it then.'

'See you. Thanks again.'

I hear Camilla and Abe speaking in Dutch behind the door but my language skills aren't quite good enough yet to understand what they are saying.

Thank goodness I hadn't given him an answer to the date yet. I knew Camilla was hanging around and I should have listened to my head rather than my heart. I was right to be cautious. Anything could be going on between the two of them.

I hadn't expected to be back home so quickly, and when I walk in, I realise just how cold it is. The temperature isn't much better than outside. The heating is struggling now. I throw my jacket off and put a cosy onesie on to stay warm. I need comfort and *cwtches* right now.

Then I pour myself a glass of wine and try to relax with a book, which is proving difficult. My mind keeps wandering and I can't stop thinking about how I missed something so obvious with Abe. He is so bohemian and cool. Of course Camilla likes him. I never even asked what the relationship was between them. Perhaps he is not the monogamous type and thinks nothing of dating Camilla while trying to woo me. I suppose I have also played hard to get, so what if this is all just a playful challenge for him?

If there is one person that I need to speak to right now it's Debbie. She met Abe and Camilla and will tell me straight out what she thinks. It will be lovely to hear her voice too. I dial her number and desperately hope she picks up.

'Hey, you. How's fabulous Amsterdam? I'm already missing the waffles,' she says.

I try my hardest to keep my chin up and sound cheery.

'Yeah, all fabulous. I went to the Sunday market yesterday. There are so many great stalls there, so yeah, all good.'

'Are you sure? You sound a bit down.'

As much as I try not to, I can't help but burst into tears as I hear the concern in her voice.

'Oh, it's so silly. I'm getting homesick again. I missed you when you left, then I felt a bit better after going out to the market and now… I don't know what's wrong with me. The thing is that I knocked on Abe's door and Camilla answered and now I feel so stupid.'

'What do you mean, she answered the door?'

I explain and am surprised when Debbie is so supportive.

'Just because she was there and he was in the bathroom doesn't mean she's dating him. I mean, he's all over you in front of her. I don't think he'd be like that if anything was going on. She seems quite pushy with him; she's probably made some excuse to go over there.'

'Yeah, but answering his door?'

'She may have seen you approach and is trying to frighten you off. I didn't get the impression anything was going on when I saw them together. All I see is someone trying hard to chase him. It's embarrassing, if anything.'

'Yes, but I don't know for sure. I need to be cautious. I'm just glad nothing happened between us.'

'Well, like I said, you don't need anyone anyway. Look, why don't you come back to Wales for a few days? Have a look at the house before the contracts are exchanged? Maybe you'd get your fix of home and not miss it so much. It takes time to settle in somewhere new, no matter how wonderful the place is.'

'Thanks, Debbie. I'll think about it. Oh, I don't know, it seems to come in waves. One minute I am over the moon being here, then I start missing home and, well, it's mostly you I miss really.'

'That's perfectly normal. You went over there on a whim and now the honeymoon phase is probably starting to wear off. I'm not going to twist your arm, but if you want to come over and stay with us, well, it would be lovely to see you.'

'I appreciate it. I'm just not sure. I promised myself that I'd said my goodbyes, and there's still so much to do on the boat. The registration is due to come any day for the new name and then I can get that painted on. I guess I need to focus on the things I should be doing here and crack on with it. You're right; I suppose it's just normal to have these unsettled moments when I'm in a new place, especially when Camilla seems to hate my guts.'

'Oh, ignore her. Of course it's all natural. Maybe in the summer, when you're settled completely and after all the work is finished, you can take a break and come and stay next year.'

'That sounds like a good idea. I think I need more time to settle, or I may not want to come back. Thanks, Debbie.

You're a great friend. Anyway, how has Nigel been since you got back?'

'Do you know, he's been so much more appreciative of me – and me of him.'

'I'm glad to hear you're back on track, yet here I am complaining and on a downer. I need to get on with completing my life goals and stop moaning. It's just one of those days, or weeks.'

'Everyone has them. It's easy to complain. We just take things for granted. I mean, how excited were you about living on a houseboat, and now you live on one, perhaps the novelty is wearing off slightly.'

'I wouldn't say it's wearing off – I do love life on a houseboat. I guess it's just my social circle and those little teething troubles. I'm sure everything will be fine. It's a silly blip.'

However, as I try to perk myself up again, I hear a big clonking noise coming from the boiler. That will be because it is working to keep up with the colder weather, I tell myself as I try to ignore it. It reminds me that I still haven't chased up Abe for the number of the boiler guy. However, instead of worrying about the boiler, I go online and have a last look at the estate agent's listing for my old house. The buyers want to exchange contracts next week. I look at the advert saying 'Under Offer' and for some reason, seeing it on there, knowing that I will no longer be the owner, makes me burst into tears again. There are so many memories in that house. This is the final moment. Now there really is no going back.

I let myself feel sad for a moment and then, as I always do, tell myself not to dwell on it. Nothing is going to change by feeling down about saying goodbye to the family home once and for all; besides, I have so much to be grateful for.

It's a new start with my first Dutch class tonight. If I want to reach my goals of having a stall at the market and meeting new people, then I must get on with my language lessons.

—

In a large classroom with white desks and plastic chairs, I introduce myself as I sit beside a young Spanish student. The native Dutch teacher doesn't seem to have much time for frivolities and gets straight to the point. She is almost on the verge of scary, but I know that if I want to learn this language, it is not about sitting here making friends and having coffee breaks. This is about getting serious.

We chant words out loud, answer each other's questions and it is full-on from the outset. I am grateful that I picked up those books to learn a few basic words, or I would probably start to panic.

'*Hoe gaat het met jou?* How are you?' I repeat to the class.

I can do this. I know I can.

'*Alstublieft,*' I say out loud. How can 'please' sound so different in Dutch?

By the time the intensive class is over, my head is a jumbled mix of Dutch words, and I am relieved that it is done for the night. Nothing ever came from taking the easy route. I'll get back to my books in the morning and look at the workbooks that the language teacher has given us to complete by next week.

It is a relief when my head hits the pillow. However, I wake up at three thirty a.m. to the biggest clonking noise and realise that the boiler has got a lot worse overnight. I finally fall asleep and wake up again at eight a.m., but I can feel something is drastically wrong. The timed heating hasn't come on and it is freezing, even under my thick duvet. My nose is cold, and my cheeks are red as I go to the old engine room and check out the diesel-generated boiler. A gauge sits in the red zone, and I realise that I have no idea what is wrong, but I do know that the boiler is no longer working. It seems that on one of the coldest days of the year so far, the boiler has packed up. I put my head in my hands, remembering Nigel's words once again. B.O.A.T. Bring Out Another Thousand. How many thousands will this set me back?

Chapter Twenty-Six

I learn the hard way that owning a houseboat isn't always a bed of roses. Then again, I did buy an old one that isn't energy efficient and needs a lot of work. You get what you pay for and I probably deserve everything I get. My first instinct is to run over to Abe's and ask him for the number of that boiler specialist he always mentions, but after seeing Camilla over there, I am staying well clear. Instead, since I know Gerrit will be at his desk, I pick the phone up and ask his advice.

'Hi, Gerrit. I'm sorry to bother you. I promise not to make a habit of calling you every time something goes wrong, but my boiler's packed up. Do you know of any engineers, by any chance?'

'Ah, of course. This is such a common problem this time of year. Shall I give the company I know a call and ask them to come round?'

'You're a lifesaver. I'd be so grateful.'

'No worries. It must be cold for you. I'll get someone around as soon as I can.'

While I wait for the engineer to arrive, I try to stay warm with my hot-water bottle and every layer I can find, while praying that I don't have to wait too long.

Two hours later, I finally get a knock at the door. Oh, thank goodness.

The guy, who rambles in Dutch, has overalls with a company name and a toolbox with him, so I presume he's the engineer. I tell him I don't speak Dutch, and he switches to English for us to converse. It makes me embarrassed at how bad I am at Dutch and I am determined to get on with my Dutch lessons, although I'm not sure that the language books or my classes necessarily teach phrases such as 'my boiler has broken'.

I welcome the engineer in and offer to show him where the boiler room is located but he seems familiar with the barge.

'I've been servicing it for years, when the old owner lived here,' he explains.

'That's great. Hopefully you know your way around it and what must be wrong, in that case.'

'I'll try but it's a very old boiler. When I did the last service, I expected it to be the final one.'

I don't like the sound of this already.

'Okay, well, let's hope you can fix it one last time, hey?'

The engineer doesn't look too convinced, and I leave him to inspect my decrepit boiler.

It takes him all of five minutes to tell me that a part is not working, which he tries to describe to me. But his words mean nothing, as I don't know enough about boilers to even slightly comprehend what he means.

'The boiler isn't worth saving. I'm sorry, but the time has come for a new one.'

'Oh no. I suspected this would happen. How much do they cost?'

'I can get one for around thirteen hundred euros. We have some back at the depot. I can fix it by tonight, and you'll have this place warmer than before, for sure. The old boiler wasn't economical and was unable to work hard enough any longer.'

My goodness, he makes my boiler sound like the way I feel some days!

'If you could get that done by this evening, that would be fantastic. I'd be really grateful. Thank you.'

'Okay, I'll be back as quickly as I can.'

I close the front door behind him, desperately trying to keep any heat in as I wait for him to come back. I consider doing some star jumps to stay warm, but decide that the old houseboat might not be too supportive of that idea. Since I am feeling so cold, my subconscious gives me the urge to start knitting a jumper. My hands are too cold to hold a needle in my hand to do any felting. But I figure knitting might help my hands from turning blue if I can keep the circulation going.

I haven't done any knitting since I arrived here, focusing more on my felting. The clickety-clack of the needles feels comforting immediately. I follow a pattern for a jumper that I think would sell at the market. It's something I had planned in my mind as my first trial piece to see if I still have the knack. The first few rows feel promising, but I haven't got the arms knitted yet. It's early days, and anything could happen.

I have knitted around thirty rows when there is a knock on the door. I assume it must be the engineer returning. I almost fling the door open to welcome him in but, as I near one of my windows, I can see that it's Abe on the doorstep. Quickly, I jump down to the floor and hide. I have nothing to say to him after yesterday. I mean, he could be asking me if I want to go on a date with him and Camilla for all I know! Although, thankfully, I can't imagine Camilla agreeing to that and nor would I.

The problem with the houseboat is that it is a bit like a goldfish bowl, and if Abe was to look in at one of my windows, he would easily see me. So, I crawl under a table and stay as still as possible. I stay mortally quiet until, eventually, I hear the sound of footsteps getting further way. I poke my head up and sneak over to the window to see Abe leaving and walking back towards his place. Phew. That was close. I know I'm going to have to face him at some point, but I don't know what to say to him at the moment.

I return to my knitting and then, an hour later, the door goes again. This time, I am more cautious. I slowly creep around but see that it is the engineer.

'I'm so glad you're back. I don't know how much more of the cold I can take. I'd have had to stay in a hotel tonight if you couldn't have returned today.'

'It's okay. We have priority for older people. We won't let you get cold.'

Older people? Does he think I am a pensioner?

The engineer whistles happily away to himself as he heads off into the boiler room. I was going to ask him if he wanted a coffee, but now he can stuff it! If I wasn't so desperate to have heating in here, I'd find someone else. Do the Dutch have to be so direct? There was no need for that.

I sit on my bed and look at my reflection in the mirror. It's true that I don't look my best today. I mean, I couldn't shower because I have no hot water, so my hair is a little limp and the grey streaks perhaps show more noticeably, but still. Where did my youth go? It feels like it all went in the blink of an eye. My reflection is like a reminder that for my next big birthday I will be sixty, even if I do have a few years to go yet. As always though, I like to think of myself as a positive person and so, instead of dwelling on this fact, I resolve to make the best of my life. I'll go into one of the fancy department stores and find a new eyeliner, have a bit of a makeover and get my small business off the ground. I can't do anything about ageing, but I can do something about fretting about it.

Having calmed down over what the engineer probably thought was an innocuous comment, I finally offer him a coffee as I make one for myself.

He gladly accepts and then tells me that he has to go to his van that is parked by the canal to get something.

Unfortunately, when he returns with some extra tools, he isn't alone.

'Someone's here to see you. He was outside,' he says.

I look up at Abe. Why did the engineer have to let him in?

'Hi, what's happened here?' he asks.

'Oh, nothing I can't cope with. The boiler's packed up. No big deal.' I don't admit that I was almost having a breakdown this morning. He doesn't need to know that.

'Ah, no. I promised you the number for my guy. Sorry, I forgot.'

'It's no problem. I can arrange things by myself, thanks.'

'I'm happy you found someone. It's needed replacing for years. It's probably best before the worst of the winter weather comes.'

'Yeah, well, it's done now. Anyway, did you want something?' I might sound sharp, but I can't hide yesterday's disappointment at seeing Camilla.

'I came to apologise about Camilla answering the door. I hope you don't think she makes a habit of it.'

'Oh, no. I don't know what I thought.'

'Her husband left her a few months ago. I think she's a bit lonely on her own, and so she's always calling over. I'm sorry, I don't think I thanked you properly for the lovely dog. It's so thoughtful of you. It's the most beautiful gift. I told you before how talented you are.'

'Oh, well, thanks, but anyway, I'd better be getting on here. In case the engineer needs anything.'

'I don't need anything,' shouts the engineer. Oh my, does he listen to everything?

'Of course. Yes. Well, it's just that I came over to say… how do I say this… to make it clear that Camilla is only a friend, but perhaps it didn't look like that because she answered the door.'

'It's fine. I don't know what I thought. It's no problem. You're free to do as you please.'

'Good, because she was just trying to be helpful while I was in the bathroom.'

'Right. Helpful.' That sounds so wrong, and I can think of other words more suitable than *helpful* for her.

'She just wanted to offer me some special dog food she found. Ted has some pain in his leg, and she said it could help his joints. She came over with it and I offered her a coffee.'

'Well, I hope it helps him. That was very nice of her. Yeah.'

'So, anyway, I was hoping that you'd come over yesterday to tell me you'd decided to go on that date that I asked you for? I guessed perhaps you didn't want to bring it up with Camilla there.'

'No, you're right.'

'Well, I'm so sorry it was a bad time. Can I ask you now? Or do you want to take a rain check?'

As Abe asks me the question, the engineer drops a wrench, and the vibration reverberates around us. Is he still listening? I lower my voice in case.

'You know what, Abe. Yes. Okay. I'd love to go on a proper date with you.'

'Really?' Abe's face lights up and we smile at each other. All the chemistry between us, that I sometimes try to deny exists, is clear to see from the look on both our faces.

'Yeah. Life's too short to worry about what can go wrong. Let's go on a date and see where it leads.'

'I'm so happy to hear that,' says Abe, smiling.

Then, we both turn our heads as a loud hissing sound comes from the boiler room and water and steam spurt everywhere. If only the engineer wasn't so busy listening, he might not have opened the wrong valve.

It isn't the most romantic moment to agree to a date but, then again, Abe and I are hardly conventional people, and we both see the funny side as the steam begins to surround us and we start coughing and spluttering.

Chapter Twenty-Seven

A new day can bring so many possibilities. My home is finally cosy and warm and I am going on a date, although I have no idea where to. The problem is, how are you supposed to know what to wear for a first date when you don't know where you're going?

All morning, I am a bag of nervous excitement. I have done lots of nice things with Abe but now that it has turned into an official date, it's a lot more formal. I try to take my mind off my pre-date nerves by knitting. Then I try to do some felting, but my hands shake too much. I must calm down. I have a coffee but that makes me feel even more jittery. What is wrong with me?

By the afternoon, I practically jump out of my skin when I realise that Abe is at the door to collect me. I take at least five deep breaths before I calm down enough to greet him. He looks as gorgeous as ever with that shaggy coat he wears, and his ponytail. His eyes crinkle at the sides as he smiles at me. I look up at him and feel as though I am about to hyperventilate. He's such a handsome man. While I am a nervous wreck, Abe is his usual confident self as he finally tells me where we are going.

'As you may have guessed by now, I love going around markets. So, for our first date, I wanted to take you to a very special marketplace. Don't worry, I'll also take you for dinner afterwards.'

I am relieved that I chose to stick to jeans and a jumper and didn't get too dressed up.

'Oh, I wasn't expecting dinner. Honestly, just going round a market with you is always fun.'

Although I am intrigued as to what sort of market he has in mind. It could be a meat market or even a fish market. I hope it's not. I didn't spray on my favourite perfume for it to be masked by the strong smell of herrings and mackerel.

Abe gives nothing away as we walk down the canal in the opposite direction to the market we usually go to. He strides ahead with his long, muscular legs and casual walking boots.

'Are you cold?' he asks.

'Yeah, I am a bit.'

He holds out his hand to take mine and moves in closer to me. It feels amazing being so close to Abe, and I realise what I have been missing by being so reticent. Here on the streets of Amsterdam we look like any other couple, and I catch our reflection as we pass by the shop windows. It feels strange not seeing Paul as part of the couple in the reflection, but Abe and I look good together. Really good.

It doesn't take long until I see some stalls in front of me and Abe tells me this is where he wanted to bring me for our first date.

'It's a special place for me. Welcome to Amsterdam Boekenmarkt,' says Abe.

'A book market? How wonderful.' Thank goodness it's not a fish market after all.

'I could spend hours here. Look at all these books! It's my favourite place to visit. Did you know that booksellers come from miles away to sell vintage books, first editions, and you can find cheaper paperbacks here too.'

Around the stalls, people gather browsing the books that are all laid out in organised piles in crates and on tables.

'You can find out-of-print books – everything is here. It's a book lover's paradise.'

But then Abe suddenly looks at me as though he has just had a terrible thought.

'Do you like reading? I just realised I presumed everyone does. I never asked you before.'

'Yes, I love reading. I honestly couldn't have asked for a better place to come on a first date.'

'That's a relief. I didn't think about it. Just because it's my favourite pastime, it doesn't mean it has to be yours too. Can you see how long it's been since I've been on a date with someone? I didn't think to ask,' says Abe, as his face relaxes.

'It's perfect, honestly.'

'So happy to hear that. Then let me show you my favourite stall.'

Abe holds my hand tightly among the crowds as we dash across to the other side of the market. The stallholder recognises Abe immediately. They speak in Dutch and then Abe introduces me.

'This is Marty, he owns the stall.'

'Hi, Marty. Good to meet you.'

'You too.'

'I found that book you wanted,' says the stallholder.

'It's my favourite Dutch writer,' Abe explains to me.

'Sounds exciting.'

The stallholder bends down under his table and pulls out an ancient-looking green leatherbound book. Abe is delighted with his purchase, and I love how happy finding this precious book makes him.

'Take care of Abe, he's my favourite customer,' says the stallholder as we leave.

'I promise I will.'

We weave in and out of the stalls selling both old and new books, and stop at one with a sign in English above it.

'You know, it's not just Dutch books here. There are all languages. Let's find some English books for you.'

I stop and look at the interesting selection of paper-backs, but decide that I probably have enough back home. My reading pile is already quite big, although these books give me an idea.

'You know what, I'm desperately trying to learn Dutch. Perhaps I should look for Dutch books instead.'

'In that case, follow me.'

Abe seems to know his way around all the different stalls as he shows me one with children's books.

'I think I know just the thing to help.' I am beginning to wonder if he thinks I should start off reading toddlers' books when we pass by the stall and find another. Here he hands me a thin book.

'Here, it's a book of Dutch short stories. Why don't you try that?'

'That's a great idea. I'll take it.'

'Ah, let me. I insist on paying,' says Abe.

'Oh no. You can't do that.'

'Of course I can. Please, let me treat you. I spend all my money in this place. I like to support the different stallholders. I mean, where would we be without book-sellers?'

'Yes, indeed. The world would be a very sad place without them. Thank you, that's really kind. I'll treasure it. Now, can I buy you a drink in return?'

'Why not? I know a great place nearby,' says Abe.

'How did I guess? You know all the best places.'

Despite being huddled up to Abe with his arm around me as we walk to the bar, it's still bitterly cold. The warmth of the pub is a welcome relief as we enter. The place is just Abe's style, with memorabilia hanging everywhere. Black-and-white Sinatra prints are intermingled with a Punch and Judy set. It is truly bonkers and fun in here. On one side there are muppets, on another historical legends like Elvis. A jukebox in the corner plays the last words of a Scritti Politti song and a small black pug dog runs under my feet as I order.

'What do you recommend here?'

'Dutch beer on draught. It's a must.'

'Let's go for it then.'

I order two pints of Dutch beer, and we take a round table in the corner.

'*Proost!* Do you know that one yet?'

'I'm ashamed to say I don't.'

'It means *cheers*.'

'Oh, yes, of course. How could I not know that?'

The beer tastes refreshing after walking around the book market and once again Abe's recommendation is spot-on.

'I meant to say that Beatrix asked if you wanted to join her book club? She said you might enjoy it. Now that I know you're a reader, I may as well mention it. I wasn't sure if I should ask, but they read a lot of English books, not only Dutch.'

'That's so kind of her. Yeah, that would be nice. I like Beatrix and it'd be a great way to make new friends. She seems very kind, just like you.'

'Ah, she's a good person. She always takes care of her younger brother. She always did when we were small, too.'

'I'm glad to hear it. It's important to have close family. How old is she? She looks quite young.'

'Sixty-one, but don't let her know I've told you.'

'Really? I thought she was around...' I stop myself from saying 'my age'. I don't want to bring that up just yet. I'd say Abe is in his fifties, but he might be younger than me. It's difficult to tell nowadays with everyone looking so good. My gran looked as though she was 120 by the time she was sixty-eight. People age so differently now. They could be thirty or sixty. You can never tell.

'Yeah, she's two years older than me. She still treats me like her baby brother though.'

'Well, you must have great genes. I'd never have guessed how old either of you were.'

'It's the Dutch way of life. I'm sure I wouldn't be this way if I'd stayed in corporate life. I'd be a stressed old man.'

'Hmm, stress definitely ages people. We're so lucky to be able to live like we do.'

I might have had my teething troubles over the past few weeks, but sat here in a quirky bar with this gorgeous Dutchman, I couldn't wish for anything more. Life is back on track again.

'Talking of living well, perhaps we should eat something. Did you want to drink up and go for that dinner?'

'I guess we should, although I love it here so much, I don't want to leave.'

'Me too. Who needs somewhere fancy? In that case, how about we order some snacks to share and stay here?'

We are always on the same wavelength. Do I confess to Abe that I have been eyeing up the delicious snacks coming out of the kitchen?

'Well, I have seen people ordering some lovely-looking *bitterballen*.'

'*Bitterballen* to share it is. They do the best here. Oh, am I being presumptuous? Did you want to share? Or do you want your own? It's hard to stop once you start.'

'Sharing is fine.'

The beef and gravy croquettes complement my Dutch beer perfectly and I sit back and take in the atmosphere. I relish every bite of my meal as I slowly get used to this easy-going pace of life. It seems that a stroll around a book market, followed by a pint and some *bitterballen*, is the recipe for the most wonderful date I have ever been on. Just shows how you don't need to spend a fortune to have the best day ever.

Chapter Twenty-Eight

I am still on a high after my date with Abe by the time Beatrix's book club comes around. I love that our relationship stays so casual. There are no expectations to live in each other's pockets, and no hurry to move things along. I feel so relaxed in his company. Although, as Abe takes me round to Beatrix's flat for the first time, I confess how nervous I am of being there and meeting her friends.

'You've got nothing to be nervous about. There's no need for that. You'll love Beatrix's friends.'

'But will they love me?'

'Of course they will. Why would they not? They're going to adore you just as much as...'

Abe doesn't finish his sentence as Beatrix opens the door with the same smile her brother has.

'Sandy, so good to see you.'

She hugs me and gives me such a warm welcome that the nerves soon dissipate.

Beatrix's first-floor apartment is exactly what I'd expected. It's small, cosy and filled with her character. A collage of photos with Beatrix and her many friends hangs on the wall, and her bicycle with the customary wicker basket leans below it in her hallway. Further along the wall, a wooden coat hook holds the weight of a pile of thick jackets. It seems there are quite a few people here from the number of coats hanging up. I can already hear the chatting from the hallway.

'Can I get you a glass of wine or beer?' asks Beatrix.

'Wine would be lovely, thank you.'

Beatrix takes Abe and I into the living room where people are sat on bean bags and a white wooden egg chair, just like Abe's, hangs in the corner. I assume that must be where Beatrix was sitting as it is still swinging slightly as though there is a ghost sat on it. Like her brother, she also has an impressively stocked bookcase too. A dark-haired man, wearing big tortoiseshell glasses immediately makes a beeline for me and introduces himself as Willem, Beatrix's new boyfriend. He seems as lovely as Beatrix with his similarly warm welcome. I can't help but take to him immediately.

The book club is a mix of male and female readers of different ages – young and old. They all smile and say hi to me, and one woman asks me where I am from and then proceeds to tell me how she is originally from Southampton. It is so nice to meet someone from the UK who has moved over here too.

'I'm Theresa. Please, come and sit here next to me,' she says, gesturing to the empty bean bag beside her.

Beatrix returns with my wine and heads back into the kitchen to get some snacks. Abe follows her to help and so I sit down beside Theresa and introduce myself.

'How long have you been here?' she asks.

'Only eight weeks. I'm still a complete newbie and finding my feet. How long have you been here?'

'Ten years now. I met my husband on a hen night in Amsterdam. He's sat over there.'

I look at the studious-looking Dutch guy in brown cords and wire glasses sat opposite her.

'How wonderful. I bet you're glad you went on that hen night.'

'It was a bit awkward, to be truthful. You see, I was the bride, but it still makes for a good story.' She shrieks with laughter.

'Wow. That sure is a story. So, a Dutchman swept you off your feet, did he?'

'You could say that. A little birdie tells me that you may have been swept off your feet by one, too?'

I look over to Abe, who is dishing out some crisps into a bowl in the open-plan kitchen.

'Well, I'm slowly being convinced. It's very early days yet. Very early!'

'You won't regret it. Dutch guys are the best and, in case you didn't know this, but the sex… Oh my god, well, let's just say you won't get better. No inhibitions.'

The wine I've just sipped spits out of my mouth and I almost choke. Everyone in the room turns to look at me as I cough everywhere and turn bright red. I don't think Theresa has any inhibitions either.

'Oh, now, I wouldn't know about that,' I say.

'Wouldn't know what?' asks Abe as he puts down the bowl of crisps. He smiles at me innocently as I cringe at Theresa's topic of conversation.

I look down at the floor and try to shrug off his remark.

'Sex, Abe. She doesn't know that Dutchmen are the best. Or so she says,' Theresa says, winking at him.

My cheeks can't possibly turn redder, and I don't know where to look. Abe obviously picks up on the fact that I am mortified.

'Hey, come on. She's a lady. Let's not embarrass her.'

I look up at Abe with gratitude as he stands above my bean bag.

'I'm just kidding. Come on, sex is natural. No shame in it.' She shrugs her shoulders and fortunately shuts up when Beatrix sits down on her egg chair and officially introduces me to everyone.

'This is Sandy. My brother's girlfriend.' I feel my cheeks flush again at the mention of *girlfriend*. Is this what he has told Beatrix? There is no time to ask as she moves straight on to discuss the book they have been reading.

'So, let's talk about the book. What did everyone think?' Beatrix holds up a copy of *Zangvogels* by Christy Lefteri. Even though the Dutch name isn't familiar, I recognise the cover as the wonderful *Songbirds* book. What luck! It's one of my favourites.

'So emotional,' someone says.

'Tragic,' says Theresa, shaking her head.

'Moving. It's written so beautifully,' says Theresa's husband.

Everyone agrees that the story is beautifully written, and we discuss the topics of grief and the life of a house-maid. Eventually, the conversation moves on to who is due to choose next month's book. A woman in cream flared trousers, braces and a striped shirt announces that it is her turn.

'I suggest Wilbur Smith?'

'Ah, we did Wilbur Smith last time it was your book. Every time you say the same thing. Do you not have any other authors you read?' says someone.

'No. He's my favourite author.'

'Can you have a think about a new author? We need some variety,' says Beatrix.

'If you don't like my suggestions, why don't you ask Sandy to choose? She's our new member here,' says the woman wearing the braces.

Everyone in the room turns to look at me.

'Would you like to choose something?' asks Beatrix.

'Umm, yeah. I'd love to, if that's okay. I know this might not be to everyone's taste, but would you mind if I suggest a classic to shake things up a bit?'

Everyone around the room nods and smiles politely.

'*The Canterbury Tales* by Geoffrey Chaucer. What do you think?'

'A wonderful classic. I think it's a great idea. Something we can get our teeth into,' says Abe.

Beatrix nods her head in agreement, and everyone happily accepts my choice. For the rest of the evening, we enjoy our drinks, eat all the crisps and mingle with each other. Abe puts his arm around me as we move to chat with a professor and her husband. She tells me that she teaches history at the local university. Someone else I meet works in an antiques store on one of the streets near the canal, and the woman in the braces works in fashion. I love how so many different people are under one roof here thanks to their love of books. It is a grown-up and civilised evening as we all have adult conversations about subjects ranging from politics to the latest television adaptation of Jilly Cooper's *Rivals*, which we all agree was wonderful. Theresa, especially so.

By ten p.m. we say our goodbyes and the lovely people I've met tell me how wonderful it was to meet me. I feel as though I am part of a whole new social circle, and I look forward to our meeting next month.

'That was a great evening. Thank you for introducing me to so many great people,' I say to Beatrix.

'You're so welcome. I'm glad you could be here. It's great to see my kid brother so happy.'

'Hey, I've told you, I'm fifty-eight. When will you stop calling me your kid brother,' teases Abe.

The three of us laugh and Beatrix and I hug each other goodbye before Abe and I head back out into the night. The street lights reflect down on the water in the canal as Abe puts his arm around me and we snuggle in close all the way home.

'Thanks for such a great night, as usual, Abe.'

'Anytime. I love being with you, besides, I need to keep up my English,' says Abe, jokingly.

'You put me to shame. I need to practise more of my Dutch. I should have used it tonight, but I'm never brave enough. Besides, I've another few weeks of classes yet. I'm spending the day catching up on my homework tomorrow.'

'Ah, does that mean I won't see you?'

'Hmm, studying or seeing you? Please don't give me such a hard decision.' I playfully tap his arm.

'Well, I'd hope it would be an easy decision,' he says with a big, teasing smile as we reach my houseboat.

'Yeah, it is.'

Abe pulls me to him and kisses me outside my front door. I return the kiss and hold him tight, although something has been nagging at me all night.

'I guess I should get home but, if you have a chance, I hope I'll get to see you tomorrow,' says Abe.

'I'll make sure I can fit you into my busy schedule,' I tease him.

'I appreciate it.'

As he turns to head home to his barge, I stop him.

'Abe. Can I ask you something?'

'Yes, sure.'

'Is it time I found out? I mean, are Dutch guys really the best at... you know?'

Abe looks at me, smiling, and then laughs.

'At *you know* what?'

'So, you didn't hear what Theresa said then?'

'Hmm.' Abe starts laughing and has a twinkle in his eye.

'You do know. You overheard the conversation, didn't you?'

'Okay, maybe I did. I just wanted to watch you squirm a bit,' says Abe with a big smile.

'That's naughty.' I laugh.

'Yes, sorry. It was a bit, but regarding your question... Of course, if you want to find out if she was right then there's only one thing to do.'

'In that case, are you coming in?'

'How can I refuse such an offer? I mean, I always believe you should fully immerse yourself in the experience when you're in a new country. I'm only too happy to help,' says Abe, as he wraps both his arms around me and we giggle together. Then he kisses me under the Amsterdam moonlight, and I melt into his arms.

Chapter Twenty-Nine

Everything has been a learning curve since I arrived here and, as I lie in bed, with the morning sunlight filtering through the curtains, I think I may have had my final lesson. Every word Theresa said was true. How have I lived so long without a Dutch guy in my life?

Waking up with Abe sleeping beside me, I smile at the sight of his strong shoulders peeping out from under the duvet and his hair loose over the pillow. I can't help but stare at him as I remember last night. He stirs as I stroke his hair and he opens his beautiful, mesmerising eyes to look at me. My stomach does a little somersault as he smiles.

'Good morning.'

'Good morning, Abe.'

'So, I guess last night wasn't just a nice dream, huh,' he says.

'Nope. It wasn't a dream.' Abe pulls me closer and I kiss his chest.

'Maybe we should have done this sooner,' he says. He might have a point, but I still think it was better we waited and let all this tension build up between us.

'Oh, I don't know. I think it was perfect timing.'

'But look how we missed out. Last night was incredible.'

'It certainly was.'

'Now that we know how good we are together, I want to make the most of every moment with you. How about we have a repeat?'

'Sounds good to me.' I smile.

Just like last night, everything is perfect. If I was pessimistic, I would think he is too good to be true. How can someone have it all? He's gorgeous, kind, educated and so selfless in bed. But the best bit is that, right now in this room, he is all mine. Although I still worry that it might not stay like that, I try to push those thoughts out of my mind and not spoil this magical moment by thinking about the future.

I have to drag myself away from him so that I can make us some coffee, but quickly rush back. We cuddle up, clutching our drinks, and it makes me remember how nice it is to be snuggled up in bed with someone. I feel as though I have been alone for so long that I forgot about these glorious, lazy moments. I could stay in here all day with Abe.

'What time is it?' asks Abe.

The one thing I haven't got around to doing is getting a clock in the bedroom. I don't exactly need one when I have no set itinerary each day. That is the luxury of being retired.

I check my watch on the table beside the bed.

'It's almost nine a.m.'

'Oh, no. I need to open up.'

'Can Beatrix not do it?'

'Nope, it's my day to open. I'm going to have to run. I'm so sorry to leave you like this.' Abe puts his coffee down on the side, letting some spill out as he's in such a rush. I watch as he jumps out of bed, taking in his naked body as he throws his jeans on from last night. I have never had a man send so many shivers down my body.

'So, will I see you tonight? I don't want to keep you from your Dutch lessons,' says Abe.

'Of course. Maybe when I get back you can teach me some extra Dutch. It would be a lot more interesting, and you already taught me some pretty nice words last night.' I smile.

'I'm no teacher, but you're a good learner. In fact, I'd say there's not much anyone can teach you,' says Abe, with a mischievous smirk. Then he rushes off, letting himself out, as I sink back into bed. I can smell the scent of his aftershave on the sheets and I want to revel in it a while longer.

–

It's an hour later before I manage to take myself away from the memories of last night and this morning. I don't know how I am expected to do any studying today; I can't focus on anything except Abe, and I keep getting glorious flashbacks. So, instead of getting the language books out, I decide to head out to the flower market to pick up some more fresh tulips. Fresh air and tulips are much more my mood than studying this morning. I could almost do a happy dance as I wrap my scarf around me and walk down to the market, passing Abe's coffee shop on the way. The windows are steamed up and it looks busy. I'm not surprised he had to rush off; I hope he didn't have too much of a queue waiting for him.

I find myself smiling at everyone around the market as I pick up a bunch of bright red tulips. They totally match today's disposition. I consider heading to Abe's for one of his lovely hot chocolates but decide I might seem like a stalker if I turn up there after he's only just left me, so I head home instead.

As I pass Camilla walking past Abe's, her presence doesn't faze me. She pretends not to see me as I attempt to smile at her. Perhaps Abe has told her that we are seeing each other.

Feeling revitalised after the fresh air, I pop my flowers in a vase and am singing to myself when someone arrives at the door.

I am surprised to find Beatrix on the doorstep with a plate of sandwiches that I recognise from the cafe.

'Hi, Abe asked me to bring you these. He said you'd be busy studying and was worried you wouldn't eat.'

'That's so sweet. Thank you.' His kind gesture makes me feel guilty that I haven't done any of the homework that I promised myself I would complete today.

'Did you want to come in? I was just going to make a coffee.'

'Umm, you know, I should get back... But it would be nice to get out of there for a bit. We've been run off our feet today.'

'Well, come on in. I'll make you a coffee and you can take the weight off your feet.'

'Thank you.'

I put the kettle on while Beatrix rests her legs.

'Hey, what's this you're making? It's gorgeous,' says Beatrix, looking at my work-in-progress on the table.

'Oh, it's going to be a jumper. Yeah, I'm doing a bit of knitting. It's hard to stay focused sometimes but, when I put my mind to it, then it doesn't take me too long to do something like this. It depends on the felting orders, though.'

'Ah, yes. Abe showed me the amazing miniature Ted you did. Would you be able to make one of my cat, Percy?'

'Of course. I can make practically anything. Dogs, cats, unicorns…'

'That's awesome. You have some serious talent.'

'Thank you. I guess I've always been a little creative, but when you have to work in an office it kind of stifles things a bit.'

'Too right. What do you do with your pieces once you make them? Do you sell your things? I'd love to have a jumper like that. Do you knit scarves, too? Sorry, I just love knitwear. I'm getting overexcited. I wish I could knit.'

'I'd be happy to teach you. But you might need a bit of patience.'

'What a great idea. Knitting classes. Why don't we do that? We can have sessions around mine, or you can do them here. Knitting classes on a houseboat sounds fun.'

'That's not a bad idea at all. I'd never thought of anything like that, although my dream is to…'

I consider admitting my dream to Beatrix. I know Abe previously mentioned that she has some contacts at the flea market, but I would hate to get a stall there due to favouritism.

'I was thinking of opening a stall, once my Dutch is a little better. That's my dream, anyhow.'

'That's a great idea. I have some contacts down at the market. The one we went to when we first met. Would you like me to ask them if they have anything available? You might have to join a waiting list.'

'Oh, I don't want any special treatment, but I'd be interested in knowing how long the waiting list is.'

'Leave it with me. I'll find out for you.'

'Really? That would be wonderful. I wouldn't mind being added to the list because maybe by the time something comes up, I could be ready. I still need a bit more time.'

'For sure, I'll do that. What name shall I call your enterprise?'

'Ooh, I hadn't thought of a name.'

'Every business needs a name.'

'Hmm. It would have to be something crafty,' I admit.

'Yes, something to do with knitting and crafts,' agrees Beatrix.

'Get Knotted? No, that sounds a bit negative. It's hardly welcoming!' I say.

'How about something like Spin a Yarn,' says Beatrix.

'Hmm, people might think I'm some kind of liar.'

'Okay then. Let's keep it simple. Cosy Creations by Sandy?'

'I love that idea. I can see it now. Perfect.'

'Great. So, you have your business idea, now we need to find you a stall.'

'If only it was that easy.'

'Have faith. I'm sure something will come up.'

'Thanks, Beatrix. You're as amazing as your brother. You two really are so helpful to people.'

Beatrix smiles and gets up to leave.

'Talking of being helpful, I'd better get back to that brother of mine. I'm not being very helpful now.'

For the rest of the afternoon, once I've finished my homework, I focus on my goal of launching Cosy Creations by Sandy. I finish off the jumper and start on a new piece of felting since I will no doubt need samples to persuade the market to have me there. It's going to take time to get all the stock made up, but, if there is one thing

I have learnt on my journey here, it's that reaching your goal takes hard work and tenacity and that is something I am not afraid of.

Chapter Thirty

Two weeks later, Beatrix has spoken to her contact at the market and put my name down on the waiting list. They said that when a place opens up, they will need to meet me and discuss what I'll be selling. It isn't as straightforward as giving me a stall simply because I know someone. This is great news, though as I want to be given the stall on merit, and it leaves me enough time to create some nice pieces that will hopefully convince them to choose me.

In the meantime, Beatrix has managed to get together a knitting group for every other Monday evening at my houseboat, which starts tonight. My new life seems to be coming together, and it is all thanks to Beatrix and her friends. She even knows someone who is selling a second-hand bike I can have. Tomorrow, I will finally have my own wheels so that I can cycle around the city just as Abe and Beatrix do.

As Abe potters in the kitchen, helping me get everything ready, I have some last-minute concerns about starting a knitting group. I have never taught anything in my life. What if they don't understand a word I'm saying and can't grasp my advice? Despite trying to remind myself that these are Beatrix's friends, and they are all very lovely, the thought of teaching people something new still fills me with some dread. However, I soon have ten ladies in my living area, including Beatrix and Theresa, who have all brought a pair of knitting needles and some wool and are ready to cast on. My voice shakes slightly at first as they all stare at me, awaiting instructions.

'So, if we start with a few easy loops around your needle, which is called casting on. This will be like the foundation of your project,' I say.

I do a demonstration with my own needles and then watch everyone closely as they copy me. Theresa manages to get into a muddle immediately.

'Now what do I do?' she asks me in a panic.

'Unthread it all and start again, it's fine. Take your time.'

'I really want to crack this. It's so important. I'm going to make a willy warmer. I thought it could be a Christmas present for Frankie.'

Oh, good gosh, I wasn't expecting that from my knitting group on the first night, but then again, that is what happens when Theresa's around.

Everyone is laughing and Abe, who originally only popped in to give something to Beatrix, looks at me, smiles, and then grabs a bottle of wine to top everyone's drinks up. Even though he didn't mean to stay, he ends up being so helpful, and the perfect co-host as he remains in the background making sure everyone is fed and watered. In hindsight, I'm not sure wine and knitting are the best combination creatively, but it is huge fun.

By the end of the evening, we are all merry and Theresa has managed to do a basic knit stitch and get the hang of binding off. If I can teach Theresa to knit, then it feels as though I can conquer the world. I look in amazement at this group, who knew nothing about knitting when they arrived and are now excitedly chatting about creating their first item. I did it! I managed to take my first knitting class successfully.

I am delighted as everyone leaves and thanks me for such an enjoyable evening. 'I can't wait until the next one,' says Theresa as she heads out.

'I'm so glad you enjoyed it.'

As I say goodbye to Beatrix, Abe comes behind and puts his arms around me.

'That went well. You're a big hit with Beatrix and her friends, you know that?'

'Am I?'

'Oh, yes. And a big hit with me, too. Do you need me to show you quite how much I think of you?' says Abe, kissing my neck.

'Yeah. Maybe I still have some doubts. You might have to convince me a little bit more.'

'Oh, do I now? Then you'd better follow me.'

I follow Abe into my bedroom where he proves once again just how wonderful he is.

—

My social calendar is quickly filling up with knitting classes every other Monday, usually followed by an amazing night of passion with Abe, and book club on the last Friday of every month, which is also followed by a night of passion. In between, I have my Dutch lessons, ride my second-hand blue bicycle to go shopping, and create more items for my future stall in the hope that one day it will become a reality. I now even know how to say knitting in Dutch.

Then, one bright sunny morning before Abe and I take Ted out for his walk to the beautiful Vondelpark, my post arrives. I open the official-looking letter, wondering what it says. I hope I haven't fallen foul of any houseboat rules that I didn't know existed.

I open the envelope and see that it is my request for planning permission. Even though I only want to replace a few windows, do the outside painting and change the name, I had to go through all the legal channels and this is the letter I have been waiting for. I can finally do the outside work on the barge.

'I have the permission!' I shout to Abe.

'That's wonderful news. Shall we start painting soon?'

'Are you sure you don't mind helping me?'

'Seriously, you have to ask that? Of course I don't mind helping you. Is there anything more therapeutic than painting a houseboat?'

'Well, I'm not sure yet. I suspect it's going to be hard work, but it'll be fun having you help me. I'm just so excited that I can finally change the name. I can't wait to see what it's going to look like when it's all done.'

'It's going to be perfect. It will be the final touch to reflect its new owner.'

Ted is getting impatient for his walk so we head off hand in hand to Vondelpark, excitedly chatting about where we will start on the outside renovations. We walk straight through the orange and gold leaves that are littered along the path. Ted seems to enjoy the noise and is in his element scrunching the leaves beneath his paws. It's funny what makes us happy. For Ted it's a walk in the park, crushing the leaves; for me it is this moment, as I prepare to finish the houseboat and walk along here with my handsome Dutchman and lovely little Ted. How quickly my life has changed.

Cyclists and joggers whizz past us as we stroll along by the lake and a man runs by us in his workout gear with a sleeve of tattoos visible.

Abe notices him too.

'I liked his tattoos. You don't have any tattoos, do you? What's your opinion of them?'

'I don't mind them. It's not something I've ever thought about. I feel I'm a bit old to have one now. Hannah has one; it's a little map of Australia on her wrist.'

'What? You're never too old for a tattoo. It's something I've often thought about, but it has to be special. I don't know what I want yet. It's my goal to get one before I turn sixty. Australia sounds like a good choice for Hannah. I'd love to meet her one day.'

'Wouldn't that be lovely? I wish she wasn't so far away, but I can't blame her for wanting to living there. I'm pleased she's happy and healthy; that's what's important. Maybe one day she can come to Amsterdam, or I can go over there. Perhaps one day you could come with me to Melbourne and meet her.'

'I'd like that very much.'

It feels heart-warming that the man I am seeing takes an interest in Hannah and wants to meet her. Even though I don't see much of her, it's important that Abe cares so much, as we take our relationship day by day.

'So, when shall we start the painting, now all the permissions have come through?' says Abe, changing the subject.

'As soon as possible. I can't wait to put my mark on it.'

'How about we start next week? I'll ask Beatrix to cover for a day or two. She can always get Willem to help.'

'Really? We can start that soon?'

'Absolutely. I know a place we can get the marine paint. If you like, I can pick up some paint colour charts for you. I don't believe in waiting for anything you want. Do you?'

As Abe looks at me, with his kind smile, I can't help agreeing.

Why wait when you know something is right?

Chapter Thirty-One

True to his word, Abe turns up, as promised, with a chart of paint colours before rushing off to work. Over a coffee, I look at the shades of red and green that he has picked out. They're all gorgeous. It's going to be so difficult to choose between them. What colours were used for the houseboat on *Rosie and Jim*? That is the exact colour I want. I'm tempted to write to the BBC and ask them if they have the details in an archive somewhere.

The reds are all fabulous. Do I choose flame red or signal red, so that I look like a traffic light? Then there is emerald green, moss green, grass green and leaf green. How green do I want my windows and surrounds? Who would have thought choosing the right colour would be so difficult.

I eventually narrow it down and get my choice between two reds and two shades of green. I decide to get Hannah's opinion since she is good at things like this.

I send the photos across on WhatsApp and hope she picks them up soon. In the meantime, I practise some of my Dutch.

'Rood,' I say. I'm sure that's red in Dutch.

'Groen,' I say to myself. Then I check back in my book that I've got the word for green correct. My Dutch is finally getting somewhere, and I am understanding quite a bit and able to speak a lot more each day. Having a strict teacher has paid off.

As I'm making another coffee and am about to move on to the next level of Dutch, I see that Hannah has messaged back.

> Hey, hope you're having fun there. I think Rosie and Jim's boat had a darker green shade. Go for the darker one.

> Thanks, love. Everything okay there?

> Yeah, good. I held a party for Dad's birthday. I'm still a bit hungover.

> Oh no. Must have been a fun party though.

I have been so busy socialising that it hadn't occurred to me that it was that time of year already. Paul would have been fifty-eight yesterday.

> Well, tell him happy birthday from me, hey.

> I will. I told him you're having the time of your life in Amsterdam.

That's nice. Were many at the party?

I can't help wondering if Hannah invited Paul's new girl-friend. Do they all cosy up together now and play happy families without me? I try not to let it get to me. After all, Hannah is grown up and Paul is my ex. But it still hurts to think that another woman gets to see Hannah more than her mam does.

Yeah, about twenty of us. Anyway, I'd better go. Off for an interview at a new bar that's opening. Hoping to pick up some work. My backpacking days are over and I can no longer sofa-surf with Dad's family. I may do a part-time interior design course.

I'm glad you're getting life sorted. Give the family my love.

Will do. Love ya. Take care.

Hannah finishes the conversation by sending a photo of Paul's party.

I recognise the house. Hannah must have arranged to hold the party at Paul's sister's place where she is temporarily staying. It's been modernised since I was last there but the fireplace in the background is instantly recognisable. However, it isn't the fireplace I'm worried about. The photo shows everyone happy and smiling, and Hannah is standing with her arm around her dad. On the other side of Paul is a woman who looks around the same age as him, perhaps a bit younger. She looks sporty and surfy and everything I am not. I never did enjoy water sports like Paul did. I suppose he was brought up with surfing the Australian waves, whereas I only had the local community swimming pool to visit. Paul looks happy in the photo. I can't help comparing how he looked in photos with me. Was he smiling as much as this? Perhaps not. Moving back home seems to suit him and, if I am honest, his new girlfriend is probably more suited to him too.

I put the phone down, realising that our relationship coming to an end was hard but ultimately it was better for both of us. We are free to live our best lives now, with people who are more suited to us at this stage.

After my conversation with Hannah, I grab the paint chart and scribble a ring around the colours I have decided upon. Hannah was right about the darker green. I can't wait to share my decision with Abe, so I rush down to the coffee shop for a chat and a hot chocolate. I can hardly contain my excitement as I hurry down the canal on my bike.

With a big smile I open the door of the cafe and see Abe at the counter, talking to a woman in her forties. His perfect smile dazzles as he jokes with her. I can't help but feel a pang of jealousy. I tell myself not to be so silly. He is nice to everyone; it is the way he is. The woman laughs back with him and he hands her a coffee without charging her. Abe is so busy chatting in Dutch to her that he still hasn't noticed me standing near the door. I shouldn't be nosy but I can't help listening in and trying my best to translate what they are talking about. I can understand some of the words. Slowly I digest each word, repeating the sentence in my head and then translating it in English to myself.

Did Abe really just say, 'Let me give you my number and we'll arrange a date'? I must have misinterpreted a word somewhere. Abe surely wouldn't do that to me. I trust him. I watch closely as he gets a piece of paper, writes something down and hands it over to the woman. I stare at them, not able to believe what I have just witnessed, when Abe spots me and waves like he doesn't have a care in the world. How could he be so brazen?

I drop the paint chart and walk out the door. To be fair to him, I guess we never had a conversation about being exclusive with each other, but I assumed he wouldn't go around giving his number out to random women who come into the coffee shop. Was all that talk about him not having been on a date with anyone for a long while the truth? Perhaps he is a serial dater. What if he wasn't truthful about Camilla? It could all have been one big lie.

I rush back out into the street and cycle straight across a bridge, oblivious to everything around me. I hurry down the streets until I feel my heart racing and finally find myself near Dam Square. I stop my bicycle to catch my breath and lean against a shop window. Surely there must be some explanation? Could I have got the translation wrong? But then my brain reminds me that he handed his number over and didn't charge her for the drink, so it corresponds with what I think I heard. Does Abe make a habit of giving out free drinks to women he likes? As much as I want to convince myself that this is all some kind of linguistic mistake, I have to accept the truth. I may have thought we were exclusive, but I got it wrong.

What surprises me is how disappointed I feel, despite promising myself that I wanted to keep things casual. I begin to realise that I had started falling for him; something I promised I would never do. How could I let myself get hurt like this? I am so annoyed with myself for not seeing through it all after Camilla. Perhaps she and I have more in common than I thought. He probably did the same to her, but I was the other woman, and now he's moving on to the next.

I pass the street organ near Dam Square, which always makes me smile, but not today. Instead, I find myself fighting back tears as I rush through the crowds, realising that I am not living the dream with a handsome Dutchman by my side; instead I'm an invisible woman in her fifties who thought she could have it all.

Chapter Thirty-Two

Once I am home and close the door, any bravery I tried to show outside is long gone. I start sobbing and once I start, I can't stop. I fling the Dutch homework that is still on the table across the room.

'Damn you,' I shout. Stupidly I think that if I hadn't understood what Abe was saying then I might not be so hurt. Truthfully, though, I know that I needed to find out. What was I thinking? Abe is a handsome man who has everything. It's time to admit that I got swept away with the romance of a houseboat and the charming guy from next door. Abe lives his life so freely that thinking he only wanted to be with me shouldn't have even occurred to me. I should have known better. Just because he makes me feel like the only woman on earth when he is with me, it doesn't mean that is how he behaves when we are apart. I suppose it is lucky I found out now, before I get even more hurt. So much for him wanting to meet Hannah!

In between tears and trying to work out why I didn't spot any red flags earlier, I turn to my knitting. It feels cathartic, taking my anger out with the clicking of the knitting needles. They go ten to the dozen as I clack away in a temper. My mood ranges from sad to angry and then to one of annoyance. Although I don't know if I am more annoyed at myself or at Abe. After all, did he promise me anything? I merely assumed everything. It's not like he ever said that he wouldn't ask anyone else out on a date now that we were casually seeing each other, although surely that's not the done thing unless he is polyamorous and has forgotten to tell me that little nugget of information. Perhaps I have read this whole thing wrong. Abe never promised me anything; we were simply having fun together.

However, I think about how Beatrix called me Abe's girlfriend when she introduced me at book club. She must have thought there was something to our relationship. Which suddenly reminds me that tonight I am due to be at book club and it is my pick! That's all I need. Abe will be here at seven p.m, all smiles, ready to walk over to Beatrix's. I don't want to tell him what I saw and act like a jealous ogre. Quite honestly, I don't know how to handle any of it.

By the time Abe comes over to collect me for book club, I decide the only thing to do is feign a headache. When I hear him knock on the door, I answer him in my dressing gown. I only hope he doesn't look at my puffy eyes.

'Hey, did I catch you early?'

'No, not at all. I can't make it. Sorry.'

'Really? Are you sick? You look a little...'

A little what? Sad?

'Got a bit of a migraine, that's all.'

'Do you want me to stay in with you? We can have a quiet night if you prefer. I'll let Beatrix know.'

'No, you go ahead. You know what it's like when you have a headache. Bed is the best place.'

'Are you sure you're okay? Because you dropped your paint chart and seemed to run out when I saw you earlier.'

'Oh, yeah. That. I had to rush off suddenly. Felt a bit faint. Maybe it was the migraine coming on then.'

'I wondered what was wrong. You looked like you'd seen a ghost.'

Seen a ghost? He must realise that I saw him giving the woman his number but he doesn't seem to care. Is he that blasé that he assumes something else must be wrong? I don't know what he thinks about free love and open relationships, but it's certainly not for me.

'Oh, no. It's just this headache. Look, you go over to Beatrix's, and please give her my apologies. I am terribly sorry for not being there when it was me who chose the book.'

'It's fine. She'll understand. The most important thing is that you rest.'

'Thanks. Enjoy yourself.' Perhaps I'm doing him a favour. After all, if I'm not there then he can call the woman for a date even sooner.

'I won't enjoy it as much without you.'

I give him a fake smile and pretend I am gullible enough to think he means it, and bid him goodnight.

Then I return to the knitting and clickety-clack until I get cramp in one of my hands and feel the start of a genuine migraine.

—

In the morning, when I am still in bed sulking, I hear a knock on the door. The last thing I want to do is answer it, but I need to check in case it's the postman with a parcel I'm expecting from Debbie. She said she was going to send me some of my favourite tea bags.

I throw on my dressing gown but find Abe at the door.

245

'Good morning, I brought you some pastries. They say sweet things help migraines. Are you feeling any better?'

'No, not really. I'm still in bed.'

'Sorry I disturbed you. Take these, and I'll leave you to sleep a while longer. You get back to bed. Shall I pop over later to check on you?' says Abe, handing me a plate of various pastries.

'No, don't worry. You go and enjoy yourself doing whatever you fancy. I'll only be here, miserable, with a headache.'

'I don't mind. I'm happy sitting on the sofa with you.'

'It's fine. Thanks. Maybe we've been seeing a lot of each other recently, anyhow.'

Abe stands back.

'I thought you liked spending time with me. I'm sorry if you felt it was too much.'

Oh, Abe. It was never too much. I have loved every moment with you, but I have to protect myself here. I am not about to get myself into some polyamorous relationship. I just don't know how to say it out loud.

'It wasn't. I just feel that maybe we should cool things down a bit, you know?'

'Wow. I wasn't expecting that. So do you really have a headache, or are you trying to get rid of me?'

He might be direct, but I am not as confrontational.

'No, I do have a terrible headache. I just also think we need a bit of space between us.'

'Well, that's difficult when we live next door to each other, but I get the hint.'

I look at his face. It surprises me that he seems so disappointed.

'Thanks anyway for bringing this over.'

Abe doesn't answer and storms off. Looking at the delicious pastries with blackberries and blueberries, I feel a teeny bit guilty for upsetting him, until I remember the reason behind it. Perhaps it is just his pride that is hurt and not because he cares.

For the rest of the weekend, I keep a low profile. I don't want to bump into Abe until things have cooled down a little, and so I stay within the confines of the houseboat to ensure I avoid him.

As my mind is consumed by Abe, how much I miss him and how we should have started painting *New Beginnings* today, it completely slips my mind that it is also knitting Monday until I hear a knock on the door and chattering outside. Oh, heck.

I quickly throw some magazines on the shelf under the table and try to clear up. There isn't enough time to get the place as I'd like it but, following another knock on the door, I have no choice but to answer it.

'Beatrix, hi.'

'Hi, did you forget it's knitting tonight?' she says, looking at me as I put my hand through my hair to tidy myself up.

'Yeah. Sorry. The weekend went so fast. That's what happens when you're not working, I suppose. You don't realise what day it is.'

'You look like you just got out of bed. Anything you want to share? Where's Abe?' says Theresa, laughing as she peeps out from behind Beatrix.

'He's not here. It's nothing exciting. Just had a bit of a headache. Anyway, now you're all here, come on in.'

Fortunately, I have a bottle of wine in the fridge and so I get them all a drink and start where we left off during the last session. Beatrix has already made half a scarf, her friend, Alex, has half a side of the body of a jumper and Theresa has half a willy warmer knitted up. At this rate, she will be able to fulfil her wish of giving it to her husband as a Christmas present. I just hope he likes it.

As the ladies chat and sip their wine, I try my best to remain jovial with them, but I feel so flat that I am finding it difficult. I go to pour more wine when Beatrix approaches me, looking concerned.

'Hey, I didn't want to ask in front of everyone else, but are you okay?'

'Yes, of course. I'm sorry about tonight. I honestly lost track of time. It's been a bit of a mad weekend.'

'Yeah, Abe said that he hasn't seen you and you didn't make book club. I was worried about you.'

'Oh, yes, I'm sorry about book club. That was unforgivable when it was my book choice as well. I had a terrible headache, but I should probably tell you now that I don't think I'll be able to make the next one. I might not be able to come to any of them, actually.'

'Why not? Have my brother or I done something to upset you?'

'No, Beatrix. You're so sweet. You've not done anything to upset me. You could never upset me.'

'Then my brother has upset you. Is that what's happened? I must be honest, he confided in me and said you didn't want to see him. He can't understand what went wrong. And neither can I. But I don't know the facts, and you don't have to tell me. I think it's a shame, that's all. You seemed so perfect for each other.'

'Yeah, well, I also thought that but I guess we weren't.'

'We all did. I'm sorry you changed your mind about him.'

'I didn't change my mind about him. He's a great guy, it's just we are in different places in our lives.'

'You're both on houseboats in Amsterdam. I'd say you're practically in the same place,' says Beatrix, smiling.

'It's just that sometimes one of you wants more from a relationship and someone may want less. I guess you need to find that balance and, for us, we weren't on the same page. My feelings changed over time, and perhaps I got too involved.'

'Okay, well, that's a shame because I know Abe was serious about you, but I understand if you don't feel the same way. Anyway, this is not my business. Although, so you know, I'm also here as a friend, not just Abe's sister.'

I listen to what Beatrix is saying. Abe was serious about me? It's probably best I don't tell her the truth about what I witnessed. Perhaps she doesn't know.

'So, anyhow, I spoke to the guy at the market. They think something is coming up very soon. A stallholder verbally gave notice, and management is waiting for them to give it in writing and then they'll open up the waiting list. You might have that chance to get your stall.'

'Really? That's wonderful news.'

'Yeah, isn't it great? Let's keep our fingers crossed it can be yours. Once I hear something, I'll arrange a meeting for you.'

'Amazing. How on earth can I thank you for this? It really would be a dream come true if it comes off.'

'You don't have to thank me. You've taught me to knit, something I always wanted to master, and look how much fun we have together.'

I look around at the ladies in the room as they chat and laugh with each other and my enthusiasm for our biweekly Monday-night knitting returns. No matter what happens between Abe and me, these ladies have become my friends.

'Come on, let's have another glass of wine,' I say, as I put my friendship with Beatrix and the rest of the knitting group before any drama with Abe.

Chapter Thirty-Three

Since Beatrix told me that I might not have to wait too long for the market folk to get in touch, I fill my days with getting jumpers and more needle-felted animals ready in case I get my stall. I figure that I can always sell them online if all else fails. There is always someone looking for a felt cockapoo somewhere in the world.

By the time I have much of my stock ready, the spare room looks like it is waiting to be part of a jumble sale as I fill it up with miniature dogs, cats, unicorns and mohair jumpers and scarves. Perhaps it is for the best that I don't have Abe to distract me. It is more important that I impress the management down at the market. I have never been more determined about something in my life, and I am going to make this stall work no matter what.

Four days pass and I have yet to see Abe, thanks to staying in and getting on with building my furry empire. On the fifth day, I have no choice but to go out and, as I know I have to pass the coffee shop to get to the supermarket for my weekly supplies, I feel a knot of dread in my stomach at the thought of cycling past. I try to convince myself not to worry, that he will be rushed off his feet as usual and busy behind the counter. In which case, unless he is staring out of the window, there is no chance of him seeing me. Still, I pop my hood up, so that I can try to remain incognito. As I start getting closer to the coffee shop my stomach does a somersault. That's the problem with break-ups, you dread seeing someone for the first time. Perhaps I should just get it over with and then I will have nothing to worry about in future.

As I approach the coffee shop, I see the woman he gave his number to standing outside with a dog on a lead. They didn't waste any time. Ted is playing with the woman's dog and I realise how even Ted has happily replaced me. Then Abe walks out with a coffee in his hand and gives it to the woman. They sit down at an outside table. I can't help but stare as I watch them chatting and laughing about something as the dogs play together. I want to keep on cycling as fast as I can, but find myself automatically slowing down as I watch, especially as I then see Beatrix coming outside and sitting down with them. So, Beatrix is in on this too. I almost feel a little betrayed, but I guess blood is thicker than water.

I have to stop my bike before I lose my balance as I am going too slow to keep pedalling. I stare over in their direction despite knowing that it is pointless watching them all. It only makes things more painful. But then Abe sees me from the other side of the street and waves at me. It is not his usual friendly wave but at least he is being pleasant. Sheepishly, I wave back and then start to cycle away slowly. Then I hear Beatrix shouting my name. She must have spotted Abe waving at me. At first, I pretend not to hear her and wobble about on my bike, but she runs up to me as I get stuck behind some pedestrians.

'Hey, we're just having a coffee break. You want to join us?'

Do I want to join them? Well, this is awkward!

'I'm just rushing off. I have to get somewhere.'

Beatrix looks at the reusable shopping bags in my basket.

'If you're off to the supermarket, it doesn't close for another few hours. How can you refuse a hot chocolate? I'll make it with your favourite cream and a chocolate flake, on the house. Just the way you like it.'

I think about making up some spurious appointment I have before doing my shopping, but a part of me wants to see Abe and break the ice. I may as well get this over with.

'Well, okay, if you insist.' I smile and take a deep breath before I reach the table with Abe and his lady friend.

'Sandy, hi,' says Abe.

'Hi.' I look at Abe's mysterious friend and greet her too. It's not her fault she was unwittingly involved in this love triangle.

I sit down with them in silence as Beatrix heads inside to make my drink. I hope she won't be long; every second is excruciating.

'So, how've you been?' asks Abe, finally.

'Yeah, good. I don't know if Beatrix told you, but it looks like a stall is coming up, so I've been busy getting stuff ready. You know, in case I'm lucky enough to get it.'

'She did tell me. I'm keeping my fingers crossed for you. I know how much you want it.'

'Yeah...'

'And here she is,' says Abe, looking at Beatrix as she carries the hot chocolate with cream overflowing from the top threatening to spill over.

'Thanks, looks lovely.'

'Sandy, have you met Johanna before?' says Beatrix.

So, her name is Johanna.

'No, I don't think so.'

'Abe, you're terrible for introducing people,' says Beatrix, rolling her eyes at Abe.

'Sorry.' Abe shrugs his shoulders.

'Sandy, since my brother is so bad at introductions, I'll do it. This is the amazing Johanna.'

'Good to meet you, amazing Johanna,' I manage.

'Johanna does a lot of work for a local dog rescue. In fact, we are joining forces and doing a rescue day here next week. We're just planning the last details. I love that Johanna dedicates her life to finding lovely homes for shelter dogs, and we want to be a part of it.'

'Well, now I can see why you call her amazing. That's great.' How am I supposed to compete with a saint like Johanna? No wonder Abe was so keen to give his phone number to her!

'Ah, it's not just me that can take all the thanks. My wife started the shelter before we met, and she did all the groundwork,' says Johanna.

Her wife?

'We arranged the date for next Saturday. Maybe you can join us? Let's hope we can get lots of people in on the weekend,' says Abe.

Arranged the date? Could it be that I have got it all wrong? He did try to explain that Camilla was just lonely and there was nothing going on. I jumped to conclusions then, too.

I feel the blood drain from my face. I had thought that because Abe is so fun-loving, he didn't take our relationship as seriously as I was beginning to. How could I have presumed such a thing, just from overhearing a conversation in a cafe?

Johanna's dog starts getting excited as a woman approaches the table and my hot chocolate almost tips over with all the excitement.

'Oh, here's my wife now. This is Famke.'

'Hi,' she says.

I want the ground to open up and swallow me. I don't think I have ever got a situation so wrong in my life.

I can't look at anyone. I am so embarrassed for thinking that Johanna liked Abe and that something was going on between them. I can't even speak, and drain what is left of my hot chocolate and make an excuse to leave.

'Well, thanks for the hot chocolate. I guess I'd better get going to the supermarket, otherwise there won't be any of my favourite bread left on the shelves. I'll see you around then.'

'Yup. See you around,' says Abe.

I stroke Ted goodbye and pick up my bike and ride away, feeling like the most mighty idiot on earth. How could I possibly sabotage something so good because I assumed the worst? I didn't even speak to him about my suspicions when, if I had, he could have told me all along about the dog shelter and why he was giving this wonderful woman his number. How could I misjudge something so badly? He has already told me once that I need to speak to him about things and not assume stuff.

As I walk around the supermarket in a subdued daze, I wonder how I can possibly put things right. Is it really over? Or can he somehow forgive me for being such a fool? But as I think about wearing my heart on my sleeve and telling him about the ridiculous assumptions I've made, I realise that would mean admitting how silly I've been. The thought of telling him how wrong I was is mortifying.

Chapter Thirty-Four

I dump the shopping at home while becoming more and more angry at myself for being so untrusting of Abe. So many different thoughts are running through my head as I blame myself for everything. Did I fear the worst because secretly I have lost confidence over the years? Has being a wife, mam and a carer for my mam when she was ill, left me somehow feeling unworthy of happiness for myself with such a wonderful man? It doesn't take long before I can no longer face staring at the walls of the houseboat all alone, so I put my coat back on and walk down to my favourite bar further down the canal. I feel the need to be with people as I don't want to wallow in my own company. I am longing for a distraction.

Sitting under a patio heater with a blanket over me, I order a bottle of wine. It isn't often that I go through a bottle on my own but, then again, it isn't often that I make such a fool of myself. I don't stop pouring the wine until my glass is almost full. I must look like a complete loser sat on my own, filling up my glass like someone desperate, but tonight, that would be an accurate description of how I am feeling. What difference will it make if I look the way I feel?

I watch couples chatting together and friends gathering, making me feel uncomfortable alone. My mind is playing tricks, telling me that everyone is staring at me, that they are feeling sorry for the woman on her own with a bottle of wine. Although the truth is that everyone is having far too much fun with their friends and partners to even notice me. But with every sip of wine my self-consciousness eases a little more. When I am three glasses in, I no longer care what people think of me.

I am about to pour myself my fourth glass of wine, knowing full well that I will have a terrible headache when I wake up in the morning, when I spot Abe walking in the direction of home. Perhaps it's the wine, or maybe the guilt I feel for thinking the worst of him, but I badly want him to join me. The truth is that I miss him desperately. I cough loudly to get his attention, but in the busy street he doesn't notice, so I call out his name, shouting, and the four women on the table next to me stop talking. Perhaps I shouldn't have hollered quite that raucously but at least it gets him to notice me. He waves but looks as though he will continue walking home, so I gesture for him to come over. Slowly, he walks towards me, and I thank the wine for giving me the courage to summon him over.

'Wow, bumped into you twice in one day,' I say.

'Yeah, just on my way home. It's been a busy day.'

I look at the bottle of wine with another glass left in it. I might end up in the canal if I finish it, so I gesture to it and ask Abe to join me.

'I don't know. I really should be getting back.'

'Oh, come on. I honestly can't finish this by myself, please help me out.' I give him what I hope is a pleading look.

Abe looks hesitant about joining me and I can't blame him, but the wine is making me persistent. As a waiter passes, I ask him for an extra glass and Abe finally joins me.

'So,' he says.

'So,' I reply.

Abe drums his fingers on the wine glass, making no effort at conversation whatsoever.

'It was nice to meet Johanna today,' I say, attempting conversation.

'Yeah. She's cool.'

'Yeah, she is.'

Abe looks down at his wine glass, then at the boats going along the canal. He gazes everywhere except towards me.

Since small talk isn't working, I figure only an apology for my strange behaviour will save any relationship between us, even if we are left with just a friendship as neighbours, going forward. I will accept his decision whatever he chooses.

'Abe, since you're here with me now, I wanted to apologise about the other night. I had a terrible headache and wasn't really thinking straight. I never meant to upset you.'

'Thanks. I appreciate it. I don't know what I did to upset you. I think that's the hardest thing. I've gone over it in my mind, wondering if I did something. One minute we were getting on so well, and the next you said you wanted a break. Am I really that annoying?'

'Oh, Abe.' I lean over to touch his hand, but he pulls it away from me. 'You are the least annoying man I've ever met. It doesn't matter what we do, or how much time we spend together, you could never get on my nerves. I love being with you.'

'Then why did you decide we should take a break?'

I take a sip of wine and then another. There is nothing else for it: I will have to confess.

'You're going to think that I am completely bonkers, but do you remember when I walked into the cafe with the paint chart?'

'Yes, and you dropped it on the floor. You were acting weird.'

'Yeah, it's just that I saw you talking to Johanna. I was so excited, coming to tell you that I'd chosen the paint, and then I heard you talking to her about a date. I managed to understand what you were both saying from my limited Dutch, and then I saw you giving her your phone number.'

'Yes, for the dog homing day. She needed to check with Famke.'

'I get that now. I got completely the wrong end of the stick. I thought perhaps you wanted some kind of open relationship. I'm so embarrassed.'

Abe looks shocked. 'Are you serious?'

'Well. I mean, Johanna is a very attractive woman. I just thought you might be more interested in her than me.'

'Why didn't you tell me this? Why didn't you speak to me, instead of making me think you didn't like me?'

'Oh, Abe. I like you more than you can ever imagine. That is why I didn't dare bring it up. I just admitted defeat. Johanna's younger and way cooler than me. I didn't think I could begin to compete.'

'Wow.' Abe sits back and looks at me.

'So, there you go. I've told you the truth.'

'Thanks for telling me, but I just wish you'd been straight with me from the start. Maybe you need to remember to say what's on your mind instead of making excuses.'

'I know, but I felt stupid admitting my suspicions. I thought perhaps you assumed there were no commitments between us and that you felt we were free to see whoever we wanted. You did say right at the start that you weren't asking me to be your steady girlfriend. So I didn't want to demand to know who the woman was.'

'Sandy, I'd never want to be sleeping around with other women. I can't believe you would even think that of me. We had such a great thing, why would anyone want to spoil that?'

'Had?'

'Yeah. We had a brilliant thing.'

I take a big drink and ask Abe the question that is burning inside me.

'Do you think you could forgive me for being so silly? Could we try again?'

Abe doesn't respond immediately, and makes me wait for his reply as he slowly sips his wine. My heart is beating so fast as I wait for his answer that I fear he will see it jumping out of my chest.

'I'd hate to lose something so good, but if we have any hope of things working out between us then you need to be more open with me,' he says.

'I will, I promise.'

'If something is bugging you about me then you must tell me. Otherwise we can never know what's wrong.'

'Of course. I'll never keep my fears to myself again. If I have a problem, I'll tell you straight.'

'Good. Then let's start again. Come here. I've missed you.' Abe pushes his chair close to mine and hugs me. I snuggle into his neck and kiss his lips.

'Oh Abe, I've missed you too. I'm so sorry. I promise never to be so suspicious and silly again.'

'It's okay, I forgive you. Although you may have to make it up to me.' Abe gives me one of his naughty grins, and you don't have to be psychic to work out where he is going with this one.

'I'd say we have a lot of making up to do,' I agree.

'Good, then your place or mine?'

'How about yours for a change?'

Abe agrees, and takes my hand in his and kisses it. Then he calls the waiter for the bill and once again I find myself walking hand in hand along the canal with Abe, which is the best feeling in the world.

Chapter Thirty-Five

Ted jumps up on the bed, waking me with a start as I remember that I stayed in Abe's houseboat. It is the first time I have stayed over here, rather than let him come to me. His bedroom is more masculine with a black cabinet of drawers and plain blue curtains that match his bedsheets. His jeans are thrown on the floor beside the bed, a reminder that nothing else mattered more than being united again last night.

'Ted, can you get your butt out of my face?' says Abe, laughing.

'Who says romance is dead?' I laugh.

Ted pushes between the two of us, creating a barrier.

'So much for snuggling in together this morning,' says Abe.

'Ah, it's fine. It's cosier with Ted,' I tease.

I can't help grinning to myself as I lie in Abe's cosy bed with Ted already snoring beside me.

'I just want you to know that's not me,' says Abe.

'I know. You never snore because you're just perfect.'

'And so are you.'

We both reach over Ted, to hold hands and gaze at each other.

'What a lovely way to wake up,' I say.

'I couldn't think of a better way to start the morning.'

'So, what shall we do today, once Ted decides it's time to get up?' asks Abe.

'Don't you have to get to work?'

'Nope. Beatrix is in. It's my day off. I was thinking, if you like we could sort the paint out? I was worried about that as I knew you wouldn't know where to pick exterior boat paint up from. We can go together and order everything, if you want. We might even be able to start painting later today. At least we can do the base coat. What do you think?'

'That would be amazing. Why not? If you're sure you have nothing better to do.'

'Oh, I can think of something better to do but, unfortunately, Ted got in the way. Maybe we can get back to that later,' says Abe, grinning.

'Sounds like a plan.'

As Abe gets up to make us coffee to start the day, Ted follows at the sound of his food bowl being filled up.

I sit up in bed as I wait for Abe to return with our morning coffee and smile. I can't believe I almost lost all of this because of assuming something so ridiculous. From now on, I promise myself that I will never doubt Abe's intentions again.

After dashing back home to change, Abe and I head to the paint store on our bicycles and collect the first items we need. Abe recommends a primer for the wood, and we take the pots back to the boat in our respective baskets. As soon as we get back, he puts on those paint-splashed overalls that I love so much and together we start work on the outside.

Abe and I make the perfect team as we begin sanding down the barge. I soon realise how much more fun it is doing renovations when you have someone you care for doing it beside you. We sing along to the Eighties radio station that blasts out from my small radio as we paint on the primer. This job is going to take a lot of time and hard work, and I am already impatient for a quick result and wanting to start painting on the colour. Thankfully Abe is more patient than me, and reminds me of the importance of getting it right from the off if I want a good result. When we finally use the body filler to cover some uneven bits, I see what he means.

'You see why you can't just gloss over things?' he says.

'You're right. We have to start from the foundations. It's just tedious when you can't wait for the end result.'

'It will be worth it. Just you wait.'

By the end of the following week, Abe is right. It is so worth it. With the pots of green and red paint in front of us, we can finally start painting the boat together. By this stage, even the neighbours are involved and Pieter and Lotte pop over with some fizzy drinks to keep our strength up and motivate us by reminding us what a wonderful job we are doing. Even Camilla walks past and smiles at me while she introduces us to her new, younger boyfriend, Rick. The happiness around *New Beginnings* is contagious.

It takes another week before it is almost complete. The previous name of the boat has been painted over in red. I pick up the stencil so that I can write the new name with precision across the side. Now this is the moment I have been waiting for.

'I'm so excited, Abe.'

'It's going to look wonderful. So, what are you waiting for?' says Abe, looking at me with the thin paintbrush in one hand and the stencil in the other.

'I'm scared I'll make a mistake.'

'Do you want me to help you do it?'

'No. Thank you for offering, but it's something I have to do myself.'

Taking a deep breath, I start painting the first letter. Then the second and the third.

I look at the first word, painted in a white fancy scroll: *New*.

'Looks good,' says Abe.

'It does. Now for the rest of it.'

I paint in the B and then the E and the G and then my mind goes blank. It must be my fear of getting it wrong, but I have some kind of brain fog from nowhere and forget how to spell *beginnings*. I look at Abe in disbelief.

'What's wrong?' he asks.

'My mind's gone. I can't remember how to spell beginnings. I mean, is it two Gs and one N or the other way around? The pressure of getting it right has got to me.'

'One G, two Ns.'

'I can't believe you can spell better than me and English is your second language.'

Abe laughs and then dips his finger in the white paint and splats me on the nose with it. I wave my paintbrush in the air to give him a warning.

'Just wait until I'm done. It's paint wars now,' I tease.

'Sounds fun to me,' says Abe.

'Right. No more messing about. I'm going to have to concentrate now.'

I focus so hard on getting the spelling correct that I bite down on my lip. Then slowly, I remove the stencil from the front of the boat and step back. There are no mistakes as I feared and thankfully the name is in a straight line.

'*New Beginnings*,' I say as I read it out loud.

'Beautiful, well done,' says Abe, giving me a kiss.

We stand back with our arms around each other and admire the houseboat.

'You've done a great job,' says Abe.

'*We* did. It was a joint effort.'

'Ah, it was all your idea. The colours, the name. I was just the assistant.'

'I could get used to having you as my assistant. You know what would be nice now, my assistant Abe? A nice cold beer.'

'I think we need something more than that. I have just the thing.'

I take a photo of the completed houseboat as I wait for Abe to pop over to his place to get whatever he has in mind. Then I send the photo to Hannah and Debbie. I am astonished that I have managed to get it all so beautiful in so little time. If I could have dreamed of the most idyllic houseboat to live in, it would be this one. There is nothing I would change about it.

As Abe walks back towards me, I can see him carrying a bottle and something red that I can't quite make out. I try to squint but have no idea what it is.

'Here, the final piece to make it home,' says Abe. I look at what he has in his hand and realise that the red item is a little pair of wooden clogs for me to put out on deck.

'Oh, Abe! This is the final touch? They're so cute.'

'I thought they'd be a nice decoration for you. They used to always be on the deck, by the front door. When they cleared Henrik's place after he died, I couldn't bear the thought of someone throwing them out, so I took them to keep safe. It's up to you, but I thought perhaps they could be a memory of the last owner. A mark of respect to him? Perhaps you can even use them to grow flowers in. Some people do that.'

'I absolutely love that idea.' I throw my arms around Abe and thank him once again. 'What would I do without you?'

'You'd be fine without me, although maybe you wouldn't have quite so much fun,' says Abe, handing me the bottle he's brought over.

I look at the fancy bottle of champagne in my hand.

'Wow, this looks expensive.'

'It's the last memory of my old life and the one thing I didn't leave behind when I came here. It was a gift for reaching a target at work. It was too nice to open. All these years, I've been saving it for a special occasion. I think it's time to open it. After all, we are celebrating *New Beginnings*, right?'

'Are you sure? Once it's open it's gone forever.'

'I'm sure. Just make sure you don't drop it on the way in.'

I pretend to let it slip, but truthfully, I am holding onto it for dear life.

Together, we walk inside, and Abe opens the champagne while I search for a suitable glass. Unfortunately, I don't have any champagne flutes, and I quickly realise that I shouldn't have sold all the crystal glasses I had back home. We will have to make do with the tumblers.

Just as Abe is talking about the history of the champagne and where it comes from, someone knocks on the door. It makes me jump and I am relieved that I no longer have the bottle in my hand.

'You expecting anyone?' says Abe.

'No. Not at all. That's strange.'

I open the door to find Beatrix standing on the doorstep.

'Hi, can I come in? I have something urgent to tell you.'

'Yeah, of course.'

'Ah, Abe. You're here too. That's good.'

'Is everything okay?' I ask.

'It's more than okay. I have the most amazing news. The stall is yours. I had a call from my contact there. It's yours, but you will have to arrange your market pass and street market licence first, or they'll have to give it to the next person on the waiting list.'

'Seriously? Does he not need to meet me or see my stock? I haven't been to see him yet.'

'I told him how talented you were, and I showed him a photo of that jumper you made and the miniature Ted. He'd not seen felt animals before and he loved them. So, he said for me to come and tell you that it's yours if you want it.'

I look at both Abe and Beatrix, who have the biggest smiles on their faces.

'What a day this is turning out to be. We were just celebrating *New Beginnings* being finished, and now this. Beatrix, you're going to have to join us for some of Abe's special champagne.'

I pour her a glass and we all squeeze together on my sofa. As I sip the champagne, I realise that it doesn't matter what kind of glass I am drinking out of. It is who is sitting beside me that is important.

Chapter Thirty-Six

When I arrive at the market, the stall manager, Fabien, is waiting in the office for my pass, along with the other documents he has requested. I have been quite impressed by how easy it is to get all the required documents in the Netherlands, whether it has been for the houseboat or setting up a market stall. The country is so efficient compared to other places. Beatrix comes with me to meet Fabien for moral support and to ensure there are no hiccups. Fabien is a jolly man. He is friendly but doesn't beat about the bush when it comes to the rent.

'So, you must pay by the first of every month, or the stall comes back to us. There are no excuses.'

'I understand, that's okay. I'll make sure you get the rent.'

'And if you want to give notice, you have to give one month.'

'Okay. No problem.'

'Good. This is your contract. It's in Dutch, are you okay with that?' says Fabien, handing it across the table.

'It's fine. My Dutch isn't too bad, although I can speak it better than I can read it. I'm sure Beatrix can help me if I get stuck.'

'Good. Okay. If you can read and sign it by tomorrow, then you're good to go. Shall I take you to see where the stall is before you sign? I want you to be satisfied with your pitch.'

I am so excited at the prospect of having a stall that its positioning hadn't occurred to me. It could be somewhere with terrible footfall. I can feel myself doing it again; rushing in feet first, just as I did when I bought *New Beginnings*.

'Oh, of course. I think that would be a wise idea.'

Beatrix and I follow Fabien out of the office towards the stalls, although the market is now closed and they stand empty. The tables have tarpaulins pulled over them but, come Sunday, it will be busy here again. A Sunday market will be perfect for me as it will give me time to replenish my stock during the week. Even with the coverings over the tables, I recognise the layout from when I have come here with Abe. As Fabien races along, I pass the place where my favourite organic wine stall usually is, and then we stop near the woman who sells the teddies. I guess this must be the crafts section.

'This is yours,' says Fabien, pointing to a stall.

I can't believe my luck.

'This is great. It's exactly the area I wanted to be in. It couldn't get any better than here.'

Even though the market is now like a ghost town, I picture what it will be like when my stall opens amid the crowds, and it is once again the usual busy atmosphere. I wonder if there is any camaraderie with the other traders, or if it gets competitive?

It isn't long until I find out. The following Sunday, with all the paperwork completed, I am allowed to open my stall.

It is early, and a frosty morning. Abe helps me bring the stock down on our bicycles. With both our baskets loaded up, we arrive to find the other traders busy setting up. I notice the woman with the teddies and smile at her. She gives me a friendly greeting and busies herself arranging her bears. Other traders nearby say hello and I start unloading the baskets until Abe leaves me to set up while he dashes back home for more stock. The only problem with not having a car is transporting stuff. One of the other traders whistles to himself as he sets up a stall selling home-made candles, and another sings a Dutch song. I needn't have worried about the other traders welcoming me as the newbie; everyone is helpful and the guy on the stall next to mine introduces himself as Jose and asks if he can get me a coffee. I gratefully accept as I desperately need something to warm me up. As I display the felt animals and some of the knitwear I have managed to finish in time, I find myself humming a tune too. By the time Abe returns with the final bits of stock, I am grinning like a Cheshire cat.

'You look happy,' he says.

'I am. This is just what I've always wanted. I was born to be a market trader. It's so much better than being stuck indoors in an office. I should have done this years ago.'

'It does seem to suit you. You need one of those market trader's aprons you can tie around your waist to keep money in. Where will you keep the cash?'

'Oh, no. I knew I'd forgotten something. My float!' I start to panic. I had so much to remember, I knew I would miss something.

'Okay. Don't worry. I'll go back and get it for you.'

'Are you sure? You don't mind all these trips back and forth?'

'Of course not. Keeps me fit. I'll cycle over and walk back with Ted. I'm sure he'd love to see you on your first day here. It's a big day, for all the family.'

Abe's words warm my heart.

'Thank you.' I hug him and find it hard to let go. His embrace is so comforting. I could have chosen to snuggle in bed with him on a Sunday morning, but there is plenty of time for that later. Now I have a big day ahead of me.

My first customer arrives just as Abe returns with Ted. It is a woman with two children, who adore the felt animals. She excitedly tells me that she has never seen them before. Perhaps felt animals aren't a trend here yet. So far, I have no idea whether the knitwear will do better, or the felting. It's hard to judge this early on but it seems to be the felting that everyone is attracted to. At least it works to draw in the crowds and then perhaps they might see some knitwear they like. Isn't that how luring customers in works? I should know this more than most.

The woman takes two pink and white unicorns for her daughters, and I work out how many euros in change she needs. At first, I find it hard to work it out. I promise myself by next week I will set up a card machine. It is all a lesson. I thank them for their custom and, once they leave, I finally have a moment to chat to Abe and Ted.

'Great start,' says Abe.

'Thanks.' There is no time to chat as a man immediately comes up and admires one of the stripy scarves that hang on the side of the stall.

'I'll take this one,' he says, in Dutch. Proudly, I manage to answer him in his own language, and I have another happy customer.

Ted starts getting bored hanging around the stall, so Abe heads off in search of breakfast, with promises they will be back soon. It is so busy, however, that I forget I left home before breakfast. I don't even notice my stomach grumbling. By mid-morning, crowds of people are milling around and many head over in the direction of my stall. I want to pinch myself as another family comes along and buys matching jumpers for their twins. By lunchtime I am almost sold out. When Beatrix arrives to see how I'm getting on, there are only two scarves and a couple of felt dogs left.

'I'd say this was a sell-out. Looks like a great morning,' she says.

'It's flown out. I can't believe how much has gone, and so quickly,' I say, as I stamp my feet up and down to try and stay warm. Now that the crowds have dispersed a bit, I realise how cold I am.

'Have you had a fun day? That's what's important.'

'So much fun. It's brilliant here. The other stallholders have been so kind, and we keep an eye on each other's stalls when we have to pop to the loo or grab a coffee or whatever. I feel like I've made so many friends in one morning. Customers are saying they'll be back next week. I even had someone ask me to knit them something bespoke!'

'I knew they'd love your stall, and your knitting is perfect for the Dutch weather. So, what time are you going to pack up?'

'Not long. The crowds are thinning out a bit, plus I've only got these items left. I'll give it another ten minutes, and I think I'll call it a day.'

'Great. Then perhaps we can go somewhere to celebrate your success?'

'That would be lovely. Although I may need a shower to warm up a bit first.'

Once I pack up the stall after its successful inauguration, I cycle back home, with only four pieces of stock left in my basket. I feel as though I am a fledgling Dutch resident now. I've learnt enough of the language to get by, I have a proper Dutch bike and I am cycling back home to my houseboat with a smile on my face. I am living the Dutch dream!

I dump my bike on deck and rush inside for a warm shower, which slowly defrosts me and makes me grateful for my shiny new boiler. Then I go over to Abe's so that we can meet Beatrix at a pub for a bite to eat.

Willem is meeting us there and is already sat down, waving over to us as we walk into the busy bar.

'Hi, I heard you cleaned up at the market today.'

'Ah, I wouldn't say that, but I didn't do too badly,' I say, as I think of the 200-euro profit I made.

'So, you'll be back there next week then.'

'Oh yes, and I can't wait. Although I'm going to be busy trying to restock everything and making a bespoke jumper for a customer. Who'd have ever thought I'd end up getting requests like that?'

'You'll be opening your own store next,' says Willem, as Beatrix returns from the bar with some drinks for us.

'Well, I don't know about that. I am supposed to be in retirement, after all. I was supposed to come here to chill a bit. But, if I'm honest, I love it. I could never sit still all day. Everyone needs some kind of mission in their lives.'

'What's that you're talking about?' says Beatrix, sitting down with us.

'We were just saying about me opening a shop. I think that would be a bit too much for me right now. Once a week at the market is good enough.'

'Too right. Who wants to work all the time? You've got to have some work/life balance. That's the good thing about being your own boss.'

'Yeah, but it also means you work harder than ever for your business,' says Abe.

'True, but you know what they say about choosing a job you love – you never work a day in your life. I think that's what we did with the coffee shop, Abe,' says Beatrix.

'Yeah, now that is true. It's hard work, but so rewarding.'

I watch Beatrix and Abe as they chat about the cafe and smile at Willem. I love how close everyone is. Since I arrived here, they have opened their arms and welcomed me into the comunity, and now their circle of friends. Although I miss Hannah every day, I suppose this is how she feels when she is with her dad and his family. For her, Melbourne is where she belongs. The longer I stay here, the more I feel as though this is where I belong. This was my destiny.

I think back to the very first time I came here with Nicky and fell in love with the place. It felt so relaxed, yet also buzzing with life, and there are so many things to do. It mesmerised me right from the beginning and, today, having started at the welcoming market where everyone embraced me, I love it even more. I adore the culture and the Dutch people, and most of all I love Abe and his family. Perhaps it's time I told him that.

When we finish our evening with Beatrix and Willem, I ask Abe if he would like a nightcap back at mine.

'Why not. One for the road, as you always say.'

'Great. I wanted to have a little chat with you, and since it's been such a long day it would be good to unwind a bit. I think I'm still on a high from the market.'

When we return to *New Beginnings*, Abe pours me a small glass of *stroopwafel* liqueur and I take it from his hand, putting it down beside me. I stop and look him in the eye.

'Abe, I wanted to tell you something. I know it's only been a few months, but I think I've fallen in love with you. I never expected to find love a second time around, I didn't even think I wanted it. But how could I stop myself when I met someone as wonderful as you? I love you, your family and everything in Amsterdam. I am so happy and content. My life here really is a dream come true, and you've helped to make it that way.'

'I'm glad to hear that. I was worried for a moment about what you wanted to say. I love you too, and I want you to know that this isn't something I would ever say unless I really mean it. So, I want you to know that I really, really mean it.'

Abe takes hold of my hand and kisses it.

'You know, it's like we were made for each other. You are the yin to my yang,' he says.

'I love that. We were made for each other, and you are my yang. Goodness, everything is so perfect. I never imagined things would fall into place like this. It's incredible.'

'Maybe it's this houseboat. I always felt like it had a nice energy. Henrik had many happy years here. He was ninety-eight when he died, and that was on holiday. Nothing bad ever happens here. I know this sounds strange, but I believe this houseboat chose you. It knew you needed a new start in life and now you have it.'

I look around at the houseboat and almost start to believe Abe's theory. It did pop up at the strangest moment, and everything started changing from then.

'Yeah, at the time it felt too good to be true, how it found me all the way over in Wales. Stranger things have happened, I suppose.'

'If it did choose you then I want to thank it. The best thing you ever did was move in next door.'

'Isn't that the truth? I can't even imagine what I would have missed out on if that advert hadn't popped up. It doesn't bear thinking about.'

'It's quite spooky how it's all worked out. There had to be some luck involved.'

'Abe, maybe you're right. This is a lucky home.'

I take my glass from the table and make a toast to Abe and thank him for everything he has done for me. Then silently, I make a toast to the houseboat too.

'Thank you, little houseboat, for everything.'

Chapter Thirty-Seven

Eighteen months later

Debbie stands by the canal with a big smile on her face. I run down and give her the hugest of hugs. Oh, how I have missed her. It feels like forever since she was last here.

'I can't believe I've had to come to you again. That's what happens when you refuse to come home, even for a holiday,' says Debbie.

'Well, I'm busy with my stall. Don't want to let my regulars down, plus I'm having far too good a time with this one,' I say, looking over at Abe.

'I can see that. Look at you! Doesn't she look well, Nigel.'

'You do look well, Sandy. Great to see you here. Finally, I can see where you ran off to when you sold up.'

'Yup, welcome to Amsterdam and *New Beginnings*. You are going to love it here, just like Debbie and I do.'

'Well, I must admit my first impressions aren't bad. I've already heard there's a Heineken tour somewhere around here. I'm looking forward to that, and the Sex Museum. I'll have to visit those two places.'

Debbie and I grin at each other. How did we guess those would be first on his list of attractions to visit?

'But, anyway, first things first, let's see this houseboat of yours,' says Nigel, still standing on the side of the canal. 'You going to invite us in then, or what?'

'Of course. Sorry. Do you want Abe to give you a hand with your bags, Debbie?'

'No, it's alright. I can manage them all.' Nigel looks at Abe and introduces himself, speaking very slowly.

'I am Nigel. From Wales.'

'You can speak properly, Nigel. Abe speaks very good English.'

'Oh, tidy.'

Debbie rolls her eyes, and it is just like being back in Wales with the two of them. Nothing has changed since we were last together.

Abe and I take Debbie and Nigel inside the houseboat and show them around. The decorations have been revamped slightly since Debbie was last here, as I have moved the furniture around a bit. This time she can stay in my room as I'll be on *Aquaholic* with Abe.

Nigel has a good look around the living room and kitchen area as he brings in the luggage.

'I have to say, this isn't quite what I expected. It's much better and, fair play, it doesn't even smell of damp.'

'Nigel!' scolds Debbie.

'Well, I'm just saying it as it is. I'm being nice. You've done a lovely job, Sandy. Much better than I expected. Ooh, yes. Now, I could live somewhere like this.'

'Could you?' Debbie and I look at each other hopefully.

'Oh, definitely. It would be a bloody lovely way to live now I'm retired.'

I wonder when Debbie is going to tell Nigel that *Aquaholic* next door is for sale. I suspect she will take him on the Heineken Experience and ply him with samples there first.

'Can you go out on the roof there?' asks Nigel inquisitively.

'Oh, yes. Go and have a look.' When he sees the rocking chair and the scenery, Nigel is going to be sold.

Debbie is about to whisper something to me when Nigel comes back down.

'Debs, have you seen it up there? Brilliant view over the canal.'

'Yes, I know. I saw it the last time I was here.'

'Imagine smoking a pipe up there in your dressing gown, rocking back and forth,' says Nigel.

'Oh, for goodness' sake, you can't stand pipe smoke.'

'No, true. But what I mean is, it's very relaxing up there.'

Debbie winks at me, delighted that Nigel is already falling in love with the place. I hadn't expected him to be this easy to win over but, then again, *New Beginnings* has that effect on people.

'Right then. We'd better leave you to settle in for a while. I'm sure you want to unpack and freshen up before tonight. Anyway, I have an important appointment to attend with Abe now. We'll have to rush, or we'll be late.'

Abe looks at Debbie curiously.

'Do you know where she wants to take me? She's been planning this for ages and won't give anything away,' says Abe.

'Nope. Sorry, only just arrived, I've no idea.'

Abe shakes his head.

'We'll be back at seven p.m. to collect you for dinner. I thought we could go to a fabulous Chinese restaurant on the water tonight. It's not too far from here. Is that okay with you, Nigel?'

'Oh, yes. I do like a chow mein.'

'Great. They have robot waiters and everything. It's so much fun there.'

'Oh, I don't know about robots. They're putting people out of work, aren't they?'

'It's okay. There are still lots of staff there. Don't worry. I promise you'll like it.'

I shake my head at Nigel; he is so set in his ways. I do hope Debbie can talk him into moving next door like she believes she can.

'Maybe we should have let them stay on *Aquaholic* so they could get a feel for it. See if they like it,' I say to Abe, as we head to the appointment I have made for us.

'No, we did the right thing. Let them experience some of the magic on *New Beginnings* first. That'll make sure they want to move in next door.'

'True. I like your thinking. Oh, I can't wait for you and Ted to move in with me. It's going to be wonderful. Ted will be back where he came from. Isn't that lovely?'

'It is. Who'd have thought it would work out with him moving back in? He'll be glad to have us back home this afternoon. I must say I'm surprised you wouldn't let him come with us today. Where is it that you're taking me that we had to leave Ted at home? You know how he likes to come everywhere with us.'

'I know, but Beatrix is with him. We're almost there now.'

'It's a good job I trust you.'

Soon enough we arrive at the place I have planned for the surprise.

'Right, since it's your fifty-ninth birthday, I thought you might like a tattoo. I've researched this place and it's one of the best. No pressure, we can always back out if you don't want one. I've already explained the situation to the staff, and how this is a complete surprise, and that you might not want to go along with it. But I remembered how you said you wanted a tattoo before you hit sixty. You still don't look a day over forty, by the way. But, yeah… Would you like a tattoo for your birthday?'

'Seriously? You remembered me saying that?'

For a moment, I am worried my plan is going to backfire. How stupid of me to book a tattoo as a surprise. In hindsight, perhaps it isn't the most sensible birthday gift. I watch as a big grin reaches across Abe's face, and he pushes the tattoo parlour door open.

'I love it. I think it's the best birthday present ever.'

'Really? You're not just saying it?'

'Nope. It was on my bucket list, and I needed someone to give me a push. It's brilliant, and so thoughtful. I mean, I only have another year left to get one by sixty, so I'd better get on with it.'

I breathe a sigh of relief as a tall man with piercings through what seems like every orifice greets us and sits us down with some artistic drawings. The pictures are incredible. They are so beautiful that they look like they belong in one of the art galleries around the city.

'I also have this book,' says the tattoo artist opening another large plastic-backed book.

'Many who come in for couples tattoos choose from this one. You can have the same tattoo or half a jigsaw piece, for example, and the partner has the other side that fits. There are so many choices.'

A female tattoo artist walks in and introduces herself to me saying that she will be doing mine.

'You're booked in for a tattoo also?' says Abe, looking at me.

'Yup, I could hardly leave you to do it on your own.'

'Shall we choose a tattoo from the couples book then?'

'I'm happy with that if you are.'

'Wow. I always said it had to be the right tattoo, and this is perfect. Let's have a look and see what we can find.'

'You do know a tattoo is for life,' I remind him one last time.

'Well then, I guess now we're committed for life. Is commitment really so bad?' he asks.

'No, not when you've found the right person.'

We browse the tattoo book together and point at the same one at the same time.

'That one?' we say jointly.

We laugh at our synchronicity as we both tell the artists which tattoo we want.

'Yin and yang. It has to be that one,' says Abe.

The tattoo artists prepare us both and we place our wrists out ready to be inked. As they sterilise the area and the coldness hits my skin, I realise there is no turning back. The noise of the tattoo gun starts up and I think to myself how commitment comes in all different forms. It doesn't always have to be about a fancy ring. But just before the artists can begin, Abe grabs my other hand from across the bed he is lying on and squeezes it tight.

'For life,' he says.

'For life,' I agree.

'Good, because now that I've found you, I want it to be forever,' grins Abe.

A Letter from Helga

First, a huge thank you for picking up a copy of *A New Life in Amsterdam*. I truly hope that you will enjoy your trip to a fictional houseboat on a canal in beautiful Amsterdam.

I first went to Amsterdam when I was cabin crew with Gulf Air (a very long time ago!) when I fell in love with the place immediately. The Dutch people are so laid-back and wonderful, the food is divine (I mean, have you tried those Dutch waffles?), the scenery is sensational and there is so much culture and history all around the city.

The last time I visited, I took a ride down the canal on a boat serving champagne, and there is a pancake boat I need to try the next time I go. On each visit to Amsterdam, I have found something new. I have tried to put some of the amazing sights and activities into this story, but I am sure I have hardly scratched the surface. There is so much fun you can have in this city.

I do hope you enjoy the story of lovely Sandy and Abe and the adventures they get up to as they get to know each other. I fell that little bit more in love with Abe every time I worked on his character. Sadly, he isn't based on anyone in real life!

I am always very responsive on social media, so please feel free to contact me if you enjoy the story. You can contact me via:

www.twitter.com/HelgaJensenF
www.facebook.com/helgajensenfordeauthor
www.instagram.com/helgajensenauthor

Acknowledgements

The hugest thank you to Keshini Naidoo at Hera Books, who gave me my first book contract all those years ago. Also, a big thank you to my wonderful editor, Jennie Ayres, who whips all my books into shape. My thanks also go to Lindsey Harrad for the copy edit and Jenny Page for the proofread. Diane of D Meacham Design, thank you for the cover as always. Book covers are so important, and I am always grateful for the time and effort involved in the design of them.

As I always say, it takes a team to get a book noticed and out into the world, so I want to acknowledge the wonderful publicist Kate Shepherd, the Hera/Canelo sales team, the book bloggers, librarians and, of course, the bookshops. To the amazing bloggers who take part in my blog tours through Rachel's Random Resources, your support means the world to me. You are truly amazing. Also, a big thanks to the wonderful Gemma for telling me about houseboats and floating key fobs!

On a personal note, thank you to JK for ferrying me around in your lovely new car, and to Mr B who is the perfect passenger. They will always be magical memories.

To my supportive friends, special people, the one who sends me jokes every day and is always there for me through thick and thin, I love you lots. To my writing bestie Jenny, thank you as always. I hope seven books of acknowledgements shows you just how much I appreciate you being in my life!

Finally, my heartfelt gratitude to each and every one of my readers. I can't thank you enough for choosing to read my books.

Happy reading X